I0731812

CONTENT WARNING

This novel contains adult content
and is not suitable for children.

What is the Wyrdwood Project? Learn more.
(http://wyrdwoodangel.com/about/)

Sign up to receive the Wyrdwood newsletter.
(http://wyrdwoodangel.com/newsletter/)

DEDICATION

One of the themes of this novel is family, both the one we're born into and the ones we choose. Family molds who we are in so many ways, and for me, my greatest influence has been my brother. Matt has always been my #1 supporter and inspiration. His strength and steadfastness have made him my anchor. I would not be the person I am today if he weren't in my life. Love you, Matt!

◆

Wyrdwood Welcome #2

Jumping
the Moon

by Angel Leigh McCoy

◆

*"All things must change,
to something new,
to something strange."*

—Henry Wadsworth Longfellow—

CHAPTER 1

I recently learned something important—that when you're on an adventure, your natural inclination is to face forward. Each developing moment brings new information, new sights, sounds, and feelings, so there's no possible way to look back without missing out on something.

As the plane taxied toward the airport—Portland International Airport a.k.a. PDX—I heard someone say that our flight had been "uneventful." On the contrary, it had been so full of events, I hadn't closed my eyes once. I'd never flown before.

My Mom sat on my left, Corona at the window, and Jake was across the aisle from us. The flight from Peoria to Chicago had been scary. The plane was small, and we'd hit heavy turbulence. Then O'Hare was enormous. We all had to stay together, which wasn't easy between Mom's lack of attention and Corona's attention to everything. Jake took charge of Corona, and I kept hold of Mom's jacket.

I'd never seen so many people in one place in my entire life, all different, all living lives that felt—to them—just as solid as mine felt to me. All were going places, talking about things important to them, loving each other, working, thinking, breathing... and yet not once did I see a collision of bodies. It was miraculous.

When we got on the big plane, the flight attendant said, "Hi," and smiled at me. I beamed right back.

We found our seats, stowed our carry-ons, and settled in. Then we flew two thousand miles across the country. I looked out the window and saw clouds below us. *Below us! There was a time when people would have called me a god for looking down upon the world from such a height. Or they'd have laughed me out of the village—maybe even locked me up in an institution. And yet there I was.*

My eyes weren't big enough to take it all in.

We crossed the Rockies, and I saw mountains for the first time in my life.

Corona commented, "I always knew I was short, but I never knew I was so tiny." I couldn't have agreed more.

Why, I wondered, had I never left Illinois? Not even for vacation. I was almost to my thirties, and I'd spent the first third of my life stunted, hemmed in by schedules and duties. That ol' tick-tock of the clock. I'd never known what I was missing.

Everything changed the moment my car went into the lake. My eyes had opened even as I was drowning. That was when Colin Aubrey, my fiancé, was ripped from me, and when the machine that had been my life fell apart. The gears grinded. Springs sprung. And the cuckoo flew away.

To Wyrdwood.

Still looking out the window, Corona asked,

"How's Colin going to know where you went? Aren't you worried he won't be able to find you?"

I wove my hands together in my lap, and my pin came to mind. I shoved the thought aside. With more confidence than I felt, I said, "He'll find me. If he shows up at Abram's door, Abram knows to tell him where I am. And I left a letter for him."

"You must miss him."

An ache, now familiar, made me look down at my hands. I nodded almost absently. I missed him. Being separated from Colin was like having a darkness sitting in your peripheral vision. I was always searching for his face in crowds, always on alert for his voice, scanning the skies for his winged silhouette. He was the last thing I thought about at night before sleeping and the first thing when I woke up, usually with alternating emotions of sadness and anger. He'd abandoned me. Twice. Three times if you count when he dropped me from a gajillion feet in the air.

For years, Colin had tried to tell me he could fly, and I just thought it was a delusion caused by his amnesia. To say that he'd surprised the hell out of me when he'd proven he had wings and could fly was the understatement of the century. That was the moment I knew for sure that I was either insane or there was much more to the story. I still couldn't think about how majestic he'd looked without a portion of my mind trying to sweep it under a rug.

"He'll show up," said Corona.

I rubbed my hands over my face and said, "I

know," but I didn't know at all. I let my hands fall limp onto my lap. "Only thing is, I'm not his first priority, and I don't think he's safe with me."

Corona rested her hand on mine. "His family won't be trying to kill him forever. I hope. You have no idea where he is?"

"None. He went one way, and I'm going to Wyrdwood."

Corona was silent for a moment before asking, "What do you think it'll be like there?"

"Your guess is as good as mine," I admitted with a nervous chuckle. "We'll be in a brand new place."

"A place called *Wyrdwood.*" *She emphasized the "weird."*

"We'll fit right in," I joked with a goofy shrug I didn't quite feel. It was a platitude meant to ease both her anxiety and my own. Trouble was that I saw through it.

"True!" She leaned in, playing along, and then lowered her voice. "And peeps there have lived their whole lives without ever once thinking about us, looking at us. Judging us. I'm pretty fucking psyched about that." Her brown eyes shone. "It's a brand-new start, Viv. We can be squeaky, fresh out of the box." She did a little wiggle in her seat that drew a laugh out of me.

"When you put it like that," I said, "it does sound kind of exciting."

◇

After a while, the pilot announced that we'd begun our descent into Portland, and we slid down through the clouds. The landscape appeared below us. I realized that this was the layer we lived in.

The suburbs of Portland sprawled across the land, each a maze of streets lined with houses. The area wasn't flat like Chicago. Hills covered with green trees forced mankind's structures to go over and around them. A thick river—the Columbia—snaked through it all. Portland was a vast hive of humans, buildings, and parking lots. Skyscrapers clustered together. Long bridges crossed between land masses. Cars ran along them in solid streams, their headlights glowing.

I watched out the window as we approached the runway, pushing down my fear. The ground rose up to meet us. We were going so fast, and then there was a bump, a bounce, and the roar of the engines. A thrill rose up from my gut and made my chest feel full. My heart.

We had landed.

Rain spattered the window, and it felt like a special welcome.

I said, "Hello, Portland."

We took down our carry-ons and followed the crowd off the plane, up another tube, and into PDX. It was smaller than O'Hare and much less chaotic. The people weren't in as much of a hurry. They sat around reading or looking out the giant windows at the planes criss-crossing between land and sky. No one was shouting or even talking loudly.

As soon as I was back on land, I whispered, "Simon?" I'd been doing so whenever I thought about it—ever since my invisible friend had left—checking to see if he was back. He wasn't. Or if he was, he wasn't declaring it. I had neither seen nor heard Simon since leaving Malum Center. He'd been my constant companion ever since I was thirteen. For so long, I'd thought he was a figment of my imagination. He'd been my guardian and guide throughout my toughest years. When I learned he was real, he left—or so it seemed. He wouldn't tell me where he was going or why. The silence he'd left in his wake made me feel sad and vulnerable.

Our little group walked through the Portland airport, past shops selling smoked salmon, fleece, and Trail Blazers' basketball souvenirs. Jake had done all this a thousand times before, so we followed him like ducklings to Baggage Claim. He tried to get us to walk instead of riding the moving sidewalk, but he lost that vote. Corona and I each took one of Gisèle's arms and guided her on. Then we streamed along, the breeze in our hair. When we walked too, it felt almost like flying.

Baggage Claim was in the underbelly of the airport. The energy there was different, the crowd impatient and anxious, everyone searching for something or someone. They surrounded large carousels with suitcases carried around like nigiri at a sushi bar. The people checked out each morsel to see if it was what they wanted.

A hole in the wall gave birth to suitcases, the newborns riding the merry-go-round. They all had that well-traveled look. It made me happy to see them claimed and reunited with their owners.

As we waited for our suitcases, a pair of women approached Jake. He greeted them with smiles.

"How was your trip?" asked a tall redhead with strong bones and a voice like melted butter. Something about her sparked my curiosity. She was a striking beauty, despite the ragged scar that cut down one side of her face. Dressed in a peach crocheted sweater, skinny blue jeans, and white sneakers with no socks, she had a cosmopolitan style that screamed self-confidence.

Jake replied, "Good. I'm glad it's almost over though." He launched forward to nab one of the suitcases.

The woman let her gaze drift over the rest of us, evaluating. She caught my eye, and I looked away.

The second woman was older, with black hair caught up in a French twist. A narrow streak of white grew from front-and-center, just above her forehead. Her dark eyes were warm and welcoming as she held her hand out to me. "You must be Viviane," she said. "I'm Rio. Welcome to the Pacific Northwest. We're your ride to Wyrdwood."

I shook her hand. "Thank you. It's nice to be here." I indicated my mother and Corona. "This is

Gisèle and Corona." I was feeling shy.

Corona bounced, "Do you work with Jake? Are you from Lost Lambs?"

The redhead took a step toward Jake, helping him move the bags onto a big cart.

Rio answered, "Yes, we are. You're going to love it there. We've got the ocean, the forest, mountains, a river... everything you could want."

It was as if a cork had popped from Corona's mouth, and she started talking a mile a minute. Truth be told, I was grateful. I felt so overwhelmed by everything that I had no words. I don't think I could have made rational small-talk if I'd tried.

A girl with piercings all over her face walked by, as did a man with blue hair and a couple dressed in rags, wearing socks inside sandals. One woman had her blond hair all in knots, dreadlocks. People played with hand-held devices and talked to thin air, an earbud in one ear. I saw a man in a turban, a group of Japanese people in suits, and an eagle.

An eagle. It flew down from a beam overhead and landed at the redhead's feet.

Corona gasped. *I gasped. No one else noticed.*

The eagle pecked at a nearby man's loose shoestring, pulling it undone.

The red-head laughed, deep and rich. "The looks on their faces!" she said.

Jake laughed, too. "Guys, this is Hilda, and that's Hugs, her familiar. She's harmless."

"Who?" Corona asked, "Hilda or Hugs?"

Hilda raised both eyebrows.

Jake said, "Both."

"Don't you believe it," Hilda said under her breath.

Corona asked, "No one but us can see Hugs?"

Jake nodded. "That's right. Hugs is the kind of magickal creature that Normals can't see."

That brought my overwhelm to a whole new level. I latched onto my mother, the noise and sights of the airport forgotten. I was so engrossed in watching Hilda and her familiar that I walked into someone's luggage and tripped. A strong hand captured my upper arm and kept me on my feet. When I looked up, a man with tusks looked down at me. *Not a man. My insides began to vibrate at a low resonance. His eyes were kind, his smile gentle. He said, "Careful there."*

My every instinct was to get away from him, and I stumbled again.

Jake was at my side in a heartbeat. "Thank you," he told the man, helping me himself. "She's new to the Sight."

The tusked man rumbled a sympathetic hum and released me.

I realized I was holding my breath.

Jake put an arm around my shoulders. "You're okay. Let's get to the van."

I nodded, staring back at the man-not-man, trying to wrap my mind around him. He was watching the carousel for his luggage and had forgotten all about me. I would never forget him. His body was thick, not fat, and he stood over six feet tall. His bald head had tattoos that resembled a pit of snakes or Celtic knotwork—it was hard to tell which as we moved away from him. He wore loose jeans and a blue windbreaker. If it weren't for the sharp tusks growing upward from his lower jaw, protruding from the corners of his mouth, I'd have thought he was just a sun-leathered world traveler.

We caught up with the others.

I asked, "What was that?"

Hilda answered me, her tone clipped. "Who. *Who was that. He's a person, like you and me.*"

My cheeks grew hot. "I'm sorry. I didn't mean..."

Rio said, "You might say he's a nature spirit. They're a race known as Orcneas. They've been around longer than humans."

Jake asked, "Where's Gisèle?"

"What? Mom?" I asked, turning in place to search for her. "Where is she?"

"Shit," Jake said. "Did you guys see where she went?"

"Oh holy crap," cried Corona. "I was watching the Orcneas!"

I took off into the crowd, searching for her.

"Viviane!" Jake called. "Wait!"

But I couldn't wait. Not a second. My heart was hammering. She could have been... But then I spotted her going out the exit doors. I took off running, pushing people out of my way. When I got to the exit, the automatic doors opened too slowly, and I squeezed through the moment the gap was wide enough.

Mom was crossing the sidewalk, making a bee-line for the curb. She stepped right into traffic.

"Mom! Stop!" I flew toward her, bent forward to reach for her. I grabbed a fistful of her sweater and yanked her back just in time. A car of laughing teens went by inches in front of her. I tugged her into my arms. "Mom! Don't do that!"

An instant later, Jake was at my side, guiding us both back to safety.

"Well," said Hilda dryly, "that was unexpected. Note to self: buy leashes."

Rio commented, "Ah, the complexities of family life."

I wanted to glare at them, but for some reason it struck me funny, and I started to laugh. It wasn't the good kind of laugh, but the edge-of-hysteria kind.

Jake stayed by my side, one hand on my shoulder. "Breath with me."

It took me the entire walk to the van before I had myself under control again.

◇◇◇

CHAPTER 2

The drive to Wyrdwood would take us a little over three hours. We stopped about every hour to stretch our legs, use the restroom, and eat fast food—tacos and burgers. Whenever we stopped, Hilda's eagle flew down to join us. Corona tried to share her french fries with it, but it turned up its beak at them. I began to relax again.

We passed through a series of quaint towns, evergreen forests, and wide fields, many of which had horses. My attention was always captured by horses. I loved riding, though it had been years since I'd done so.

Rio noticed and commented, "This isn't Kentucky, but we've got our fair share of horse ranches here."

I smiled.

With less than an hour to go, we pulled into a rest stop, nestled in a forest of pine and cedar trees. It smelled amazing, like wet earth and scotch, with hints of Christmas. Corona and I sat together at a picnic table, drinking hot chocolate from the vending machine. Gisèle was sleeping in the van, having reached her limit of activity for the day. Even Corona had begun to wind down.

Jake joined us. He said, voice serious, "I want

to go over a few things with you guys before we get there, okay?"

We nodded. Corona asked, "What?"

"I know it's been a very long day, but I wanted to tell you—"

"Warn you," Hilda interjected, mostly to herself.

Jake shot her a sideways glance and continued, "...a little about Wyrdwood before we get there." He had our attention. "Wyrdwood isn't like the towns you're used to. It's a haven for people like you, but also for people the likes of which you've never seen before."

"Like the Orcneas?" Corona asked.

"Exactly like that. Most Normals think the only race is humanity, but that's never been true. Sadly, many of them reject the very idea of magick, and they have a predilection for persecuting anyone who's different." Jake watched us both in that way psychiatrists did when they weren't sure how a patient would react. I was reminded of Richard, and the memory sent a shiver through my shoulders. Jake continued, "Magickal beings—we call them 'magick wielders'— have to stay hidden from Normals for their own safety."

"Awesome!" said Corona, eyes shining. She clutched my upper arm. "Like Simon."

I patted her hand.

Jake said, "All over the world, there are pockets of protected space. Wyrdwood is one of the oldest—

that we're aware of."

"How do they do it?" Corona asked.

"Do what?" Jake tilted his head.

"Keep the Normals from knowing. There are so many of you."

Jake met Hilda's gaze for a moment before he said, "Wyrdwood has one prime rule that we must never break. It's forbidden to reveal the true nature of Wyrdwood or magick wielders to anyone who isn't magickal. You must never out anyone else."

"Or they'll chop off your head," Hilda finished for him with morbid undertones.

Corona nodded. "I get it. Mr. Smith must never find out that we took the red pill."

Returning from the restroom, Rio took a seat on the bench beside me. "Giving them The Talk, huh?"

Jake nodded to her, then held his hands out to Corona and me, palms up. "I need your promise before I can take you there."

Corona sat up straight, put one hand over her heart, and rested the other across Jake's palm. He closed his fingers around it. "I promise." She looked down at their clasped hands in surprise, then laughed.

When I only nodded, Jake looked right at me and said, "I need you to say it out loud, Viv. And I need you to take my hand. It's a binding."

"A what?" I asked.

Rio explained. "It's a sacred binding. A promise so strong that if you break it, the pain of that break will eat at your soul from the inside."

"If we don't cut off your head first."

"Hilda, please," Jake scolded quietly.

Corona said, "Like putting your hand on a Bible."

They all watched me, expectant. Flame-haired Hilda with her eagle familiar standing on the table in front of her, Rio with her eyes as black as tar, Corona wide-eyed and nodding to encourage me, and Jake—evaluating me with every passing second.

I reached out and took Jake's hand. It was warm and calloused—strong. "I promise." A streak of tingles passed into my hand and up my arm to my chest. It surprised me, and I gasped, attempting to pull my hand free. Jake's grip tightened, and he held on for a second more before letting it go.

"That," Hilda said with smug satisfaction, "is magick."

I rubbed my arm.

Jake slapped his palms onto the tabletop. "Let's hit the road."

We bundled back into the van with Hilda at the wheel. For the next while, we drove through trees, evergreens on all sides. Oregon was so different from Illinois. There, the trees were all round blobs on top of sticks. In the Pacific Northwest, the trees were emerald pyramids, fat at the bottom and pointed at the top. Some were very tall. I yearned to smell them, so I lowered my window a crack. With the air came droplets of rain. I inhaled. It smelled different, too. Peoria smelled like farm animals and growing vegetables.

The aroma coming into the van was a mingling of water and earth, ancient trees and tribal fires, and just when I was thinking that, the trees parted, and the ocean came into view. We turned onto a road that ran perpendicular to the shore.

Corona squealed. "Is that the Pacific? Oh my god, oh my god! I've never seen the Pacific!"

Neither had I. For that matter, I'd never seen any ocean before. It was vast, stretching to the edge of the world. The sun was setting at the horizon, painting the sky a blend of pink and orange. I was overwhelmed with awe.

Corona asked, "Can we stop? Please!"

"For a few minutes," Jake agreed, and Hilda found a place to pull over.

As we piled out, I could smell the ocean—the salty, fishy tang of it. The waves rushed in and out, bouncing and rolling across the rocks. There wasn't much beach, just a narrow stretch, and Jake took hold of Corona's arm to stop her from running down there. "We'll come spend some time here later, during the day, okay? Not tonight."

We all settled into silence, watching the sky blush as the sun sank closer and closer to the edge of forever. A bird with long legs stood out on the rocks—a crane of some sort. It was gawky and pretty with its knobby knees and graceful neck. Seagulls circled overhead, calling out to one another.

Jake said, to no one in particular, "Sometimes, the seals hang out here on the beach." He came to stand beside me, our shoulders brushing, and I felt a swell of gratitude overtake me, bringing tears to my eyes. I thought about what my life had been like up to that moment. Hiding my supposed psychosis, my hallucinations, working in the hospital laundry—those long nights of noise and sweat—and my dreams of marrying Colin and everything righting itself. In that old vision, he was well, I was well, and we were living a normal life. It was almost laughable how naive I'd been.

I wasn't meant to be normal. Neither Colin nor I were ill. We were different. Jake had rescued me from Vince Malum Residential Living Center—the mental health facility where I'd been committed after my car went into the lake with Colin and me inside it. So much darkness.

Yet, I'd survived it all. I let the sunset ease my eyes and my heart with its beauty, soaking it in as it faded to a rich blue.

"Time to go," Jake said, touching my elbow.

Corona whined. "But I love it here sooooo much."

Jake opened his arm, and Corona stepped into its circle. He guided her toward the van like a caring uncle. It was so different from the doctors and nurses I knew from Malum. It felt like family—like I was a foreign exchange student traveling with a kind family.

My entire world was changing, and I knew my options. I could flee deep into myself as I'd done in the past. Hide from the world. Hide from my own truth and potential. That way was death. Or I could accept it, embrace it even, and flap my wings as hard as I could. No. I wasn't *ready to embrace it. Not then. But I could go with the flow. I turned and walked back to the van.*

◇

We passed a sign that said, "Welcome to Wyrdwood. Population 1864." Someone had spray-painted an "ish" after the number. A filigree half-moon hung above the words, beautiful and shining silvery as the headlights illuminated it.

Jake pulled out his cell phone, dialed, and put it to his ear. After a moment, he said, "We're here." He listened. "When?" he asked. The tone of his voice hardened, his mouth tightened, and his eyes went downcast. "Dammit," he hissed. "How is he finding them?"

Hilda glanced over at him, a question in her expression. He met her gaze, and they exchanged a look.

I asked, "Is something wrong?"

Jake put a tense smile on his face and shook his head. Into the phone, he said, "I have to go. We'll talk about this when I get home. We're ten minutes out. Please ask Ayu to make coffee, will you? We're going to need it." He hung up, and when he saw everyone watching him, he said, "Nothing to worry about. Just business stuff. We're almost there."

Hilda turned off the ocean-side highway and onto a smaller road that moved inland along the mouth of a river. Condominiums and beautiful homes faced out toward the ocean. Before long, we left the modern luxury of the coast and entered an older area that was medieval in style. Buildings made of stones and thick timber lined the street. A large wooden sign said, "Wyrdwood Olde Towne."

Everywhere I looked, I saw the most extraordinary mix of people. The kind of people you'd expect to see in a small town, yes. Many of them. But also magickal beings whose true essences shone from them like auras that began to solidify the more I looked, as if I were making them solid with my gaze. A man held the hand of a small child as they looked in a shop window, and both had hooves instead of feet, their knees bent backwards, and they had fur where there would have been pants. Two women walked arm in arm, one with long flowing seaweed hair, the other with a short shock of what looked like burrs on her head. They were talking, eating ice cream cones.

"What?" cried Corona. "Look at them. Jake! Are they married?" I followed Corona's pointing finger to a pair of adults herding a trio of children, one of which was in a stroller. The man was tall and slim, with a bald head and skin with mottled coloring. The woman had a curvaceous figure and a cat's tail that swished back and forth as she walked. The children were an obvious genetic mix of the two.

"I don't know if they're married," Jake replied, "but they're together. He's a dentist in town. And those are their children."

"They can have sex? With each other? Make babies?"

Jake laughed, and Hilda gave Corona a frown in the rear-view mirror. "Take care, girl," Hilda said. "Your prejudice is showing. Of course, they can."

Jake explained, "Just like human races—Caucasian, Asian, Latino, etcetera—can date, fall in love, have sex, and procreate, so can all the magickal races. As a matter of fact, we've all intermingled our DNA so much that there are very few people left who don't have a mixed genetic profile. Like you, Corona. You're part human and part magick wielder."

"Wow," Corona said. "I didn't mean to sound racist."

Jake said, "We know. It's all new to you."

We cruised past the town-square park where a group had gathered on blankets to watch an outdoor movie—*The Princess Bride. They were a hodge-podge of humans mixed with fantastic beings, and they all laughed. I saw more of the Orcneas and people of all skin colors. The majority looked "normal," but then so did I.*

Jake reached back to touch my knee. "You can close your mouth," he said with a smile in his voice, and I realized it was hanging open.

I swallowed hard.

Jake asked, "Are you okay?"

I didn't know what to say. I nodded.

Hilda explained, "Many kinds of kin live here in Wyrdwood. You can see them because you have wyrd blood. But many of those folks out there are non-magickal humans. They're unaware that their neighbors are magickal, and most will never find out."

Corona pressed her nose and palms to the window. "What if a human falls in love with a non-human?" she asked.

Hilda said over her shoulder, "We don't use the term 'non-human.' It implies that magick wielders are less-than. That is not the case. If anything, humans are non-magickal."

Rio said, "To answer your question, Corona, most magick wielders know better than to get involved with a Normal, but the heart wants what the heart wants, as they say. So it does happen. It's a complicated situation, however."

"Not unlike dating your boss," Jake interjected.

"Exactly," Rio continued. "There is always the chance of a break-up and, if you've revealed yourself to your human lover, then they could turn on you in a heartbeat. I hope you understand what a leap of faith we're taking by bringing you to Wyrdwood. The knowledge of our existence is a huge responsibility."

Corona said, "I understand."

Every third person I saw was different, fantastic. Magickal. They were all just doing regular things, and it felt like Halloween because they were so casual.

Through a restaurant window, the silhouettes

of the patrons were such an odd mix of shapes and sizes. An unnaturally thin man helped a hunched old woman into a car then walked around and got behind the wheel. A woman with midnight-blue hair came charging out of a store and strode off down the sidewalk, her wings flapping in the breeze made by her forward momentum. She skirted to one side to avoid a man in a white suit with golden curls who was looking back over his shoulder at a canoodling couple and wasn't watching where he was going.

We passed the Town Hall. It was designed to mimic an ancient Viking longhouse, though it was painted in bright colors and well kept.

I itched to get out and explore the little shops that lined the town's center. A tavern/brewery, herbalists, cafés, bookstores, and souvenir shops. I could see how tourists would love Wyrdwood. The old-town area along Main Street looked as if it had been transferred straight from the Middle Ages, from somewhere in northern Britain. To say Wyrdwood was quaint didn't quite cover it. It was beautiful, elegant, artsy, and yet earthy at the same time. Some of the buildings even had moss roofs. There wasn't a single building with more than two stories, and flowers bloomed in hanging baskets on the streetlights.

It took us a few minutes to drive from one end of the town center to the other, following the path of the river inland, and as we emerged into a more modern neighborhood, I felt as if I'd lost something. I turned back, looking through the rear window of the car, to watch the beautiful little town fade into the distance, and that was when I saw him. It was just a glimpse.

Colin.

He was standing at the end of a cobblestone alley, talking to someone. His curly red hair stood out against the mottled stone of the building behind him. A moment later, he was obscured by a truck behind us. I craned my neck to see him again, and when the view returned, he was gone.

"I just saw Colin," I said on a thick breath. As soon as the words left my mouth, I began to doubt my own eyes.

"Are you sure?" Corona asked, turning so she could look back.

"I think so." Or maybe I just wanted to see him so badly that I'd misinterpreted reality. It wouldn't have been the first time.

CHAPTER 3

We pulled into a gravel parking lot, a clearing surrounded by evergreens on three sides. The fourth side was open with a view that took my breath away. We were maybe a mile from shore, but up in the hills overlooking the shoreline. Wyrdwood spread out below us, lights golden and warm in the dark. The ocean was a mysterious void beyond.

The air was like nothing I'd ever breathed. It was food. It nourished me. It smelled so fresh with a mingling of pine, cedar, and sea. I couldn't stop breathing it deep into my lungs with purposeful inhalations.

The Lost Lambs compound was a series of houses rambling up a hillside, windows glowing. There was no rhyme or reason to their design that I could figure, but they followed the landscape willy-nilly like a stream flowing down the rise. They were part of the wilderness, part of the land, nestled in the forest's darkness.

Jake said, "Welcome to Lost Lambs. Please consider yourselves at home." He looked at Corona and me in turn, smiling.

Corona snuggled up on my arm, her entire body vibrating with excitement. She was grinning from ear to ear.

Rio said, "I'll see you all at dinner. I'm going to lie down for a while." She headed straight up the hillside stairs.

A man came down the path, nodded politely to Rio as they passed, then crossed to greet Jake. They clasped hands. I found myself staring again. This man had to be seven feet tall. He had a rough face, perhaps having spent too much time in the sun or wind, and his body was bent slightly, off-kilter, as if he were slouching to avoid hitting his head on the clouds. He was at least sixty years old, maybe older. It was hard to tell because certain elements of him looked as old as the trees we'd passed along the way. He was wearing a long, black coat—one of those oiled ones that the rain rolls off. It was stained and worn at the hem. On his feet were mariner's boots, black rubber with a yellow band at the top. He wore them with his pants legs tucked inside. On his head, he wore a brimmed hat that he'd pulled down over the tops of his ears.

The man saw me looking at him, and he smiled but only with half his mouth. The other half remained low and dead, and I saw then that he had a puckered scar on that cheek.

Jake announced, "Allow me to introduce you to Mr. Jorgenson." Jake pronounced it as if it began with a Y instead of a J. It wasn't until much later that I'd learn how to spell it properly. Jake continued, "He's been here at the haven from the beginning. You might say he's a fixture."

Corona said, "More like a landmark," looking

up several feet to his face.

Mr. Jorgenson laughed without hesitation.

Jake said, "Mr. Jorgenson is the CEO of Lost Lambs."

"I thought you were CEO," said Corona.

Jake tsked. "I'm not good with the business side of things. I'm better in the field. I'd be lost without Jorgi."

Mr. Jorgenson saluted us with two fingers.

I went to the back of the van with every intention of dragging out our luggage.

Jake said, "Don't worry about that, Viv. Booker's on his way. He'll get your luggage to your room."

My room. I had a room. The thought made me yearn to be alone, somewhere quiet with a book and a soft blanket draped over me. I was curious about my room. I'd expected something institutional, but the haven seemed different.

With the setting of the sun, the air had taken on a chilly edge. I wrapped my arms around myself and turned in place, studying my surroundings. It was nothing like Malum, nothing like Illinois.

"You must be cold," Mr. Jorgenson said. "Let's go inside." His eyes were of two different colors. One was blue, and the other—the one on the scarred side—was a surprising shade of purple.

When he caught me staring, I blurted, "Your eyes are so pretty." Immediately, I was embarrassed, kicking myself for saying something so stupid.

But Mr. Jorgenson winked at me with the working side of his face—the blue eye—and smiled there, too. "Thank you kindly, Miss. Go on now. You don't want to be left behind. The haven is where you belong."

Jake stepped up close to Mr. Jorgenson and spoke in *sotto voce to the other man, "Meet me in my study in ten. Ayu and Booker can get everyone settled in. We need to figure out what to do."*

Mr. Jorgenson nodded with a solemn expression. "Yes, we do," he said. "Before someone else gets killed."

I didn't think I was meant to overhear, so I pretended I hadn't. Nevertheless, I was troubled. Someone had been killed? Here? Who? I thought of the hag, and my blood pressure rose. Was it all happening again? Still?

I fell in behind the others, fighting the urge to look back at Jake and Mr. Jorgenson. We climbed a set of stairs made of wooden beams set into the ridge. The first house, the closest, loomed over us. Its lights lit up the windows, welcoming. A hand-carved sign by the stairs pointed at the front entrance with the words "Holly House."

◇

The house was like any house, the first time you arrive in it—new and intriguing. The interior was beautiful. We entered into a big room—rustic and made for comfort—with a high ceiling supported by wood beams. A large stone fireplace on the far wall served as the centerpiece, with seating facing it. None of the furniture matched, but that made it all the more interesting.

I was nervous, and so was Corona. She was sticking to me like a baby possum, her fingers wrapped around my upper arm. She said, "Whoa," and I knew what she meant.

My mom was unperturbed, following us without expression or reaction—as expected. At least, she couldn't walk into traffic.

A woman deeper in the house shouted, "They're here!" and then, "Carrie! Jamal! Booker! Come meet the new arrivals!" Her voice could have carried through a hurricane. She appeared in a doorway at the back of the living room, and she shouted over her shoulder, "Hustle it up!" She had an accent I couldn't identify, and she looked like the Tahitian women in Gauguin's paintings, except older and wearing modern clothes. Her hair was blacker than any I'd ever seen, cut short and sticking up in the back like a duck's tail. Her apron had a dusting of flour on it, and she was wiping her hands on a dish towel.

Jake said, "Prepare yourselves. Here comes Ayu." He laughed as if he'd amused himself.

The woman came straight to Corona and me. Before I knew what was happening, she had hugged me and moved on to hug Corona, then Mom. "Welcome, welcome."

She asked, "Are you hungry? Would you like

something to drink?" She jutted her chin over her shoulder and shouted, "Booker!" Then she looked back at us with a welcoming smile. "I made blackberry scones, and we have tea or coffee. Do you girls like coffee? Of course, you do." Again, over her shoulder, she yelled, "Booker!"

Backing away from us, she said, "Come sit down. I'll bring you a little nosh. Jake, they can sit in here for tea."

Jake nodded sagely. "Yes, Ayu. Thank you."

Ayu turned and disappeared the way she had come.

Jake said, "You can close your mouth again, Viv." He was amused.

Corona said, "I love her. Can we keep her, Viv? Huh? Can we?" That broke through some of my shock, and I smiled.

"You'll have to ask Jake," I said.

"For as long as you're here, you'll have her," said Jake, chuckling. "C'mon. We'd better do what she says. It's not smart to disobey Mother Nature." He gestured toward the collection of mismatched armchairs by the fireplace. We followed him, and Corona sat in a high-backed rocking chair made of pine and began to rock. Mom and I shared an overstuffed loveseat, while Jake stood nearby, glancing at his watch.

A teenager with Amerind features and black hair held in braids on either side of his head entered the room and came toward us. He was wearing a flannel shirt—red and black plaid—and blue jeans.

Jake said, "Booker, this is Corona, Viviane, and

Gisèle."

Booker shook Corona's hand. When he reached out to me, his hand swallowed mine, it was so big and the fingers so long.

He said, "Nice to meet you." When he leaned toward Gisèle, she didn't even look at him, so he backed away. "The others are coming," he said with a renewed smile. "I'll go get your luggage for you."

"Thank you," I said.

Corona echoed me. "Thank you."

His only response was a nod, then he was gone.

Another man and a woman came into the living room from the back. The man was thick-bodied and muscular with a chaotic afro. His eyes shone with warmth, and he was grinning. "More victims!"

Jake said, "You have to keep an eye on Jamal. He's a practical joker."

Jamal shrugged and snorted. "There's nothing practical about it." He was younger than me, though not by much.

"And this," Jake said, "is Carrie."

The woman, much more subdued than Jamal, said, "Hello." She sat on the arm of a couch and waved at us from there. She was tall and thin, and the black pants and shirt she wore made her seem fragile. Her hair was so long it hung all the way to her rump, golden blond. She pulled it around to the front and began combing her fingers through it. The movements seemed cat-like.

Carrie lined her eyes like Audrey Hepburn, just

on the top lid and thicker at the outer edges. It was pretty. I liked the dark red on her lips, too, how it contrasted with the natural canvas of her pale skin. She might have been the most beautiful woman I'd ever seen in person and made me painfully aware of how plain I was, especially after a day of airports and hours spent in the van.

Carrie asked, "Have you told them yet?"

Jake frowned at her. "We just walked in the door. Let's give them a chance to relax."

Carrie's shrug relayed an insouciance that was almost disrespectful. I found myself starting to dislike her. I assumed she was referring to the killing Jake and Mr. Jorgenson had been talking about, and a part of me wished he had told us.

At that moment, Ayu came back carrying a large tray that she set on the coffee table. On it were two white thermal coffee pots, mugs, and a plate piled high with home-baked scones. Ayu said, "I made hot chocolate and coffee. Who wants chocolate?"

Corona raised her hand and said, "Me and Gisèle love hot chocolate."

Jake said, "I'll leave them in your care, Ayu. I need to speak with Mr. Jorgenson."

"I'll see their bellies warmed then take them to their rooms," Ayu replied. "We'll have dinner promptly at eight. Don't you two get carried away. We won't wait for you."

Jake wasn't listening. His mind had already shifted to his meeting. I watched him until he'd disappeared out the far door, wishing I could eavesdrop on their conversation. I hated that my arrival at the haven had already been spoiled by a single overheard whisper. I needed to know what they'd been talking about. *Who was dead? And why?*

A heavy hand came to rest on my shoulder, warm through my shirt, and I looked up into Ayu's dark brown eyes. They were smiling, welcoming. She didn't say anything, just handed me a mug of coffee and gave my shoulder a little squeeze. Then, she moved on, serving the others. I spooned sugar into my coffee, hoping for a little extra comfort, and took one of the warm scones.

I hadn't had coffee since before the accident. I calculated it had been twelve weeks. Three whole months. The accident seemed so far away already, almost like it had happened to someone else. So much had changed since then. I thought of Mrs. Dufour and Polly, murdered by the hag that had been stalking me. It had been my first supernatural monster—and I hoped my last. According to Corona, it had sensed my magickal blood, and that was why it targeted me. At least I'd managed to kill it and to keep my sanity intact.

The past few months felt so surreal in hindsight. The world was truly a surprising place, and I'd found my way into a group of people who said they were like me. For the first time since my car went into that lake, I was feeling hopeful about the future.

◇◇◇

CHAPTER 4

D inner had been a quiet affair, with everyone I'd met so far gathered around a well-used wooden table draped with an antique white tablecloth. The dining room had pine-paneled walls, a worn wood floor, and several mismatched buffet tables that looked like they'd belonged to someone's grandmother. We were all so exhausted we could barely make conversation. Jake was lost in his own thoughts, and he and Mr. Jorgenson stayed only long enough to appease Ayu, then they returned to wherever they cloistered.

I used my Mom as an excuse to leave early, saying I needed to get her settled in. It wasn't a lie. I knew she was used to being in bed by nine, and already the time zone change was making her fall asleep at the table.

Carrie led us to our rooms in the second building, known as Cedar House. My bedroom was on the second floor, on the corner. Mom's room was next door to mine, and Corona was just down the hall. Cedar House was just bedrooms, bathrooms, and a tiny lounge and kitchen. After Carrie dropped us off, she entered the room on the other side of mine.

Corona helped me get Mom dressed and in bed. We forewent our usual hair-brushing, both of us too tired for it, and I retired to my own room.

I was delighted to discover that our bedrooms had private baths. I took a long, luxurious shower, alone. No stalls. No shared mirrors or sinks. No strange smells. It was heaven, and I was so grateful.

Dressed in my robe, towel-drying my hair, I stood at one of my windows. If I looked one way, I saw the roof of Holly House, and if I looked the other, the lights of Wyrdwood through a gap in the trees, a mosaic of houses filled with life. The moon must have been high because it cast a shimmer across the ocean far below. I turned to look across the metal roof of Holly House. Smoke curled up from the chimney.

I caught a flicker of light out of the corner of my eye and turned. At first, he was nothing more than a flapping shadow, but it was one I'd seen before. I recognized Nathan squatting on the corner of the Holly House roof—my fiancé's brother, the man who had stalked and tried to kill me when I helped Colin escape him.

The skin at the back of my neck hunched, and my heart leapt into my throat. I knew beyond a shadow of a doubt he was looking right back at me. I jumped aside, pressing myself against the wall beside the window, but then anger boiled over inside me. I'd had enough. I rushed back, opened the blinds, and lifted the window. I opened my mouth to shout a challenge, but Nathan was gone. I hung out the window and searched all around, but he was nowhere in sight.

Nathan wasn't a normal human, a fact I understood better having come to Wyrdwood than I had when I was at the Malum Center. Nathan, like my fiancé, was magickal. Colin could fly, too. Where his wings were a luminescent black alive with color, Nathan's were hard black, like the void.

Nathan was gone, like he'd never been there at all. *Did I imagine him? It wasn't out of the question. I rubbed my hand over my face. I was exhausted. I was still traumatized from when he'd tried to strangle me, and I'd stuck a pin in his eye.*

No. I knew what I'd seen. As I closed the window, I wondered if he'd lost the eye. I debated going to Jake right then and there but decided not to incite drama on my first night at the haven.

I was on my way to the bathroom when a tap on the window startled me. I jerked around, expecting to see Nathan.

It wasn't Nathan. It was Colin. My Colin, hovering in mid-air, his wings vibrating to keep him afloat. Where the night would have swallowed Nathan like its child, Colin's wings stood out against the velvet sky, and his red hair rebelled against the darkness.

I ran back to the window.

◇◇◇

CHAPTER 5

The moment the window was open, I latched onto the lapels of Colin's coat and dragged him inside.

His wings disappeared and he half-stumbled in against me, laughing as he clutched me to keep from falling. "Hey!" he said. "What's your grandfather going to say?"

"He'll whup your ass," I replied, my lips already seeking his jaw. We were off-balance. I felt his arm go around me as he tried to maintain control of our descent to the bed. We landed with a bounce, and he pulled me tight against him.

We lay there there embracing, not even kissing, for the longest time. I was too overcome with relief and love to want anything else.

"You okay, Collie?" I asked.

"Aye, Lassie," he replied. "You?" Using our old nicknames for one another, he sounded like the Colin I'd fallen in love with. The no-meds Colin.

"Aye."

And then, his lips found mine, and my head spun.

My body fit so perfectly to his. I was overcome with the aroma of him, the feel of his weight on me, and the touch of his hands on my face, my neck, and in my hair.

Near his ear, I whispered, "We do have to be quiet."

He just nodded in response then tugged my robe open. For the longest few seconds, he reared back, eyes flowing over my exposed nakedness with as much friction as a touch. He removed his own clothes with urgency. I watched, panting through parted lips that felt swollen and alive from his kisses. His body had changed, become harder, stronger. His belly was gone, replaced with ripples of muscle. His skin was light, covered with freckles that danced up his arms and over his chest. A line of red hair trailed from his belly-button down to his mound and served as a backdrop for his erect manhood.

My body was on fire for him, fueled by the fear of losing him forever. I wanted to blend his molecules with my own, and I couldn't get enough of his skin against mine. I wrapped my legs around him and pulled his lips to my throat. He groaned, and I felt the vibration of it against my neck. His hand swept around to my breast, and at the same time his mouth traveled down to it. He kissed it and rubbed his face against my skin. His tongue flicked out at my nipple, then he sucked it in with greed. My belly and below became an inferno, and my legs spread of their own accord.

"Colin," I breathed. He slid across my thigh, and I felt just how much he wanted *me too—rod hard and slick, hot. He rubbed it across my pleasure center, and I exploded with fireworks.*

When he entered me, we merged—our bodies and our atoms, our breaths, our emotions—our souls.

The climax happened quickly. We were both so primed, there was no long, drawn-out lovemaking session. We held on tightly as our bodies released. It took everything I was not to cry out. I believed it was the same for him.

Tears rose to fill my eyes, spilling from behind my eyelids onto my cheeks and his shoulder.

"Shhhh," he whispered. "It's okay, Viv. We're okay. I'm here. I love you."

I couldn't speak, so I just clung harder to him.

After a few moments, Colin rolled off me and pulled me flush against him. I rested my head on his shoulder, and he pressed his lips into my hair. I had so much to tell him and so many questions, but for that moment, I just wanted to bask in his presence, in his warmth, and in this rare intimacy that we seemed doomed to experience only occasionally.

Then, it hit me. I pushed up on one elbow, alarm clanging bells in my head. I looked at him and said, "I think Nathan's here. I thought I saw him right before you got here."

"I know," Colin said. "I saw him too. It's okay. I waited for him to leave before I came down."

"You're sure?"

"Positive."

I glanced over my shoulder at the open window shades. I couldn't leave them like that, so I crawled off the bed.

Colin protested, but he let me go, and I drew the shades. Colin turned back the bedding and crawled into it. He held them open for me when I returned.

"There," I said, crawling in against him.

He got me settled with my head on his shoulder, drawing the blankets up to my neck.

I said, "Don't you fall asleep."

"Not on your life." He pressed his lips to my forehead.

I had so many questions but didn't know where to start the asking.

Fortunately, Colin did. "Do you like it here?" he asked.

I had to think about that for a moment. Finally, I replied, "I think so. It's too soon to tell. We just got here today. It's all really weird and new."

"Wyrdwood."

I nodded. "All these magickal beings..."

"Shocking, right?"

"A little," I said, though my mind answered, *A lot*.

"You'll get used to it," Colin said, nuzzling his stubbly chin against my shoulder.

"So you knew about Wyrdwood."

"I did. But not until I got my memory back. I used to live here."

That surprised me, and yet it made sense. I asked, "How do they stay so well hidden from the world? Why didn't I know about them before?"

Lazily, Colin rubbed his fingertips against my scalp. It felt amazing. He said, "Long story short, the veil has been in place for many centuries. One theory is that, as society advanced and embraced science, people began to fear what they couldn't explain. I think it started with the Romans. They invaded magickal villages and massacred everyone, took the non-magickal humans as *citizens—a.k.a. slaves— and brainwashed them with a new religion. Some of our ancestors tried to fight, but they never won.*"

Colin moved his fingertips against the small of my back. "As time passed and it became obvious the magickal races couldn't survive a head-on conflict with the my-way-or-no-way world, they learned to hide. Wyrdwood is here because some very powerful, godlike beings moved a whole village to the new world and covered it with a veil."

"The old town," Viv said.

"Yes. As long as they're in Wyrdwood, the town's magic protects them. It's complex, and those godlike beings I mentioned are still here, maintaining the veil."

"Not everyone is in Wyrdwood, though. Why don't we hear reports of them being seen?" I knew the answer as soon as the question was out of my mouth and spoke it. "They get locked up and treated like they're crazy."

Colin nodded solemnly. "Or killed. Those who can't hide their true nature were slaughtered long ago."

"How do they hide it?"

"It's ancient magic, kind of like the coloring of a chameleon. We don't have to think about it, we just do it. Survival instinct, I guess you could call it. Only those with the Sight can see through it."

We were silent for a moment, as I thought about that. Then, I blurted, "Jake says I have magickal blood, and that's why I can see... what do I call them?"

"As a collective, we call ourselves 'kin.' Individually, we're known as wielders, because we wield magick. You *must have magickal blood, or you'd be blind to them. That's probably what attracted me to you when we first me."* He touched the tip of my nose with his index finger.

"And here I thought it was my boobs."

"Nope, definitely not your boobs. Though I've grown to like them a little."

I breathed a silent laugh and nuzzled his collarbone. "Wielders," I said. "But I don't have horns or hooves or pointy ears or wings."

Colin chuckled softly. "Not all do. Some look very human. Some are part human. Maybe even mostly human. It's genetics. You're a product of your ancestors. Abram is as human as they come, so you've got human blood in you."

"And my mom?"

"You should ask her, next time she surfaces. She definitely has some magickal blood, but it could go back generations. Since you don't know who your father is, your magick could have come from him."

I vowed to talk to Mom about our ancestry before it was too late.

Colin said, "Our population has become a melting pot of cheeses."

"Gross," I said, and we laughed.

"I like a good fondue," Colin teased, giving me a squeeze.

I said, "Chocolate fondue, maybe."

We snuggled in silence for a few minutes, then I asked, "Are you sure you're okay?" He didn't answer immediately, and I raised my face to look at his. "Colin?"

"I'm okay," he said, putting a smile on his face and looking down his nose to meet my gaze. "This isn't how I wanted things to turn out, but I'm alive. *You're alive.*"

"Barely," I said with a touch of snark.

Nathan had come after us. He'd been ready to kill me to get Colin to go back home with him. I still didn't fully understand why that was so important, but my friend Ajani had died defending us. Bella—my grandmother—had also put her life on the line. At the end, Nathan had had me in his clutches and was using me as leverage.

Colin just left me with him. Nathan was pissed and ready to kill me. He had his hands around my neck. I used one of my straight pins, pushed it into his eye. Thank goodness, it was enough to get him to go. But he'd found me again, and it occurred to me that maybe getting Colin wasn't Nathan's first priority. *Had he lost that eye? I had no idea, but if he had, revenge was undoubtedly high on his To-Do list.*

"Tell me why Nathan was after you," I said, voice low.

"It's complicated," he replied. "Family history."

I rubbed my cheek against him. "Please."

"I'll try." He squeezed me, then said, "My father and I don't get along. We don't agree on much of anything. He's old-school, you know? Out of touch with modern Reality."

I said, "I know the type. But what did you do to piss him off?"

"I disappeared." Colin sucked in a sharp breath. "He was...training—for lack of a better word—me to be a general in his army, so to speak. I had no choice. My step-mother knew how unhappy I was, and so she sent me to find Doc Bella."

"And the amnesia?"

"Doc Bella induced it to keep me hidden. If not for that, my father and Nathan could have tracked me far too easily—through my heart strings."

"Oh." It was all starting to make sense. "Nathan found you after I hypnotized you."

"Yes. You broke the spell Bella had put on me, and my memories started returning. That's why I had to leave."

"I'm sorry," I said.

"Whatever for?"

"I thought I was helping you."

Colin hugged me to him. "You didn't know, and

neither did I. It all turned out okay."

"I don't think it's over yet."

"No, I suppose not," he said with a dark under-
tone. "My father is relentless."

"Does he still want to kill you?"

"Who knows," Colin replied. "If he had the
chance, he'd drag me back to Gehenna in a heartbeat,
punish me at best, and execute me at worst. In his
mind, I'm a traitor to him and to our people."

"It's downright medieval," I commented and
felt Colin nod in reply.

We lay there for a while, each lost in our own
thoughts. I remembered my search for him, the fight
to escape from Nathan, and the battle that resulted in
my friend Ajani's death. "I found you," I said with a
little smile.

"Yes, you did." He kissed my head. "I was very
proud of you for that."

"Too bad Nathan had to spoil it and try to kill
me."

"I can't believe I almost lost you." He rocked his
body, arms tight around me. Voice thick with emotion, he said, "I'm sorry I left you with him. I thought
he would chase me."

I hadn't intended to guilt him, but I also hadn't
been aware of the seed of resentment I carried deep
inside. "No, it's okay," I replied, rubbing his back. "I
get it. I love you." I said the words, and I did love him
with all my heart, but I didn't get it—not really. All I
knew was I didn't want to spoil our reunion. I retreat-

ed into the smell of him, the feel of his skin against mine, the warmth of our shared bed.

◇

I woke in the early hours of the morning, when the sun still hadn't fully crested the horizon. The bed wasn't my bed, and the room was completely different from my room at Malum Center. It took me a second or two to remember where I was. I sat up. The light outside hadn't fully bloomed yet, although the birds were singing to encourage it along.

Colin was gone. He'd stayed as long as he could, but eventually had to go—for his own safety. He'd woken me just before dawn. We'd shared a tearful good-bye, then he'd leapt from the window and flown up into the sky. I watched until he disappeared in a swirl of early-morning fog.

I got up, showered, and dressed. I spent some time unpacking and writing in my journal, to save the details of the memory for posterity, then my stomach growled.

On my way downstairs, I peeked in at Gisèle. She was still in bed, covered to her chin by blankets. I let her sleep.

The place was so quiet, and I was glad to explore by myself. As I descended the stairs, I paused at the landing windows to orient myself. Each building of the Lost Lambs haven sat at a different level on the rise, and the natural staircase we'd climbed the night before connected them all. In the light of day, their piecemeal exteriors resembled log cabins or had redwood siding or gray stone. It gave the whole a patchwork feel, like a woodsy antique quilt. Their windows were large, and the farthest one had a tower with a widow's perch at the top. I was eager to explore them all.

I thought of Colin. I'd promised Jake I wouldn't go running off after him, but then I'd seen him in town, and he'd found me. Even though I had no idea where he was staying, *he'd found me.*

My step lightened as I headed for Holly House. To get there, I had to go out onto the brick patio. A covered walkway—what Carrie had called a "trellised colonnade"—stretched between the two buildings, so you didn't have to dodge between raindrops. It connected the first floor of Cedar House with the second floor of Holly House.

All the buildings nestled relatively close together, with rough terrain all around. The patio at the back of Cedar House was wide and lived-in, on the ground level of Cedar House but even with the second story of Holly House. Japanese maples grew in circles left open in the brick. A small stream had been directed into a waterfall on one side, the water flowing down the hill and happily gurgling as it tumbled over carefully placed river rocks. Someone had attached a basketball hoop to the wall, though playing on brick couldn't have been optimal.

The third building was Hemlock House, offset

and higher up the hill. It appeared to have three stories instead of two, and it was the one with the tower. If there were others beyond that one, then I couldn't see them from where I was.

The dawn light was chilled and groggy. Fog rolled on air currents, dampening the cries of distant sea birds, and a fine mist settled on my skin. My stomach complained again, and I yearned for breakfast. The night before, Jake had told me I could take whatever I wanted from the kitchen. He'd insisted I make myself at home, though it didn't feel like home—yet. I crossed the trellised colonnade and entered Holly through the back door.

The moment I was inside, I heard the clank of pans and dishes. I'd entered onto a landing over the stairs that descended into the kitchen. I almost turned around and left, not wanting company, but my rumbling stomach scolded me for my introversion.

The Holly House kitchen was the biggest, most beautiful one I'd ever seen—navy blue and chrome, white and clean. It actually gleamed. I had expected to find Ayu there, but it turned out to be Jake and Corona. He was stirring a pan on the stove, and Corona sat on a stool at the u-shaped counter at his back. Their heads turned to me as I entered, and they smiled.

"Viviane! You're awake!" Corona blew me a kiss, and I returned one to her.

"Good morning," Jake said.

"Good morning." I smiled too because it *was a*

good morning. I was feeling better than I had in a long time.

I moved to peer into Jake's pan. "What's cookin'?"

Corona said, "Good lookin'."

Jake laughed. "Scrambled eggs and bacon. Want some?" He looked like he just got out of bed, still scraggly, wearing a plaid flannel robe over sweats. It was his best look. "The only way I know how to make eggs is scrambled. Sorry."

"That's how I prefer them," I told him. The eggs smelled so good—like butter and bacon grease. "Thank you. I guess you know Ayu's system?"

Jake chuckled. "Ah, you've got her pegged. Yes, I know it well enough to keep her from yelling at me." He nodded his head in the direction of the coffee pot. "The brew is strong this morning. Help yourself."

I made a beeline for it, saying, "Patients couldn't have caffeine at the Center." Another wave of happiness washed over me as I took a mug and the aroma of fresh coffee hit me.

Jake said, "You're in an entirely different environment now, Viviane. All the rules have changed, but in a good way."

"How so?" I asked.

"This isn't a hospital or long-term care facility for the mentally ill. We've already established that neither of you actually need that kind of treatment."

"So what are the new rules?"

"Well," Jake replied thoughtfully. "We're going

to wean you both off your medications, for one."

Corona gasped. "Really?"

"Really. If you need them, we'll bring the levels back up, but I want to find out who you are without them first."

I took my coffee to the counter and pulled out a stool beside Corona. "What else?" I asked.

"I'd like to start working with you and Corona to develop your abilities."

"Yeah!" Corona threw both hands in the air in celebration.

I slid my mug out of her reach and asked, "What do you mean?"

He lifted both eyebrows, "Your magick?"

The words, 'I don't have magick,' rose to my mouth, but didn't make it past my teeth. I knew I had a little, but acknowledging it aloud triggered my hide-and-lie instinct. I was well-practiced in the art of hiding the fact that I was stalking the moon. It was a tough habit to break.

With Jake and Corona, I didn't need to hide, and as that dawned on me, truly dawned, I felt a surge of tears in my eyes. My world had changed beyond recognition, and as far as I could tell, it was for the better.

I asked, "What more there is to develop?"

Jake pulled plates down from a cabinet. "That's what I'd like to find out."

Corona bounced on her stool. "I'm in!"

"Excellent," said Jake. "We'll start this afternoon. Viviane?"

"This afternoon?"

"It's nothing to be afraid of. It'll be fun."

"Can I just watch Corona do it first?"

Jake smiled over his shoulder at me. "Sure. No pressure."

"You know what I'd like to do?" Corona asked. "I'd like to go down to Wyrdwood this morning. See the ocean again. Can I?"

"You're free to go wherever you want, whenever you want. We don't lock doors here."

Worry hit me. I asked, "What about my mom? Aren't you afraid she'll wander off?"

"Gisèle is the least of our worries."

"Who's the most of your worries?"

"You are." Jake didn't look at me as he said it but focused his gaze on the pan.

"Me? Why?"

"Because I know you want to go look for Colin Aubrey."

His answer surprised me, though it shouldn't have. The thought had crossed my mind. The one thing that had kept me from begging him to take me with him the night before had been my mom. I couldn't leave her, and he understood that. Jake didn't know I'd already found Colin, and I wasn't ready to enlighten him. I said nothing.

Jake took a moment to scoop eggs and bacon onto three plates.

While he did that, Corona caught my eye and

wiped her index finger around her mouth. I didn't understand, until I mimicked her gesture and felt the stubble burn there from kissing Colin. She lifted her eyebrows, questioning, and I replied with a shake of my head. It was not the time. I hid my face behind my coffee mug.

As Jake carried our plates to us, he said, "If your plan is to search for him, it's a dangerous one." He set the plates on the tiled counter, leaned on his elbows, and looked me in the face. I held my mug under my nose and breathed in the rising steam.

He said, "You have free will. You can go wherever you want. But." He paused to sprinkle salt and pepper on his eggs. "But," he continued, "just because you're in Wyrdwood doesn't mean you're safe. Your situation with Aubrey is dangerous. His family—they're serious business." His eyes came up to meet mine. "Please, Viviane. Promise me you won't run off alone. In exchange, I promise I'll help you find him. Okay?"

I wasn't keen on making any kind of promise. I hesitated long enough that Jake said, "There are dangers out there you know nothing about. Whatever's happening with Aubrey is bigger than either of us knows. If you're not here in the haven, in Wyrdwood, you're not protected. Promise me."

I believed in promises, and I believed in keeping them. I'd heard how promises plus magick could be a larger-than-life binding. But if I didn't promise, he might have locked me up or put a babysitter on me. I couldn't have that. I said, "What do you know about his family?"

He took his mug back to the coffee pot, stalling. When he came back, he leaned toward me and put his hands on mine. They were big and warm. Looking me right in the eyes—the serious psychiatrist move— he said, "All I know is they almost killed you once, and we may never learn why. Secrets in the magickal world can be...elusive. What I can promise is that I will do everything I can to keep you safe and help you find the truth. Finding people is what we do here at the haven. If we can find him and bring him here for sanctuary, then we will. I can't promise we'll succeed. I can only promise that I'm on your side, and I'll do my best."

It felt like a trick, like he was twisting grown-up words to get me to shut up and go play with my toys. But his eyes held kindness, and I was old enough to know he couldn't promise something he wasn't sure he could deliver. He was like me. He believed in promises and in keeping them. I knew because—unlike Richard, my ex-psychiatrist—he was being careful about what he promised.

I was careful too. I said, "Okay. I promise I won't go running off alone to look for him."

Jake squeezed my hands and said, "I'm really glad you agreed to come here."

I was touched. "Me too." I felt the truth in those words and smiled.

"You're safe here, you know?"

I wanted to believe him, but I remembered Nathan perched on the rooftop. I kept it to myself. I wanted no more drama added to that lovely morning. Bad news could wait, so I just said, "Thank you."

CHAPTER 6

Corona and I were just finishing up the breakfast dishes, when the doorbell rang. Jake took
a last swig of his coffee and put the mug in the
sink. "You two stay here," he said. "Thanks for doing
the dishes."

"Thanks for cooking," I said, taking his mug and
washing it.

Corona watched him go, her curiosity blooming. "I wonder who's here?"

"A delivery, maybe?" I suggested, tipping the
mug into the drainer.

Corona headed for the door, waving me after
her. "Let's go see."

I followed her down the hall to the door that
opened on the living room where we'd first arrived.
The front entrance was directly across from us, and
we watched as Jake stepped back to allow a woman
in.

She was ethereal with white hair caught up in
a blue butterfly clip and falling in straggles around
her face. She wore white linen palazzo pants and a
Boho blouse with colorful embroidered flowers on a
white background. The loose sleeves were gathered at
the wrists with elastic. I couldn't tell how old she was.
She seemed ageless.

Corona sucked in an audible breath, and I stopped breathing altogether. I knew in my gut that the woman was magickal.

A man followed her in, tall and dark skinned, wearing jeans, a smooth-fitting crew-neck shirt in red, and a jean jacket. His hair was a short, twisted afro. Removing his sunglasses, he glanced around the room as he shut the door behind him and stood with his back to it.

Jake said, "Amalia. Welcome. What brings you to our humble abode?"

The woman, Amalia, faced Jake, but didn't immediately say anything. It was spooky watching her size him up. When she spoke, her voice carried weight. "Mr. Lamb, you've had a death in your home."

Jake looked taken aback. "I beg your pardon."

Amalia turned her gaze on me.

I felt a tension in my head, a vibration spreading outward from my chest.

She said, "Kypris Rose has been silenced."

That broke me from my trance. "What?" She had used the name of the main character in my mother's stories.

Corona let out a squeak.

Amalia just continued watching me. She said, "Take me to her."

Jake was the first to move. "This way," he said and started toward us.

With a flick of her fingers, Amalia directed her companion to stay where he was. He crossed his arms and leaned against the door.

"Mom?" I said, then I too was moving. Ahead of the others, I hurtled down the hall, then up the stairs. My footfalls pounded on the covered walkway as I ran.

"Viviane! Wait!" Jake called, left well behind. Amalia wasn't in a hurry, and courtesy forced him to match her pace.

Corona, however, was right on my heels.

When we got to Mom's room, I burst in. She was still lying in bed, as she had been when I'd checked earlier. I approached, and my heart lurched as realization dawned on me. She wasn't breathing.

"Mom?"

Of all the things I'd endured, this was perhaps the most surreal. I threw the covers back and shook her, calling out to her. She was dead. She'd been gone for some time. Her skin was cold. Her eyes open, staring, and bloodshot. All I could do was plead.

A strong hand came to rest on my shoulder, pushing me to the side. The woman was there. Amalia. She leaned past me and touched two fingers to my mother's third eye. In a voice that must have only been audible to me, she spoke a string of words I didn't understand. They sounded Scandinavian and full of magick.

"What are you doing?" I asked, anxiety in my tone.

Amalia turned and met my gaze. She was naturally as pale as a ghost, with light freckles all over her face and chest. Her eyebrows and eyelashes were albino-white like her hair, and her eyes, a vibrant green, had an *I Dream of Jeannie slant—even without makeup. High cheekbones, an angled jaw, and a turned-up nose combined to give her an ethereal beauty. She repeated herself in the foreign language, then added,* "I said a blessing for her soul and for the body she leaves behind. She must travel on—for now—without this body."

Jake moved to the other side of the bed and leaned over my mom, examining her. He put two fingers under her chin and lifted it. Her neck was ringed with marks, as if something had been held tightly around it. "Hilda," Jake said, voice hard. "Call the sheriff's department."

From behind me, Hilda asked, "What should I tell them?"

"Tell them we've had a murder."

My head reeled with questions. I touched Amalia's arm as she began to withdraw and asked, "How did you know?" I received no answer.

Amalia brushed my hand off—not ungently—and pulled away.

In some corner of my mind, I heard Corona sobbing at the end of the bed.

I was aware of movement all around me, but my mind had focused on one thought: *Was killing Mom Nathan's idea of revenge?*

"Nathan was here," I said aloud to no one in particular.

Jake's face was a mask of angles and sharp lines, taut with emotion—anger, perhaps. He asked, "When?"

"Last night." My own voice was soft, melting around the edges. "I saw him outside, on the roof."

"You're sure it was him?"

I nodded.

"I'll be back," Jake said and stormed toward the door. "Move," he commanded to those in the door-way as he left the room. Amalia followed at her own pace, leaving me alone with Mom, a sobbing Corona, and Rio who had stepped up to clasp my shoulder.

I gently replaced the covers over my mom. A chill had settled into me, and I didn't want her to be cold too.

"You're shivering," Rio said. She took the throw blanket off the armchair and wrapped it around me. She offered Corona one, but Corona shrugged it off and started bumbling around the room, searching through my mother's things. Her movements grew more urgent.

"They're gone, Viviane," Corona cried. "They were here last night. Right here. I unpacked them myself."

"Unpacked what?" My head was starting to hurt from the tension of keeping tears under control. They streamed down my face, but I refused to sob. My grief would not wrack me that way—not like it had with Colin—not ever again.

Corona stood in the middle of the room, turning

in place, both hands on her head. "Her stories, Vivi-ane. They stole her stories."

I wiped my eyes harshly and swept the room with my gaze.

"What stories?" Rio asked.

Corona was distraught. "Her stories!" she shouted.

I answered, "Mom wrote stories in notebooks. Her journals. She'd been doing it for years." I began digging through Mom's belongings. The notebooks were gone. Mom was gone. Forever.

CHAPTER 7

Corona and I tore the room apart, looking for the notebooks. We pulled out Mom's suitcase and went through it, opened drawers, tossed aside chair cushions, and even felt under the mattress.

Rio said, "They must be here somewhere." She had moved to the corner to stay out of the way.

"Hey, hey!" a woman shouted, stepping into the room. "Stop whatever the hell it is you're doing. Have you lost your minds?"

That halted us.

Hilda stood in the doorway, hands on her hips, eyes sharp. "You're destroying evidence."

I gasped. That hadn't even occurred to me.

Rio moved out of the corner and joined Hilda at the door, "I guess I should step out. I've touched too much already." She slid past Hilda. "I'll be right out here in the hall if you need me."

Corona's pause didn't last, and she went back to searching. I approached her and put my arms around her. "Stop, honey. If they're here, we'll find them later. Hilda's right. We need to stop."

Hilda said, "You need to get out of this room until the sheriff can look it over."

I looked around at the mess we'd made, and my

stomach sank. I gritted my teeth and felt a deep frown pull at the corners of my mouth. Tears welled again, and my nose tingled unpleasantly. Corona leaned against me and sobbed, her body convulsing with grief. I guided her to the armchair, sat, and pulled her down on my lap.

"Not a suggestion," Hilda said. "I'm sorry for your loss, but get the hell out."

"I'm not leaving my Mom alone," I said. "Not yet." My tone brooked no argument, and Hilda was smart enough not to try.

She stood silent, just watching us, arms crossed on her chest. She looked miserable and angry, her jaw twitching with tension. Finally, she said, "Just don't touch anything. Don't mess with the blankets. The killer may have left evidence." She turned and left us alone.

I buried my face in Corona's hair and just held her. I whispered, "Were we safer at Malum?"

Corona shifted to wrap her arms around me too, and she hugged me tightly. Her sobs were abating.

I asked, "Is this my fault? For bringing her here?"

Corona shook her head against me. "No," she squeaked. "It's mine. I should-a been here, watching out. I thought...I thought..." She moaned and said, "I wish Simon was here."

Our invisible guardian, Simon, would have warned us if he'd been there. He'd have been paying attention.

"Oh god, Mom." I remembered checking in on her, seeing her lying in the bed, on her back, blankets up to her chin. Had she awoken during the attack? Had she been aware? I desperately hoped not.

"Who would do this?" I wondered aloud.

We sat in silence for a long while.

Corona stirred against me and asked, "Who could get in?"

"Anyone magickal, I guess," I replied. "Colin was here. He flew up to my window. Nathan could have."

"You have to tell Jake about Colin."

"He was with me. He didn't do it. Corona, you can't tell Jake he was here. Promise me you won't."

Rio stuck her head around the doorjamb and said, "No. You can't tell Jake. Either of you. It will make Colin a suspect."

"Were you out there listening to us?" Corona blurted.

"I'm watching over you." Rio leaned on one hand against the doorjamb.

I asked, "You know Colin?"

"Jake told me he was your fiancé. I know he'd never do anything to hurt you."

"No."

Rio twisted to look over her shoulder and down the hall, making sure no one was coming. "You and I know that, but Jake doesn't. He's protective of you, and that includes protecting you from Colin. The police won't understand either."

I hugged Corona. "Are you hearing that, honey? We can't tell. Swear you won't."

Corona sniffled loudly, then said, "I swear."

Rio pointed her palms toward Corona and me and moved them in circles to indicate us both. "I know," she said, "that your hearts are breaking. Grief and separation are the harshest torture. I lost my son too, and every day, I die all over again when I wake up and he's not there." She stepped forward and produced a silk-wrapped deck of cards from the patch pocket of her maroon-velvet blazer. She shuffled them with practiced ease. "Let's see what the cards say."

A certain gravitas controlled the rhythm of her movements as she dealt three tarot cards onto the bed. They appeared to be old, hand-painted with symbols and designs framing a central figure. On the first, a woman wearing a crown was surrounded by three animals. I couldn't see details from where I was, but they looked like a wolf, a fawn, and a peacock. The second had a dark figure at its heart, a man in a wind-whipped cape, his face hidden behind a stag skull. At his feet stood a white dog with red ears, and in his hand, he wielded a glowing sword. The last card depicted a full moon with a naked woman silhouetted against it, arms raised as if in supplication or worship.

Rio studied each one as it was revealed, then said, "Your mother did not suffer. That is the question foremost in your heart, isn't it, Viviane?"

Surprised, all I could do was nod.

Rio ran a finger over the second card. "Everyone has their own path, their own fate, and your mother is following hers. Her story is not finished." She picked up the third card and examined it closely before saying, "She wanted nothing more than your happiness, Viviane. You owe it to her to protect your love with Colin. The two of you belong together, and your mother knew that."

Actually, my mother had warned me to stay away from Colin. She knew being around him would put me in danger, and it had. But had she known we belonged together? I loved the idea; I just didn't believe it was true.

Footsteps sounded on the stairwell, and distant male voices approached.

Jamal stuck his head into the room, looked around, and whistled low. "They're on their way up," he said. "Jake sent me ahead to warn you that the sheriff is human. Don't mention anything magickal to him. M'kay?"

I just stared back at him.

Rio stepped up to me and took hold of my chin with authority. "Viviane," she said, "that means no mentioning flying lovers or murderers. You got it? Corona? This is very important."

I nodded.

"I got it," Corona said weakly.

Rio walked back to the bed and carefully gathered up the tarot cards, wrapped them in their cloth, and tucked them back in her pocket. She moved with grace, eyes downcast, hands clasped together over her stomach. I couldn't decide if she seemed more like a mother superior, a butler, or a queen. In any case, she was hiding something.

Jake stepped into view out in the hall, but didn't come in. He indicated the doorway to the people with him.

The sheriff was a large white man preceded by his belly and a scowl accentuated by a down-drooping mustache. His uniform was engineered to counter the softness of his body, perfectly pressed with official-looking badges and buttons.

The sheriff's gaze moved over Corona and me then scanned to the bed. He reached down and pulled back the blanket just enough to see Mom's neck. "Ayup," he said, looking back over his shoulder and exchanging a nod with Jake. "Doctor Beaulieu, you better take a look."

A relatively short man with pale skin and dark, oily hair, Dr. Beaulieu stepped in from the hall. He had a face with great character, not so much wrinkled as indented at the cheeks and across his forehead.

A black woman in her fifties or early sixties appeared in the doorway behind him. She was taller than Dr. Beaulieu and dressed in a pair of dark gray coveralls with a white logo on the breast pocket. Expression appropriately serious, she leaned to say something to Jake that I couldn't hear.

Behind her, a man of Polynesian ancestry leaned against the wall. He crossed his thick arms, dropped his chin, and closed his eyes. He had skin the color of a tropical tan, and his hair hadn't been cut or combed for a bit too long. His Hawaiian shirt, a sober black-and-white tableau of flowers and palm fronds, was untucked over wear-softened jeans.

The sheriff let the blanket fall back onto my mother and turned toward Corona and me. "You must be the daughter," he said.

"I am." I had to clear my throat as it came out croaky.

He removed his hat and held it in both hands in front of him. His head was large, and his short hair was receding on either side of a widow's peak. He said, "I'm Sheriff Metzger. I'm sorry for your loss."

What was I supposed to say to that? Thank you? I just stared at him.

"Ma'am," he continued. "I'm going to need to ask you some questions. It's about to get crowded in here. Mr. Nareau is gonna give this room a good once-over to see if he can find any clues about what happened. Dr. Beaulieu and Mrs. Fandelli will take care of your mother for now. They need to do their jobs. Jake? Can we move these ladies somewhere more comfortable?" His tone maintained a surprising gentleness, considering the looming bulk of him.

I didn't immediately move for a couple of reasons, the least of which was that my legs had gone to sleep under Corona's weight, and the biggest of which was that I wasn't sure how to begin moving again. It was as if my mind-body connection had been cut.

The sheriff called over his shoulder, "Jake? I think the young lady needs some help."

Jake came in and lifted Corona off me, into his arms like a baby. "I got her," he told me. "Go on downstairs. Ayu's waiting for you in the conference room with a cup of coffee."

My hands shook as I put them on the chair's arms to push up to my feet. When I wobbled a bit, the sheriff stepped forward.

"Whoa there," he said. "Nice and easy. Just stand there for a minute, get yourself orientated."

Doctor Beaulieu and the woman with him had flanked the bed. He was wearing latex gloves, which struck me as strange—cold and scientific. The woman, Mrs. Fandelli, wasn't. Her dark-skinned hand brushed a strand of my mom's hair back from her face.

"Who?" I asked, unable to form a full sentence.

"That's Doctor Beaulieu. He's the Wyrdwood coroner. The lady is Mrs. Fandelli, of the Fandelli Funeral Parlor. They're gonna transport your mother to the doctor's offices."

"You mean the morgue." My voice sounded icy even to me. The fact of Mom's death was developing a frozen rock of ice in my chest. With others involved—a coroner, a funeral director, a sheriff—I couldn't deny it was happening.

"Yes, ma'am. They'll take excellent care of her."

◇

Ayu met us at the bottom of the stairs and directed us into the conference room. We sat at one end of the rectangular table, across from each other. Ayu set a cup of coffee in front of me.

The sheriff opened a little notebook and wrote in it. His questions were vague, mostly about what time I saw Mom last, when she went to bed, when I got up, and so on. I rebuilt the previous twenty-four hours for him, leaving out the part about Colin visiting. I did tell him I saw Nathan lurking around outside—I just didn't tell him he'd been on the roof.

Jake joined us. "Corona's sleeping, sheriff. You can talk to her tomorrow. She's very upset."

The sheriff nodded, eyes narrowing.

Jake sat down with us. "It looks like the back door was forced with a crowbar."

"That so?" said the sheriff. "Explains how they got in."

"Yup," said Jake.

"You find anything missing?"

I said, "My mom's notebooks are missing. They had her stories in them."

"Notebooks?" echoed the sheriff. "Anything else? Jewelry? Anything of *value?*"

Jake said, "She had a necklace and some rings. They're gone."

I frowned. "They are?"

Jake gave me a pointed look. "Yes, I'm afraid so."

The tears returned, filling my eyes, then overflowing onto my cheeks. I lowered my gaze to the table and let them run unhindered.

"Seems it was a robbery gone bad," the sheriff said, sounding confident. "Your mother must've awokened and caught the perpetrator in the act."

"It was Nathan," I insisted. "I saw him, watching the house." My voice was rising in pitch as an unexpected hysteria cracked the surface of my demeanor. "He hates me. He did it to get back at me. At *me*."

Jake rose abruptly and came around the table, putting his body between me and the sheriff. He lay his hand flat in front of his mouth and blew across his palm. A puff of dust hit me in the face, and my nose was filled with the aroma of vanilla. I recognized the smell even as my consciousness was leaving me, my spine collapsing.

◇

Some time later, I didn't know how long, I awoke in a dark room. I lay there for several minutes, wishing the fog in my mind would recede. Memories rushed in, and the grief welled up again, this time without restraint. I rolled and pressed my face into my pillow as sobs shook through my body.

My mother, the woman who'd been denied me for most of my life, was dead. It seemed so unfair. I'd thought she was dead until I turned eighteen when a letter from a lawyer had alerted me to her residence at a local mental health facility. Ever since then, I'd been doing everything in my power to stay close to her, to fight the disease that kept her locked in her own mind. Those rare occasions when she'd surfaced and connected with me had given me hope we'd one day break her out of her darkness and be together as mother and daughter for the rest of our lives—like normal people. She'd see me get married, be a grandmother to my children, and teach me everything she knew about our family. My hopes and dreams for a lifelong relationship with her had just been cut off without mercy or warning.

I cried until my face hurt.

A part of me blamed my grandfather despite the fact that he'd had good reasons for what he did. He'd locked her in Malum Residential Living Center and had let me believe she was dead. To lose her a second time—and so soon—was beyond cruel. Coming to Wyrdwood was supposed to have been our chance. A new start.

"Grandpa," I said, sudden realization making me blink back my tears. I was going to have to tell him. There would be a funeral. Abruptly, the dark shade of days-to-come lowered over me, and I fought back a wave of terror. I didn't want any of it.

A voice inside my head said, *No, sugarkin. I'm not your grandfather. I recognized Nathan's pretentious drawl.*

I let out a small scream and scrambled to sit up and put my back against the headboard.

Nathan was in my room. He was nothing more than a shadow seated in the armchair, but I recognized his outline.

My pillow was the only thing I had to defend myself and I threw it at the voice, even as I tried to get out of the bed.

The man oofed and said aloud, "Ew, it's wet. Are you seriously going to fend me off with a damp pillow? Do relax. Just because you're my future sister-in-law doesn't mean you can splatter me with your tears. It's unseemly." I heard movement and the pillow landed back on the bed. "Turn the lamp on, if it makes you feel better."

"Help! Someone help me!" I was tangled in the blankets and struggling only seemed to make it worse.

"And do stop yelling, please. You're giving my headache a headache. No one can hear you. I put a cone of silence on the room. We're all alone."

I tried to relax, though my breathing was sharp and quick. "Are you going to kill me too?"

Nathan laughed. "The idea has appealed to me at various times in the past, but no. You've grown on me. Rather like kudzu, if I'm being honest. Besides, I don't have time to dally. One of your lackeys is even now thinking about coming to check on you, and I can't be here when that happens."

I reached over to the lamp and turned it on. The light blazed, hitting my eyes with violence.

Nathan groaned.

When my vision cleared, I could see him. He was sitting in the armchair, one ankle crossed over the opposite knee, bright orange sock visible where his pant leg rode up. He wore a black, double-breasted suit with a dark purple vest under it and a patterned scarf around his neck. What I assumed was his coat was draped over the arm of the chair.

The last time I'd been this near to him, I'd stuck a straight pin in his eye. He wasn't wearing either a patch or a bandage, so I hadn't blinded him after all.

"Yeah," he said wryly in answer to my thoughts. "It healed. No hard feelings. I deserved it."

"Did you kill my mother?" I asked, still trying to free my legs from the blankets. They were tangled up tight, and it occurred to me they tightened the more I struggled. I stopped.

"You're shivering," he said aloud, blinking to adjust his eyes to the light. "Apologies for the open window, but I need to maintain an escape route. I'm sure you understand."

"DID YOU KILL MY MOTHER?" I shouted.

"Right to business then. Okay." Nathan folded his hands on his stomach. "That's why I'm here. I knew you'd blame me, and I'm trying hard not to be offended that I was right. You wound me, sugarkin."

My mouth tensed as if I'd tasted something disgusting. "I saw you."

"Yes, your highness, you did. And I saw you. And I saw her. But believe me, if I'd done it, there'd have been a lot more blood." Nathan moved at a snail's pace, lifting his coat from the chair's arm and unfolding it. He uncrossed his legs. "And I came to give you a warning. I wouldn't bother except my brother loves you. It seems the two of you may be fated to live happily ever after. Whatever." He stood and strolled casually toward the window, slinging on his coat.

"A warning?" I asked.

"You're not as safe here as you think. Your mother has suffered an ending far worse than death, and that same ending could befall you as well."

"What are you talking about? What happened to Mom?"

Nathan raised a finger and tsked. "If I told you, it'd take all the challenge out of it for you. Just remember—neither did I touch nor in any way extinguish your mother's corpus."

Without another word, he stepped to the window and climbed onto the sill. Before my eyes, he changed, his body going smoky, then coalescing into the form of a large black bird.

"Wait!" I cried, a thousand questions all clamoring in my head. First and foremost, why hadn't he asked anything about Colin? And second, did I believe him?

With a flap of his wings and a leap, he launched himself outward and flew away.

The blankets relaxed, and I was able to toss them aside. I ran to the window and searched the sky for him. A near-to-full moon cast its cold light, and I saw him as a shrinking silhouette against it, heading for the seashore.

"Shit," I breathed out. "I do believe him."

◇◇◇

CHAPTER 8

I wasn't able to get back to sleep after Nathan's visit, so I opened my laptop and started writing down everything I could remember about Mom's stories. My prose was nowhere near as floral as hers, and I wasn't sure I was getting all the details right, but I was afraid I'd forget them if I waited. Ever since I'd found her, when I was eighteen, she'd been writing them. Occasionally, she'd read them to me from her notebooks. Most of the stories were fantastic in nature—romantic. It wasn't until recently I realized they might be about her own life in more than a metaphorical sense.

She'd talked about my father and how he'd seduced her, then disappeared. She'd said his name was "Chance," which always seemed like a made-up name to me. Chance had changed her life when he impregnated her with me. It was a sweet and charming way to describe getting knocked up by a rogue. More recently, however, her stories had made connections in my growing awareness of the magickal world. She'd talked about a place called Apfallon and said my father was from there.

In her stories, Mom had always emphasized the need to stay hidden. She'd placed wards on my grandfather's house so I'd be safe as he raised me there.

She'd had similar wards on her room at Malum. I hadn't understood the danger. I still didn't know why she'd been killed, but I did realize that she'd been safe—until I brought her to Wyrdwood.

I cried some more, but ultimately washed my face and gave in to my yearning for coffee. The sun was coming up. On the way to the kitchen, I ran into Jake. He looked as if he hadn't slept at all, and seeing him reminded me that he'd knocked me out with his vanilla powder magick.

"Hey," he said. "I was just coming to check on you."

"To make sure you hadn't overdosed me?" I put as much vitriol into my voice as I could manage.

"What?" Jake asked, surprised I knew.

I gave him a pointed look. "Never do that to me again. Never."

Jake raised both hands in surrender. "Calm down. I had my reasons."

The back of my teeth bit down hard, and my eyes narrowed. "Don't tell me to calm down," I said, quiet and threatening. "I am calm. And I'm not a child. I'm not your patient. You do not anesthetize me without my explicit permission. You understand?"

"Okay," Jake said. "Okay. You're right. I overstepped. I did it because you were getting hysterical, and I couldn't risk you saying the wrong thing in front of the sheriff."

"Hysterical." I repeated. I hated that word. No one ever seemed to use it except when referring to women. Nevertheless, I couldn't deny it. I had been upset. I asked, "Is that why you lied about the break-in? I presume the back door wasn't actually forced?"

Jake nodded. "The sheriff is a Normal. He can't know about magickal beings."

I snorted a little, derision nesting where anger had abandoned me. "I bet that makes him effective."

"How are you feeling?" Jake asked, ignoring my comment.

I knew from my bathroom mirror's honesty that I looked about how I felt—face swollen, red, and sore from crying. I didn't bother to answer the question but tried to push past him. He let me go, then fell into step behind me.

He said, "I'm increasing security. We'll have guards around until we find out who...did it. Even on the roof."

"Great," I replied, thinking about Nathan. Then Colin. I wished I had a way to warn him. "Will they have guns?"

"No, they'll have magick. It's more accurate than a gun."

"What about wards?" I asked, pausing to turn an ear toward him, though I didn't look at him.

"You know about wards?"

I nodded. "Mom had wards on her room at Malum. And on Abram's house. We were always safe there."

Jake sighed. "Yes. The haven has wards, and Wyrdwood has one massive ward over the entire area. She should have been safe here." He touched my arm, and I shied away without thinking about it until it was done. I didn't want him or anyone touching me. I felt prickly, my skin hyper-irritable.

I continued toward the kitchen, the smell of coffee rising up the stairs to greet me.

Jake followed and took a seat at the counter, watching me. At least, I presumed he was watching me. I could feel his attention on my back, but I had no desire to look at him. I wasn't ready to see whatever emotions he had—or didn't have—on his face. The psychiatrist neutrality, the evaluation, the concern. I didn't need it, and truth be told, it would only make me feel worse.

Once I had my coffee and was leaning against the counter with it cradled in both hands, Jake said, "I called Abram for you and let him know what happened. He's on a plane now and will be here later this afternoon."

I was relieved I didn't have to have that conversation with Abram. "Was he okay?"

"About as you'd expect," Jake replied. "He was upset, but his first thought was to ask about you."

"He's like that." The sentiment rang true to me. I wouldn't have always thought it. Abram and I had been at odds for years. I'd been convinced that he cared only for one person: himself. But then I discovered the sacrifices he'd made to keep me, and my mother, safe. One of those sacrifices had been a good relationship with me. He'd let me blame him in order to keep his promise to my mom.

Jake asked, "Do you want to go with me to pick him up at the airport?"

"Yes, please."

"I booked him on an air taxi from Portland to Newport, so we don't have to drive all that way again."

"Thank you." I was finding it hard to stay mad at Jake.

◇

When Corona didn't show up for breakfast, I went in search of her and found her seated on the wooden stairs at the front of Holly House, wrapped in a blanket. Her back hunched as if she carried the weight of the world.

I sat down beside her.

"Hey," I said.

She glanced over at me. Her eyes were red and puffy from crying.

I asked, "You get any sleep last night?"

She shook her head. "Too much to think about," she said.

I scooted closer and put my arm around her. "Nathan came to see me last night," I told her.

"Why?"

"He wanted to tell me he wasn't responsible... for Mom."

Corona took that in, then asked, "Do you believe him?"

I chewed my bottom lip for a moment, then replied, "Yes, I think I do."

"Fuck," Corona breathed. "Then who?"

"I don't know."

We sat in silence for several long minutes, watching clouds roll in from the horizon, and I thought about Mom. Eventually, I said, "I need your help remembering Mom's stories."

"Okay," Corona said, then added, "What do you think happens when you die?"

"I have no idea," I said. "What do you think happens?"

After a long, deep breath, Corona said, "I used to believe nothing happened. You were just gone. Poof. Void. But now, that feels like a Flat-Earther kind of theory."

"You don't believe that anymore?"

Corona lifted one hand in a dramatic gesture, as if delivering a monologue on stage. "'Energy can neither be created nor destroyed. It can only be changed.'" She slumped back down and asked, "Do you know who said that?"

"No," I replied.

"Every—fucking—body. It's one of the basic laws of existence—the law of conservation of energy." She shifted toward me. "Think about it. There's nothing in the universe—except maybe the universe itself—that has a true beginning. Everything comes from something else, and so it follows that everything becomes something else."

I said, "I'm not sure I understand."

"Name one thing that comes from nothing. You can't. People talk about there being a source to a river, but that doesn't mean the river springs into existence from nothing. The source draws from underwater streams, rain, and melting ice. And at the mouth of the river, it doesn't just fall off the edge of the earth and cease to exist. It flows into the bay, into the ocean, where it evaporates and becomes clouds, then rain, then part of that river again. Or a different river."

I was catching on. "I see what you mean," I said.

"We are like that too. Gisèle is a raindrop. Her body will return to the earth, become nourishment."

I felt tears stinging my nose.

Corona continued, "But there's more. Gisèle and Polly—all of us—we have a force in us, something more powerful than just flesh and blood, chemistry and electrical impulses."

"Our souls?"

"That's what some people call them. I don't have a better word. But that part of us, all that we learn, all that we experience, and who we become, doesn't just disappear. You know how I know that?"

I said quietly, "No."

She said, "Children. They come into the world with personalities already in place. Child prodigies are born with existing aptitudes. Mozart began writing music at five years old. Kim Ung Yong was working for NASA before he even hit puberty. Little

Jimmie Leininger remembered his past life as a fighter pilot. It's all there—a body of anecdotal evidence that's hard to ignore or discount."

Corona's tears flowed down her face. "Shit, Viviane. There's *magick in the world, and now that I know that, it's changed how I see everything." She spoke with such fatigue in her voice that I pulled her in tighter against me. I suspected she'd been up all night thinking about death.*

She continued, "The idea that we're nothing more than mechanical systems—well, that's even more unbelievable to me now than the idea that we become angels living on clouds. Do you see what I mean?"

I rested my cheek against her head. "I do."

"They're not gone," she said. "Gisèle and Polly. They're just changing, and we're lucky to have known them for a while."

I felt her shivering and rubbed her upper arm. "Very lucky," I said.

"So why...why does it hurt so bad?" Corona broke into open sobs. She buried her face in her hands, and together, we cried and rocked.

The wind gusted, moving the treetops in a swaying dance.

After a while, Corona inhaled deeply and lifted her tear-streaked face into the air. She said, "I smell the ocean."

◇

Jake and I left around noon to go to the airport but didn't get far. Jake wanted to stop for lunch at a diner along Ocean View Road.

"I try to eat here within a few days whenever I come back to Wyrdwood," he told me. "It's kind of a tradition. You'll love this place. Great food."

The diner had a blue interior with wood paneling halfway up the wall, wood tables, and home-made booths, also made of wood. It was busy, with bright-eyed patrons—mostly human as far as I could tell—of all shapes and races. They were chatting and clinking their silverware against their china. I was immediately charmed, and then the aroma of the food hit me. "I love it already," I said, trying hard not to stare at the more obviously magickal beings.

Jake guided me to a booth at the back, and we settled in. The waitress, a pretty lady with a friendly smile, appeared instantly. She gave us menus, and we both ordered coffee.

As soon as she was gone, Jake lifted his chin to look down his nose at me and said, "I have a proposal for you."

I'd been watching a pair of teenagers at a nearby table. The boy was gorgeous, in that model kind of way, his face angelic and his ears pointed. The girl with him seemed plain in comparison until she smiled, and then I understood what he saw in her. Young love had hit them both where it counted.

They tentatively touched fingertips across the

table. It made me smile.

Jake's words pulled my eyes from them to him. "A proposal?" I asked, curious.

"Well, more a request, I suppose."

The waitress returned with our coffee, putting our conversation on hold while we ordered. I had forgotten to look at the menu, so I asked about the special. Chicken pot pie. "Yes, please."

Once she'd gone again, Jake said, "I have no idea how to ease into this, so I'll just spit it out." He opened two sugar packets and poured them into his coffee mug.

"I'm listening."

"Lost Lambs is an organization created to rescue magickal people from the mundane world. For the most part, the worst situation we've come up against is one like yours, where the wielder is unaware of their gifts and so they're vulnerable to abuse or worse."

I thought back to Richard Reuter, the psychiatrist who'd treated me for most of my life. He'd convinced me I was ill, medicated me, and eventually had me committed. I, it turns out, am sane. Of course, he'd also wanted to control me for the sake of the book he was writing.

Jake continued. "Lately, we've had something worse happening. Someone is killing magick wielders who live hidden out in Reality—normal society."

My mind immediately went back to my arrival at the haven and the conversation I overheard between Jake and Mr. Jorgenson. So much had happened since then. It felt like weeks had passed, but it had only been a few days. I leaned forward. "Go on."

Jake fidgeted with the empty sugar packet. "I don't understand *why it's happening, but I'm certain the killer is not a Normal. The murders are too unusual, often in locked rooms. Always without leaving evidence behind. Whoever's doing it is basically trying to eliminate magick wielders, and they're going for the most vulnerable ones.*"

"But," I said. "Is that what happened to Mom?"

Jake pressed his lips together and shook his head. "Maybe? The fact that this murder took place in Wyrdwood sets it apart. All the previous ones happened out in Reality. I'm struggling to figure out why she was targeted and whether it's the same killer. It's possible, I suppose, that she was already in their sights in Peoria, and they just didn't give up once we moved her. Or it could've been someone else entirely unrelated."

My mind went to the awful creature that had stalked me at Malum and killed several people there. I'd managed to destroy it, but I'd never understood why it was after me. My imaginary—a.k.a. invisible—friend Simon had said she was attracted to my energy, but maybe he'd been wrong.

"Oh my god, Jake," I said on a breath, "was Mom killed by a hag?" The image of a naked, gray-skinned old woman with long stringy hair sitting on Mom's chest while it strangled her almost made me sick to my stomach.

"No," said Jake, reaching across to put his hand over mine. "No. It was not a hag."

I stared at him, shaken, my breath coming in little tight puffs. "Promise?"

"I promise."

"But she was strangled, right? That's what they do."

"Yes, she was strangled." Jake looked down at the table-top, expression grim. "But not by a hag."

"How do you know?"

"There's no way a hag could have breached our walls. Our wards are very good at repelling beings of pure chaos."

"You mean evil?"

Jake looked at me from under his brows. "One form of evil."

"Are you saying Mom's killer *wasn't evil?*"

"I'm saying..." He chose his next words carefully. "I'm saying it's complicated."

I snorted in irritation.

Our food arrived, and it gave me a chance to calm down. Jake too went silent until the waitress had moved on. Then, he said, "Listen. Another lamb has come up on our radar, and I'd like you to come with me to get her."

"Oh, I don't know. When?"

"Soon. Your mother's funeral will take place as soon as possible, and your grandfather will fly back afterward. I figure we can travel the same day he does. I think you'd be a huge help."

"I don't see how."

Jake opened his mouth to reply, then lifted his gaze over my shoulder.

A woman said, "Well, if it isn't Jake Lamb. How's your lunch, young man? And who's this lovely child?"

I turned to see an elderly woman leaning on a cane. She had silver hair caught up in an elaborate up-do of braids with silver ribbons adding a touch of child-like sparkle to her hair.

Jake smiled at her. "This is Viviane Rose, our latest arrival at Lost Lambs. Viviane, this is Lenore Gliton. She's a long-time resident of Wyrdwood."

"Hi," I said. She had the most extraordinary eyes—a dark turquoise mingled with dirty-penny copper at the edges, far more youthful than I'd have expected in a woman of her advanced age—and her ears were those of a fairy or elf, just like those of the teenage boy in love, though hers drooped a bit at the tips.

"What a pleasure to meet you, my dear," she replied, offering me a frail hand to shake. "Would you mind if I join you? I hate to eat alone."

Jake was about to protest, but the words were out of my mouth before I knew they were coming, "Yes, please. Join us. The chicken pot pie is amazing."

"Aren't you sweet," Lenore said. She leaned on the back of a chair at a nearby table and asked, "Are you using this chair?" A man at the table got to his feet, said, "No, please," and proceeded to move it for her to the end of the booth. It was quite an undertaking, but finally she was seated there, in the aisle, at the head of our table.

Jake scratched his temple but said nothing.

"You two," said Lenore, "make a lovely couple."

Jake blinked.

"Oh," I said, shaking my head. "No, we're not a couple."

"Hm," Lenore replied with a knowing smile. "Why not?"

"I'm engaged to someone else."

"Oh!" Lenore sounded interested. "Tell me about him. What's his name? How did you meet?"

"His name is Colin. We met..." I hesitated, unsure of what I could tell this woman about Colin that didn't sound horrible. That I had met him while he was a patient at a mental hospital? That he'd had amnesia when we'd met, but now remembered he was a magick wielder who could fly? That he was on the run from his own family, who wanted to kill him? "...in Peoria," I finished.

Jake cleared his throat and changed the subject. "Have you been well, Lenore?"

The woman beamed at him, her cheeks plumping into rosy peaches. "Very well, thank you." Her eyes turned back to me, smile softening, and she said, "I was sorry to hear about your mother, Viviane. You have my condolences."

"How..."

Lenore waved a fragile hand and nodded to Jake. "Amalia," she said as if that explained everything. Jake nodded once as if in agreement that it did. Lenore continued, focus back on me. "I know your grandmother," she said. "Moira. I do hope she's well."

That threw me. Doc Bella's birthname was Moira. I had only recently learned that Bella was my grandmother when my grandfather gave me a picture of her. Grandpa thought she was dead, but I knew better. She'd been at Malum the whole time, caring for my mother, and faking my fiancé's death. I wasn't yet sure how I felt about her.

"She's..." I struggled to find the right word and settled on "gone." I hated lying for her, but if she wanted people to think she was dead, then it wasn't my place to out her.

"Oh, that is a shame. She was always such a delight." Lenore looked at Jake as if sharing a joke. "Her sense of humor could knock the socks off a cat."

I asked, "How did you know her?"

Lenore considered her answer before giving it. "We share a common ancestry. Did you know your grandmother was born right here in Wyrdwood? I remember her as a child. Such a beauty, and so tempestuous. I imagine she's still making trouble, wherever she is."

"What ancestry?" I asked, realizing my grandmother's ancestry was mine as well.

Lenore cocked her head as if listening to something no one else could hear. "Oh dear," she said. "I believe I've forgotten an appointment. Viviane, why don't you come visit me at my bookstore sometime soon? We can have tea, and I'll tell you all about your grandmother. And I want to hear more about this fiancé of yours. Bring him, if he'll come." She pushed back her chair at just the right moment. A woman who happened to be passing paused to help her up. They exchanged smiles, and then the woman went on her way.

"I...I'm afraid Colin isn't here in Wyrdwood," I lied.

"A long-distance relationship?" Lenore asked.

"You could say that."

Truth was that, in more ways than one, we'd been maintaining a long-distance relationship almost since we'd met. At first, the amnesia had created a gulf between us. Then, after an ill-conceived attempt at amateur hypnosis on my part, he'd started remembering. The more he remembered, the closer his family came to finding him. He didn't want to be found. So, he'd faked his own death to escape his horrible family. I could have—maybe should have—left well enough alone. In the end, he'd left me behind, or so I'd thought.

The fact that he was on the lam wasn't something I felt the need to disclose to Lenore.

She looked at me with sympathy, both hands on her cane to support herself. "I'm sorry, kiddo. It's so hard to build a life like that. I wish you luck."

"Thank you."

"It's been lovely spending time with you both," Lenore said. Her eyes fixed on Jake for a long moment.

Jake replied, "Same here."

"How is Rio?" Lenore asked Jake, the non-sequitur accompanied by a sly expression.

"Well."

"Yes, I imagine she would be," said Lenore, turning her gaze pointedly to me. "That woman knows nothing if not how to take care of her own interests." She began to move away from the table, and after a step or two, she called over her shoulder, "Do come visit me at the bookstore, Viviane. Jake can tell you where it is."

"I will." I waited until she was out of earshot, then asked, "She has a bookstore?"

"Yes, in Wyrdwood. It's called *Poetry, Prose, and Poe. It's a nice little shop.*"

Three Ps, I thought and was reminded of my time in the laundry. The comparison certainly wasn't fair to the bookstore.

◇◇◇

CHAPTER 9

Back in the car on the way to the airport, it hit me again, another cold wave of despair. I turned my face to the window. Before the current could pull me too far down, Jake brought up the subject of my going with him on his next mission, as he called it.

"Look," he said. "I don't mean to pressure you, especially not now when you're grieving, but I think it would do you good to come with me."

For short periods that day, I'd managed to put out of my mind that I was grieving. Why was everyone so intent on reminding me of it? "You should take Hilda. Or Booker. Or Carrie or Jamal. I just don't see why you'd want me to go."

"You'll be an asset," he said. "Besides, there's so much I want to show you and teach you. Have you given any thought to exploring your abilities a little?"

My inner alarms began to ring. I thought of my straight pin, but I wasn't carrying those anymore. "I'm good," I said, trying—and failing—to put a believable lilt on it.

"I get it," he said. "You've been hiding your magick all your life, from yourself as much as from others. But suppressing it isn't the way to go. You need to learn to control it. I can't even imagine what it's like to deny your true self for so many years."

Logically, it made sense, but I wasn't ready to embrace magick. It was still *other to me, neither part of who I was nor of who I wanted to be. Sure, I'd had an invisible friend for most of my life, but I'd only recently learned Simon was real. I was great at pretending I didn't hear someone no one else could hear. Really great at it. Practiced. That was the superpower I'd embraced—hiding, becoming a productive and normal member of society, even though I was far from it. Something told me Jake would never understand the survival instinct that developed over years of tamping down the Crazy, shackling it into submission to keep it out of the limelight.*

"You were never one of the lost ones?" I asked him.

"No. I was lucky in that respect. I grew up in Wyrdwood, protected and surrounded by magick."

"Then how'd you get started doing this?"

Jake kept his eyes on the road as he drove. "I went to college in Seattle, University of Washington. When I was there, I met someone who didn't realize who she was. She thought she was just a psychic, and she hid her true self from most people. She explained the things she saw as her mind putting metaphors on the world in order to understand the psychic input she was receiving. She was always trying to save everyone, seeing every magickal revelation as a call for help. So, she neglected her own safety and health."

"You explained what was happening to her?"

"I did." Jake's face went slack. "I wasn't gentle about it, and she wasn't ready."

"And?"

He looked over at me, eyes direct, penitent, daring me to judge him. "She killed herself."

"Oh my god. I'm so sorry."

Jake shrugged. "It was a long time ago, and it put me on the path to helping others like her—and hopefully doing it better."

"You saved me."

"I hope so." Jake glanced over at me. "So, will you come with me on this mission?"

"Let me think about it." Under previous circumstances, I could've refused because of my mother, wanting to stay near her. I no longer had that responsibility.

We pulled off the highway and into the airport. It was a tiny, two-runway affair, with small planes lining the road. A large hangar sat near a copse of trees, and a double-wide trailer had a sign that said, "Office."

Abram had already arrived and was taking his suitcase from the pilot. They shook hands and Abram turned toward the car, his eyes meeting mine. I waved. He looked older somehow, face more slack, eyes deeper. It hurt my heart, and tears made my vision swim.

The moment Jake stopped the car, I got out and half-ran to my grandfather. He opened his arms to me before I got there, and we hugged. I'd never felt more at home in my grandfather's arms than I did right then. The smell of him, the weight of him, the way he patted my back. I couldn't help but cry against his shoulder, and he made soft soothing noises.

After several minutes had passed, I began to pull away, but he didn't let me go entirely. He moved his hands to my shoulders and held me in place. He studied my face.

"You okay?" he asked. "Physically, I mean. You weren't hurt by whatever..."

I waved my hands to forestall his words. "I'm fine. It was only her."

Abram nodded. "Okay."

Jake stepped forward and offered his hand in greeting. Abram took it, and they shook.

"Jake Lamb," said Jake. "It's good to meet you in person."

"Abram Rose. But then, you know that."

Jake nodded. "I need to go in and take care of something in the office, but I'll be right back, and then we can get on our way. Do you need anything?"

My grandfather shook his head, then looked down at me. "Everything I need is right here."

I hugged him again for that.

Once Jake was gone, Abram pulled me off him again and looked me in the eyes. "Viviane, I want you to come home with me." I didn't know what to say, so I said nothing. He continued, "You'll be safe there. We know you're safe there. I couldn't bear for something to happen to you."

The thought of returning to live with my grandfather, among the corn and bean fields of Illinois, maybe even working in the Malum laundry facility again, filled me with anxiety. I could've rejected the idea with great confidence right then and there, but I chose the more diplomatic route instead. I deflected.

"Let's just get through Mom's funeral, and then we can talk about what comes after. Okay?"

Not only did I not want to go backward in my life, but I was keen to find out who killed my mother.

◇

Neither Abram nor I wanted a viewing for Mom. On the night Abram arrived, we went to say our goodbyes at the Fandelli Funeral Parlor. Mrs. Fandelli met us in the foyer. She carried herself with gentle dignity and smiled just enough—not too much—to make us feel welcome despite the seriousness of the visit. She informed us without emotion that the coroner had completed his investigation, and unless we wanted Gisèle embalmed, we could hold the interment the following day. So, that's what we did.

It was harder than I expected to watch her go into the ground, realizing with finality that I'd never see her again. Though I never got to know her, and we weren't what I'd call close—considering how distant she'd been the entire time I'd known her—I'd still grown to love her, and she'd loved me. Her death left me feeling like the bottom had dropped out of my world.

The Fandelli cemetery was old and new simul-
taneously. As we walked across the rough, but maintained, lawn to where my mother would be laid to
rest, we were surrounded by tombs, life-sized angels,
and elaborate headstones. It was an outdoor art mu-
seum honoring the dead, starting with the large, ornate iron gate that marked the entrance. Afterward,
I didn't remember the details of any of the stones or
sculptures, but I remembered the feeling of being
watched.

Everyone from the haven had come out and
were already standing around the grave when we arrived. Mrs. Fandelli was there with a stocky woman
and an equally hardy young man, both caucasian. All
three of them wore matching black suits and silver
armbands—the company uniform.

Corona stayed with Jake, tucked against his
side and wrapped in the circle of his arm. She kept
her eyes down.

Much to my surprise, Lenore had come, dressed
in a lace-collared pantsuit—midnight blue—that hung
loose on her frail bones. She had a woman with her
I didn't recognize—a black woman wearing a simple
ankle-length gray dress and antique-white sweater.
She carried a folding lawn chair and stayed glued to
Lenore's side.

Abram and I had opted not to provide chairs.
We'd wanted a simple event—one that wouldn't last
long. There was no minister, no one to spew plati-

tudes about a glorious afterlife or how pain ends at death.

Abram and I positioned ourselves at the head of the grave. The coffin rested on the lowering mechanism, an arrangement of white lilies on the lid.

I looked at everyone gathered and cleared my throat.

"I want to thank you all for coming," I said. "My mom was an extraordinary woman, and we'll miss her. She and I were separated when I was young, and it wasn't until much later that we came back together. I'll never forget the first time I saw her again."

My voice broke, and my grandfather slid his hand into mine. I cleared my throat again, eyes on the coffin, and continued, "You see, she spent most of her time in a catatonic state. Occasionally, she would surface. The first time this happened, she looked at me— really looked at me—and she said, 'You are beautiful.' It was the way she said it, with so much love. I heard her. I heard you, Mom. And you're beautiful too."

Tears swelled in my eyes, and my nose began to burn. I let out a sob and turned into my grandfather's arms. He held me, rubbing my back, and a thick silence spread through the cemetery disturbed only by the sound of the wind in the trees.

After some time had passed, Abram said simply, "Thank you all for coming." He guided me a few steps back and nodded to Mrs. Fandelli.

With my cheek against Abram's chest, I watched Mrs. Fandelli and her people come forward and prepare to lower the coffin. She removed the flowers, holding them while the others worked the mechanism. Once the coffin was all the way down, they retreated again. Mrs. Fandelli handed the flowers to the other woman, then came to stand beside a ceramic jar of dirt sitting by the grave. She offered it and asked, "Do you...?"

Grandpa nodded, but I shook my head. I released him.

Abram walked to the jar, reached in and took a handful of dirt. He held it and gazed into the hole. I saw his shoulders shake, but he made no sound as he threw in the dirt. When he turned away, Mrs. Fandelli was there to hand him a cloth to wipe his hands. He nodded his thanks.

I was very familiar with my grandfather's anger, with his laughter, and with his worry. But only one other time had I ever seen him so sad—the day I told him we had to leave him for Wyrdwood. It added a decade to his demeanor, deepening the lines on his face, the gravity of grief making his body sag.

Custom suggested Abram and I make ourselves available for condolences. He and I stood at the base of the path and offered a handshake to everyone who came by. It was all a blur to me. I nodded, thanked people—most of whom I'd never met—and remembered none of them.

Only Lenore Gliton managed to pull me out of my grief stupor. She reached a frail hand out to me and I took it. It felt like a featherless bird, so small and fragile. I held it gently, looking down at its veined and wrinkled skin. Lenore said, "Viviane, may I invite you and your grandfather to dinner tomorrow night in my home? I have some old photographs of your grandmother I think you would like to have."

I stared at her for a moment, uncomprehending. When the words sorted themselves in my brain, I wasn't sure what to tell her. I didn't think I'd want to go out. I opened my mouth to reply, but I wasn't even capable of that.

"I will send a car for you, to make it easier. Just an hour for dinner and memories. Seven o'clock? I don't stay up late anymore." She patted my arm, then turned away.

It felt like I was in a dream, watching Lenore hook her arm through her silent, green-eyed companion's. A memory I couldn't quite grasp tickled my mind leaving behind a lingering sense of déjà vu. It sent a shiver down my spine. She'd known my grandmother. I couldn't help but wonder about the photos.

I glanced over at Abram, but he was shaking another hand, eyes glazed.

When the last person had passed by and begun the walk up the hill to the road, I felt Abram breathe a sigh of relief and soften, as if he'd been tense the whole time. I reached out to him, supporting him— and letting him support me—as we made our way back toward the road.

A black car I hadn't seen before was parked there with the others. It had dark tinted windows and was running. I could just make out the silhouettes of people inside, moving, watching us. As we approached, it drove away. Later, I'd think about that car and wonder who was in it. At the time, however, I just wanted to get away from the cemetery.

Jake had provided several cars to transport everyone. In silence, we all piled back into them. Jake saw me seated and was ready to close my door for me when I heard a raven caw. It jolted me. Jake shut the door a breath later, and I searched through the window for the person I knew was there. I saw him, circling overhead. Nathan in bird form—or at least I thought it was him. In retrospect, it could have been a normal raven.

◇

The rest of that day and most of the next went by in a blur. Lenore rang early in the afternoon to confirm dinner, and my curiosity won out. I agreed to go.

Abram wasn't as enthused, but the promise of learning more about his wife's past was enough to get him there.

As promised, Lenore sent a car to pick us up. The driver was a young woman dressed all in navy blue, tailored pants and button-down shirt. She introduced herself as Cinnamon and held the car door for us.

Ayu had given us a loaf of banana bread to take

with us.

"Are you all packed for tomorrow?" I asked my grandfather.

"More or less," he replied, turning toward me. "Viv," he said. "Please. Come with me. Come home."

There it was. The question of the hour.

I'd given it some thought, though it hadn't been necessary. I knew exactly what I needed to do. "No, Grandpa. I can't."

"Why not? You don't belong here." He slid an arm along the back of the seat and put his other hand over mine. "You're not safe here."

I checked the rearview mirror, but Cinnamon had her eyes on the road and didn't seem to be listening. Nevertheless, I lowered my voice to a whisper. "I have too much to do here, Grandpa," I said, looking him square in the eyes. "I have to find out what happened to Mom. I owe her that much."

"You don't owe her anything. You need to take care of yourself."

I hung my head. "This place, this town, it's my life now. Things have changed. I wish I hadn't come here, but now that I'm here, there's no going back for me." I could see in his eyes that he didn't want to accept that.

He said, "Your life doesn't have to be crazy like your mother's. You can walk away from it. Live a normal life with me." He was almost pleading.

"I want nothing more than a normal life," I told him. "But I can't right now. There's too much going on. Soon. I'll come soon. I'm sorry."

"The charms on our house will protect you," he said, "like always."

I turned my hand over to clasp his, thinking before replying. I said, "You once told me I was safe because they didn't know the sound of my heart strings, but if they ever found me, I'd be in danger." My voice sounded grim to my own ears. "They found me, Grandpa, and now the only way I can be safe is if I learn to protect myself." I heard my truth and I almost added, 'I'm not a little girl anymore,' but I refrained, knowing it would sound petulant.

"Then I'll stay here with you," Abram said.

I had a mental image of Abram lying in Mom's bed, still as death, having been strangled.

"That won't work," I told him. "I'll come visit, and we can talk on the phone every day if you want. You have your own life. What about your friends? You don't know anyone here."

"I know you."

"I have a job to do here," I said. "I'll be traveling, and..."

"What?" Abram was surprised. "What job? Traveling where?"

I met Jake's gaze. "I'm going to help Jake and the others rescue people like me. People who maybe don't know what's happening to them. It's what I want, Grandpa." I hadn't realized I'd made a decision about that until it came out of my mouth. It felt right.

Abram sat back and studied me. His eyes told

me he knew he'd lost.

◇

Cinnamon pulled the town car into a short double driveway in front of a tiny gingerbread-style house. It was painted a mix of pastel colors and had decorative trim that gave it the look of a doll house. Only a single story, it couldn't have been very large inside. The lawn was landscaped with Japanese maples and rose bushes.

"This is it," said Cinnamon as she put the car in park.

Abram was already emerging from the back seat by the time Cinnamon got around to hold the door open for him. "Madam Gliton is waiting for you. Just ring the bell beside the door."

We followed the stone walkway to the front steps and climbed onto the porch. A set of windchimes tinkled in the breeze.

"After you," Abram said.

I pressed the doorbell and heard a *brrring inside. I stepped back.*

The inner door opened, and an elderly black woman came into view. Her hair was gray, a short-cropped afro caught in tiny nubs all over her head, and the emerald sparkle of her eyes belied the wrinkles and bowed spine of age. She gave the wood-framed screen door a push and said, "Come in, come in."

I pulled open the screen door, and we stepped into the entryway.

"I am Kushala," the woman said. "I am..."

"She is my partner," came another voice. Lenore came into view through an arched doorway. "Please come in. Welcome to our home."

Kushala took our jackets, and we followed Lenore into a cozy living room decorated all in shades of cherry, antique white, and evergreen. Thick Persian rugs covered the wood floor, and all the seating was overstuffed and antique. The centerpiece was a deep stone fireplace and its mantel covered with framed photographs. Above the fireplace, a painting created the illusion of looking into a fantasy landscape, rolling hills and a flying sailing ship. I paused to study it. In the background, a chateau gleamed in the sunlight, and in the foreground, fairies were having a lawn party.

"A gift from a dear old friend—a poet," said Lenore. "It was painted by Arthur Rackham. Have you heard of him?"

"No," I said. "He was very talented."

"He was a genius," Kushala interjected.

"What a lovely gift," I commented.

Lenore guided us to the dining area at one end of the kitchen. In all, it took us fewer than twenty steps to cover the distance. "It's so much easier," she said, "if we simply install ourselves where we're going to eat instead of having to move again after our aperitif. When you're our age, you have to plan such things."

A short, round man in an apron, loose pants, and plastic clogs—hot pink—was standing on a platform designed to raise him high enough to chop vegetables at the kitchen counter. As I studied him, his true self gradually revealed itself to me. He had a full mouth, bulbous nose, double chin, and whiskers that ringed his face. Calamitous eyebrows shaded his enormous eyes. His ears had tufts of hair growing from the pointed tips.

Lenore saw the direction of my gaze and said, "Allow me to introduce Monsieur Chim. He is our chef. He trained in Paris."

The man faced us and took a dramatic bow with a hand flourish.

"Thank you," I said, and he winked at me before going back to his task.

Kushala gently guided me forward with fingertips at my back, and I tore my gaze from Monsieur Chim. The four of us took our places around the table.

Lenore poured us each a glass of white wine over crème de cassis.

"Have you had a *Kir before?" Lenore asked.*

Abram and I looked at each other. "No," I replied. "What is it?"

"It's an aperitif—a French drink that prepares your body and mind to enjoy your meal. I think you will like it."

"Thank you," I said.

Lenore lifted her glass and said, "To Gisèle Rose. May she bloom again."

We followed her in the toast. "To Mom," I said. The Kir was sweet like berries but not too much. I did like it.

Lenore, it turned out, was a talker. She carried the conversation, relieving the pressure from Abram and me. "I know," she said, "that you want to hear about your grandmother—Moira. She and I were close."

It felt odd hearing Doc Bella referred to as "Moira" again. That would take some getting used to. My grandmother—Moira Rose a.k.a. Mirabella "Bella" Rosenblum—had changed her name at the same time she faked her own death—our family's go-to response to danger, it seemed.

I'd met Moira as Doc Bella, Colin's psychiatrist. It made sense that she'd taken a job there to watch over my mother—and me too, I supposed.

I said, "What I really want to know is why my mother was in hiding? Do you know?"

"Your grandfather never told you?"

Abram said, by way of explanation, "It was never the right time."

Lenore pressed her lips together, nodding. "Well, it's a long story and one best kept short if we intend to eat before midnight." She fiddled with her napkin as she spoke. "To put it in the simplest of terms, our family has enemies, and your mother fell victim to one of them. Your biological father. He seduced her and got her with child. If he had found you, he'd have claimed you as his property and taken you away. To keep this from happening, Gisèle took steps to hide you from him."

I searched Abram's face. "Grandpa?"

He nodded, confirming the truth of the story.

Lenore said, "I'm sorry to say, your father was an evil man." She laughed softly. "Another reason I have to be grateful to you, Abram. You protected our girl here for all those years."

Abram said nothing. He studied Lenore, and we all sat in our own thoughts for a minute.

Finally, Lenore said, "Here, let's look at this." She had set a scrapbook on the table before we arrived, and she moved it in front of me. "Open it."

The book was homemade, with a padded cover of blue silk embroidered with violets and multicolored roses. On the first page, a serious young woman stared out at me. She wore a calf-length baby-blue dress with a petticoat that flared the skirt. Her body was already blossoming with womanly curves. On her feet, beaded flats sparkled. Her dark auburn hair curled around her face, having undoubtedly been set in curlers, teased, and hair-sprayed into place. Her only make-up was a little pink on the lips.

My grandfather leaned over to see and gasped. "She's so young there," he said.

"Yes," said Lenore. "That was taken at her sweet sixteen birthday party."

The date in the white frame of the photo said 1956. I turned the page to find a series of black-and-white pictures tracking a baby through several years of development.

"What was she like?" I asked, browsing through the scrapbook. In the photos, my grandmother played tennis, laughed with friends, and sat tucked in a cushioned window seat reading a book.

"Gifted. That's the best word I know to describe her. She never met a problem she couldn't solve—that is, until she met you, Abram."

Abram looked up from his perusal of the photos in the book. "What's that mean?" he asked, sounding a little defensive.

Lenore folded her hands on the table, then said, "Moira had always been fascinated with Normal society and all its trappings. She chose to go away to college because she believed Normals had much to teach us. She believed she could bring that knowledge back to Wyrdwood and change things for the better. She always said she was going to bring Wyrdwood—kicking and screaming—into the twentieth century. But then she fell in love with you," Lenore explained. "It derailed all her plans, and she decided to stay in Peoria with you."

Abram asked, "How do you know all this?" He was staring at Lenore again.

Lenore replied, "We kept in touch for a while after she left. Then her letters just stopped." She lifted both hands in surrender. "I don't blame you. Moira brought her own troubles to your doorstep. Sadly, the only people who live a trouble-free life are dead. And Moira was happy for many years. For that, I'm grateful to you, Abram. And because of you, the world was blessed with Gisèle and Viviane."

"Madam," said Monsieur Chim from the kitchen doorway. "Dinner is ready whenever you are."

"Thank you," Lenore replied. "We are ready."

I closed the book reluctantly and got up to set it on a nearby bureau.

Monsieur Chim served a wine-marinated pot roast, red potatoes, caramelized carrots, and wilted mustard greens, all with an herb-rich sauce and a glass of Burgundy. We ate in silence aside from the praise we lavished on the meal.

When we'd finished the main course, Monsieur Chim followed it with a fresh salad of mixed greens and a homemade Dijon dressing. Dessert consisted of a flan with ruby red raspberries tumbling across it.

As I stuffed in the last bite, I felt completely sated.

Monsieur Chim cleared the dishes and brought out a tray holding four short-stemmed snifters and a bottle of Jägermeister.

"That was an amazing meal, Monsieur Chim," I told him. "I feel so spoiled."

Monsieur Chim dropped his chin to his chest in acknowledgment of the compliment.

Lenore said, "It is only right that you should be spoiled, dear, and now that you're living in Wyrdwood, it can happen more often. I insist that we make this a habit."

Abram cleared his throat in protest to my staying in Wyrdwood.

"I'd like that," I told her.

Lenore poured the after-dinner drinks, and we raised our glasses to Monsieur Chim, then sipped. The Jägermeister tasted of licorice, and I enjoyed it. Abram set his glass down and didn't touch it again.

Abruptly, Lenore asked, "How did she die, Abram?" We all knew she meant Moira.

I held my breath, waiting for Abram to answer. I assumed I was the only one at the table who knew she wasn't dead.

Abram said, "I never learned the details. She and Gisèle had gone into seclusion for the birth. Then one day, Giséle arrived, out of the blue, with her newborn—Viviane—in her arms. She told me Moira was gone. Any time I brought it up, she got very upset and refused to talk about it. I never did find out."

Quietly, I said, "You told me she died in childbirth."

Abram scanned my face, perhaps looking for a clue to my emotions. I smiled a little.

He said, "In a way, it was the truth. She died while you were being born. I'm sorry. It was as close to the truth as I could get."

Conversation took a lighter tone after that, and Lenore regaled us with stories about Moira in her youth—the sock hops, the tennis trophies, the time she snuck out to meet a boy at a street race.

Before we knew it, three hours had gone by.

◇◇◇

CHAPTER 10

I t felt like I was saying an awful lot of good-byes in those days. Jake and I flew to Portland in the same puddle-jumper as Abram, then each went our own ways. Putting Abram on that second plane was harder and more tearful than I thought it would be. I didn't want him to go, but he couldn't stay, and I wouldn't leave. So there we were, saying good-bye.

Jake and I watched his plane take off while waiting for our own flight. We sat in a remote corner at the gate, side by side.

Jake said, "Here, I've got something that'll distract you." He handed me his cellphone with a video lined up to play.

"What is it?"

"It's the woman we're trying to find. This is how we found her, but it's undoubtedly also alerted our enemies. Just watch."

"It's muted. Do I need audio?"

"Hell no," Jake said. "It's just a bunch of screaming."

I cringed, then sat back and hit play.

In the video, a multi-colored crowd of people were walking around half-naked and muddy. It reminded me of videos I'd seen of Burning Man, except they were in a green field, not the desert. As the camera scanned, I saw that it was one big party. People of all ages were dancing together. It was more like Woodstock, without the stages. There was a group doing yoga, a rainbow of meditators, and a tent where a woman was bandaging a wound. The encampment was on the edge of a deciduous forest, yet still it was surprising when a large black bear ambled out of the trees and started toward a group of children playing there. I saw the panic spread across faces and affect body language. Several people ran toward the bear— which I found brave—intending to get between it and the children. The kids were scattering, running toward screaming parents, I presumed. I was glad the audio was off.

The bear reared back on its hind legs, facing off against the people trying to scare it away.

That was when one woman stepped out into the open and confronted the bear. Not with waving arms and shouts but with a steady gaze. Her hands moved in hypnotic circles at chest level, and she was speaking to the bear. Her stance was straight, but relaxed, and as the camera moved to get a better angle, I saw clearly that she was pregnant. Very pregnant. My heart skipped a beat, paralyzed for a moment with fear for her. My instinct was to look away, but I didn't.

The bear's attention was focused on her, no longer interested in the others who were already off-camera. Up on its hind legs, it opened its mouth and—I imagined—bellowed. Then, it dropped heavily onto all of its feet and turned to lumber back into the forest.

I wasn't watching the bear after that. I'd seen it—the ripple of air, the crackle of pixels, the hints of light that had appeared around the woman's hands. It looked like excellent special effects, but it wasn't that. She'd used magick to make the bear leave.

"Wow," I said aloud.

The video ended, and I saw the title, *Pregnant Hedge Witch Saves Children from Bear. The video had been viewed over a million times.*

"Gods bless the Internet," Jake replied with caustic sarcasm.

"That's a hell of a risk." I couldn't believe a pregnant woman would do that.

"Maybe," Jake conceded. "Though it's more likely she knows the bear." He was staring down at his own hands.

I asked, "How do you know that?"

Jake shrugged. "I know her. She grew up in Wyrdwood with me. She's Landvaettir. Her ancestors were nature spirits. Her name is Agate Gunn, and she left Wyrdwood about ten years ago. No one knew where she went. All she left was a note saying she was answering the call. Her mother said it meant that a land feature was summoning her to care for it." He paused a moment, then added, "She never came back." He spoke matter-of-factly, but his expression revealed he'd been hurt by her leaving. It was personal for him.

"You know where she is?"

"Not exactly. We'll start by going to that gathering."

◇

I heard it for the first time in the airport bathroom. I was in my stall, doing my thing, when a quiet whispering sounded. For some reason, it put the hairs up on the back of my neck. It sounded earnest, but formless. There were no words in it.

A rolling suitcase clicked across the floor tiles. The whispers stopped. A shiver racked my shoulders, and I hurried to finish. What was it about me and bathrooms?

By the time I got back to Jake, I'd convinced myself—out of habit—that I'd imagined it.

◇

After our plane landed in West Virginia, we wasted no time heading for the site of the gathering. The guy at the rental car kiosk looked us over more closely once we asked him if he knew how to get to the campground, eyes suspicious.

"You one-a them?" he asked, words barbed with a West Virginia twang.

Jake put a look of disgust on his face. "We're reporters, doing an article on it."

The man's interest quirked. "They come out here once a year, ya know? Take over the field on the south ridge of Bear Mountain. God only knows what them hippies do up there."

Jake asked, "What's the best way to get there?"

The man obliged, even showing Jake on a map— one printed on paper. He then gave that to Jake, and Jake handed it to me. "There you go, Navigator. You're in charge of the map."

"Back in time," I snarked. I took the map, holding it by one corner as if it had cooties. "You're Lewis, I'm Clark. Got it."

We found our car, piled our bags into the trunk, then headed out. I transcribed the camp's general location into the map app on my cellphone, bringing us back into the twenty-first century. As I watched the scenery go by, I realized how easy it was spending time with Jake. He didn't require that I talk but rose to the occasion when I wanted to. We'd come to a place of relaxed camaraderie.

"Have you lived in Wyrdwood all your life?" I asked him.

"Pretty much, aside from a few years when I went away to college. My family's been in Wyrdwood for generations. We're a tribe of wyrdos."

"Are your parents still there?"

"No. They died about five years ago. Car wreck."

"Oh no! I'm so sorry."

"It is what it is. I'm sure they're reincarnated and living happy little toddler lives somewhere."

"Reincarnation? You believe in that?"

"Yeah." Jake looked over at me, expression serious. "I not only believe, I know it happens. Anyone with magick reincarnates. We just keep going 'round and 'round, life after life. People with purely magickal ancestry often remember some of their previous lives."

I considered that for a moment, applying it to my mother. I loved the idea that she was being reborn somewhere, hopefully to a loving family.

"I don't remember any past lives," I said. "Do you?"

Jake tilted his head, eyes on the road. "A little," he said. "Bits and pieces. Things I'm good at. A sense of déjà vu in places I've never been before. My great great grandfather was human, though, so I don't have pure blood."

I said, "You don't have horns."

Jake chuckled. "Neither do you."

"Damn shame," I said with sincerity. "So, what's your ancestry?" I watched him lick his lips and suck the top one in. He was debating how much to tell me. I'd learned to recognize that about him.

Jake said, "Way back when, in the beginning, there were a handful of races who could easily pass for human with spellwork or glamours, among all those who couldn't." His voice took on its teacher cadence. "Two of them rose to prominence and ruled large tribes. One was the Tuatha Dé, and they're my ancestors. Today, we call them the Thu for short. The other race was the Fomorians. Today known simply as the Fomor."

I grunted softly, fascinated. I asked, "Am I one of those?"

"You're Thu too, I believe. Thu and human, so— you're a mutt." He grinned.

I gave him an exaggerated look of shock. "Excuse me?"

"A mangy mutt," he teased. "But I think we'll keep you."

I snorted. "Be nice to me, or I'll pee in your shoes."

"That's disgusting." He groaned.

Neither of us laughed aloud, but it was a pleasant moment between friends. I liked that we were beginning to establish a rapport. It kept the grief at bay.

◇

Arriving at the site, we found a field that had been turned into a parking lot populated with RVs, old VW vans, and cars of all shapes and sizes. Empty spots spoke to the number of people who had already left, and we passed vehicles on their way out.

"It must be over," Jake said. He found us a spot near the foot traffic, and we got out. I took a moment to look around. Everyone was packing tents and coolers into their cars. They were filthy with mud and dressed in a haphazard style that said "hippy" to me. Patterns clashed with patterns, fabrics contrasted with fabrics; and the only unifying theme was the mud. Their hairstyles were even more varied. I saw a lot of folks with dreadlocks in blonde, brown, auburn, and black. Others wore complex braids with beads, feathers, and shells woven into them. Most of the men had beards—some short, some long, and some also with braids and beads.

I saw children of all ages, in summer clothes or swimsuits, muddy and happy—little ragamuffins with loud and energetic voices. I thought, *They'll sleep well tonight.*

Jake said, "This way," and we headed toward a trail that cut through the woods. It was wide and trampled, wet and squishy, and I wished I'd worn boots instead of tennis shoes. Many who passed us nodded a greeting, and some even said hello. Others eyed us with suspicion, and I realized how different we looked. Clean, if nothing else, until a passing child slipped in the mud and put a dirty hand on my thigh to steady herself. It felt like a little blessing, a welcome, and it made me smile to see her handprint there.

After a five-minute walk through the forest, we emerged into a giant clearing. Surrounded on all sides by tall trees, the ground was trampled flat. It may once have had grass, but all those trodding feet—along with recent rains—had changed that.

A man approached us. He had purple hair that had begun to fade, and his own brown showed at the roots. Piercings decorated his face at his nose and his lip, and he'd stretched his earlobes and filled them with black open tunnel plugs. His clothes—multiple tunics layered over harem pants—were earthy cotton.

"Welcome," he said, though his face belied the sentiment. "Can I help you?" He had the posture of someone in charge.

Jake smiled. "We're looking for the woman who faced down the bear."

The man frowned. "Are you cops? This is private property."

"I understand," Jake replied, his own smile slipping. "We're not police. We're family."

I was fascinated by how easily Jake changed his story to suit the situation. It was a skill he used with great facility.

The man looked us over again, evaluating. "What's the name of the woman you're looking for?"

"Agate," Jake replied. "We know her as Agate."

I remembered only then to put a smile on my face.

After careful consideration, the man pointed us in a direction. "I think she's in the meditation circle. On the far end of the clearing. That way."

Jake looked that way, then back at the man. He nodded. "Thanks." Then he took me by the hand.

I was so surprised, I almost pulled my hand free, but then he said, "C'mon, honey." And I got it.

"Thank you," I told the man.

Jake and I headed deeper into the camp, moving along the well-worn walkways. We didn't get far before Jake looked back over his shoulder and stopped.

"What?" I asked, searching behind us. The man

who'd directed us was heading off in the opposite direction, and so began a game of cat and mouse. We were the cat. Piercing man was the mouse. "You think he lied?" I asked as we slipped around tents, keeping a low profile, and followed the man.

"Yeah, I do." He didn't release my hand. "If it was me, I'd lie. He doesn't know who we are. He's undoubtedly thinking that even if we're family, maybe Agate doesn't want to see us."

The man wasn't tall, so we occasionally lost sight of him, but his purple hair always reappeared, and we managed to stalk him through the flock of campers.

Once, when he'd disappeared, I scanned the crowd. At the corner of my eye, I caught a flash of curly red hair just beyond a group of people playing hacky-sack with onlookers clapping out a rhythm and singing. My first instinctual thought was that it was Colin. My breath hitched, but when I looked full-on, he wasn't there. I twisted to search for him. Then, I felt ridiculous.

Jake pulled me along, "C'mon, Viviane. There he is."

I decided I'd imagined Colin. It was outrageous to think he'd be there. I was missing him so much that my eyes were playing tricks on me.

We wove our way through the camp until we came to an open area where a group of a dozen or so people were dancing in the middle of a drum circle. Musicians playing percussion instruments were creating a primitive song that reverberated in my chest and got me bopping despite myself. The dancers were naked or nearly so, their bodies dirty with mud—*au naturel. There was nothing sexual about it. The ecstatic dance was another layer on the drumbeats, building a three-dimensional harmony that was almost magickal, swollen with the joy of creating something together.*

Never in my life had I felt as free as they looked. I was uncomfortable with their openness, their nudity, and their unabashed self-expression. I'd been around people on drugs and people with mental illness all my life. That kind of display had always been frowned upon at the least and punished at the worst. I saw none of that judgement and shame there in the clearing. Those people were praying with their bodies—with their entire beings. They were joyous and free from all the things we tell ourselves about our own ugliness. Free of judgment—both of the self and of others. Free to love and be loved, without sexual expectation getting in the way. That realization sat at the edge of my consciousness, teasing me, taunting my inhibitions, and daring me to open my mind a little bit more. Confronted directly by the primitive rawness of the dance and the drums, I felt some of my prejudice crack off me and fall away, to be consumed by the mud.

"There she is," Jake said. He pulled me around the perimeter of the drum circle until I saw her too. She was dancing, though not as rambunctiously as some, dressed only in panties and a scarf tied as a halter over her breasts. Her belly was large and round. She was beautiful in an Earth Mother sort of way, her light brown hair long, loose, and curly, skin sun-kissed. The pierced man approached her and whispered in her ear.

Agate Gunn glanced around. Jake and I crouched down to keep from being seen. She thanked the man with a light kiss to his lips, then left the drum circle. She went to an old stump and began pulling on a dark-chocolate broom skirt of light-weight cotton.

Jake and I headed quickly toward her.

As we got close, Agate seemed to sense us there. She looked up. For a brief moment, the urge to flee dropped her center into her stomach and put tension on her face. It didn't last. She recognized Jake, and when she did, it was as if the sun came out from behind a cloud. She smiled, and the true extent of her beauty shone through.

Jake released my hand.

As she and Jake stared into each others' eyes, I realized just how much Agate meant to Jake.

"I can't believe it," Agate said, her voice expressing a history of intimacy. "What are you doing here?"

They hugged, and I stood by feeling awkward. I turned my gaze on the drum circle again, only to find the pierced man scowling in our direction. I smiled and shrugged.

"We need to talk," Jake told her once they'd finally finished hugging and rocking and laughing and... I could hear the impatience in my own thoughts, and

I wasn't proud of myself.

Jake said, "This is Viviane. She's a colleague from Wyrdwood."

Agate acknowledged me with a nod, then went back to putting on her clothes, adding multiple layers all of the same dark, rich brown. She pulled on pants under the skirt and several t-shirts and tunics, some that snugged against her bump and a final one that hung loosely over it.

Jake watched without embarrassment, and I watched out of fascination. Agate lifted her head and caught me. When I realized I'd been staring, *then I was embarrassed.*

Jake said, "I have something to show you." He pulled out his phone and queued up the video. The two of them stood shoulder-to-shoulder as she watched it. I paid close attention to her reaction. She went from curious to numb to horrified, and every emotion in between. Finally, she lifted her face to look at Jake, eyes wide.

She said, "Fuck."

Jake nodded.

Agate picked up a hand-made bag and slung the strap across her body. Her breath was quickened, and I was reminded of a doe who's heard a stick breaking in the forest. Sure enough, on her next breath, she turned and began walking quickly toward the trees. Jake fell in behind her, and after a moment my mind caught up and I took the rear position.

"Where are you going?" Jake asked.

"Home," Agate said over her shoulder.

It was surprisingly hard to keep up with her, despite her pregnancy, especially once we entered the trees and moved off the path. I pushed on, dodging branches that slapped back when Jake released them and learning quickly to avoid the blackberry brambles. By the time we stopped, both Jake and I were winded. I had a stitch in my side and scratches on my cheeks and hands.

Agate's home was hidden from the world. It was a marvel of camouflage, built into a hillside. The front facade was covered with ivy. As we approached, the sound of barking came from within the hill. Agate stepped up onto a wooden porch that had blended with the surrounding forest. She opened the front door of her house.

A pair of large German shepherds pushed their way out and danced around her, sniffing her and licking her ankles. They were gentle and didn't jump on her, but when they became aware of Jake and me, their hackles went up, and they both took defensive postures, growling.

"It's okay, Yogi. Booboo." said Agate. "They're friends." She emphasized the word "friends," and both dogs calmed immediately.

Amused, I asked, "You named your dogs Yogi and Booboo?"

Agate smiled. "It suits their personalities. This is Yogi. He's the beta to my alpha. And this is Boo. They're inseparable." She petted their heads, then shooed them outside. "Do your business," she told them. Holding the door open, she welcomed us inside.

The interior was dark, but not as dark as I'd expected. High angled windows—almost skylights—let in streams of light and provided a view of the treetops. The walls were like those of a log cabin, and the floor was covered with mismatched stone tiles in varying shades of gray. We entered into a large room with a fat cast-iron stove in the corner next to a pile of logs. Its iron chimney merged with a brick chimney on the wall.

The ceiling was about seven feet high, supported by thick beams. Drying herbs hung from nails in one of the beams. A low king-sized bed occupied the center of the room, covered with layers of pillows, sheets, and blankets. It had neither head- nor footboard. Long tables set beside the bed made me think it was used for seating as well as sleeping. A two-person dining table with two chairs stood against the wall that stretched into a small kitchen area. A double sink occupied a cabinet counter, but there were no appliances other than a tiny refrigerator. I could hear the purr of a generator coming from somewhere out of sight. *So, I thought, electricity and running water. As if to confirm, Agate turned on a lamp in the corner.*

Jake asked, "Have you lived here since you left Wyrdwood?"

"Once I stopped moving around, yes. Though

I didn't always have the house. It was built by my predecessor." Agate opened the door on the pot belly stove and poked around inside it. She took a log off the pile and set it in upon the glowing embers. "I spent a year following the call. It led me here."

"The call?" I asked.

Agate shut the door and stood up, brushing her hands together. She studied me. "My people have a strong tie to the land. Some of us more than others. Our purpose in life is to keep and protect it. I was called to this hill and to the river that flows under it. This is my land now. I spent my life savings to buy it once I realized it was my home. It called to me, and I answered. I'm married to it." She turned her back on me and walked to the sink.

Silently, I mouthed, "Married?"

Jake heaved a little shrug. Aloud, he said, "Agate, you're in danger."

Agate didn't even look up. She focused on filling a large, old-fashioned teapot, and said, "And you're here to save me?"

"Um," Jake hedged. "Yes? Look, there are things you don't know. Someone is killing wielders."

The teapot closed with a clack, and Agate carried it in both hands to the wood stove. The log inside began to crackle, and I felt warmth spreading from it. I stepped closer.

"You may sleep here tonight," Agate said, finally facing us. "But tomorrow, you must go."

Jake turned his palms up. "You don't understand."

"I understand. I'm outed. That video has put my face all over the Internet, and the Internet is forever. It doesn't matter. No one can find me here. I'll lay low for a few years. I can live off the land—off the grid. People will forget." Agate moved to the bed and crawled upon it. She sat back, legs crossed yogi-style in front of her, and rubbed her belly with both hands. I wondered how she was going to manage giving birth while hiding off-grid.

Jake walked over and perched on the edge of the bed. "It's not the Normals you need to fear this time. It's a wielder. I haven't figured out who yet or why, but I know they're dangerous."

I pulled out a chair at the dining table and sat. No way was I going to climb onto the bed with them. That would've been weird.

We had the most delicious tea I'd ever tasted, and Jake brought Agate up to speed on his life, his work at Lost Lambs, and what he knew about the killer—which wasn't much. As they talked, I felt myself drifting off. Twice, I jerked awake when my chin hit my chest. Finally, I crossed my arms on the table, rested my head on it, and gave up on staying conscious.

◇◇◇

CHAPTER 11

J ake shook me alert in time for dinner. The sun had gone down, and the house was lit with electric lamps, none of which matched. The stove radiated a steady heat that felt cozy and not the least bit too hot, though I did remove my jean jacket. Agate's tiny bathroom had a regular toilet and a small shower stall, much to my surprise, though only a curtain to offer privacy. I held off as long as I could, but by the time I was doing the peepee dance, I had heard Jake and Agate pee more than once, so I shoved aside my modesty.

In the kitchen, Agate poured hot water into a basin for me. She offered me a chunk of homemade soap, and I washed my face and hands.

Yogi and Boo came in from outside, their nails tick-tocking excitedly on the stone tiles, tails wagging. They brought the smell of the outdoors with them.

Agate brought a pot of venison stew out of the mini fridge and heated it on the wood stove. She moved several piles of books and her laptop off a worktable and scooted it up against the bed. She and Jake ate there. I ate at the kitchen table.

"I can't believe you get wifi out here," Jake said, breaking a large piece of bread off the loaf.

"I have a satellite dish," Agate told him. "I need

it for my work."

Feeling tired of being left out, I asked, "What do you do?"

"I'm an activist," Agate replied with pride. "I lobby politicians on behalf of the environment. Many of these guys are simply unaware of the situation. You'd be surprised how many times I've heard, 'I didn't know that.' Somebody needs to educate the legislators. Of course, the truth doesn't matter to all of them. Some are just plain evil." The passion came through in her voice, and I found myself liking her a little more.

"Well," I said, "thank you for doing that."

Agate seemed almost to blush as if embarrassed.

An owl hooted outside. Jake's head came up.

"It's okay," Agate said, resting a light touch on his arm. "If the dogs don't react, then you don't have to worry."

Jake and I cleaned up after the meal, letting Agate rest propped up on pillows.

"What are we going to do?" I asked him under my breath as I handed him a wooden bowl to dry.

"We'll stay here tonight, but we gotta convince her to come with us tomorrow."

"We can't force her to leave, can we?"

"No, but we can make a damn good argument for it." He winked at me, and I smiled.

Once the dishes were put away, we found that Agate had fallen asleep with the dogs lying on either side of her legs. Silent, I watched as Jake covered her with a blanket. "You can get in the bed with Agate. She won't mind. She's a puppy-pile kind of person."

"Where are you going to sleep?" I asked.

"I probably won't." He went to the stove and added a log to the fire. "Go on. Get some sleep. You can drive tomorrow."

I took off my shoes and crawled into the king-sized bed. There was plenty of room for all four of us, and it felt good when one of the dogs—Boo—rested a chin on my ankle. My last thought was that Boo probably felt a kinship with me since we were both omegas, last in the pecking order, and then I was out like a light.

◇

I awoke with a start, hearing quiet whispering nearby. My mind immediately went back to the airport bathroom, and I lay there, heart hammering, listening. Then words emerged from the hissing, and I realized it was Jake and Agate. They were seated at the dining table, talking in low voices so they wouldn't disturb me. I pressed my face into the pillow.

"You could have told me," Jake said.

"No," replied Agate. "I couldn't. You'd have talked me out of it or insisted on coming with me. It was something I had to do alone. The call—it's not just a feeling. It's an urge that rises from *so deep in who you are that it's almost like it's coming from your ancestors. And I suppose it was. I had to go all in. It was that or nothing. I'm sorry, Jake."*

I thought about making a noise, letting them know I was awake, but the longer she talked, the harder it got. Not because I wanted to eavesdrop, but because I didn't want to interrupt.

"I wasn't right for a long time after you disappeared. Everybody searched for you. We scoured the hills and beach. We thought you were dead." Jake kept his volume low, but the emotion in his voice was palpable.

"I'm sorry. It had to be that way. Kinda, my old self did die."

"You never wanted to come home?"

I heard the clink of a teaspoon in a mug, then Agate replied, "No. The moment I found my land, Wyrdwood stopped being my home. This is my home."

"It's not—" Jake's response was cut off when the dogs suddenly started barking. They were outside, close to the front door.

I sat up. "What's going on?"

Jake said, "Stay here." He was up and halfway to the door when the barking abruptly stopped. All that remained in its wake was silence.

Agate gasped and started to push up to standing, baby belly in the lead.

I climbed out of bed and tucked my feet into my shoes.

Jake went to the front window, pulled back the curtains, and peered out for a moment.

"You see anything?" I asked, bending to tie my

laces.

"Nothing."

"Yogi and Boo?" Agate asked, sounding afraid.

Jake reached over his shoulder to the middle of his back and produced a short black sword out of nowhere. Literally nowhere.

"Holy shit," I said under my breath. Up until that moment, I hadn't seen Jake do anything magickal.

"Viviane, stay here with Agate." Jake went to the front door, pulled it open, and stepped to the threshold.

The two dogs lay motionless on the porch, and my heart caught in my throat. Agate screamed and before I could stop her, she'd rushed forward and out. I hurried after her.

Jake had continued out into the yard and was looking around.

Agate knelt beside the dogs, frantically checking them for wounds. When she found none, she sobbed with relief. They were breathing.

I crouched down beside them and caught the distinct aroma of vanilla. It was becoming annoyingly familiar. Someone had magicked the dogs asleep. I was relieved. It could have been so much worse.

Jake cried out as an unseen presence barreled into him and sent him sprawling on the ground. The man became visible the moment he hit Jake. He landed hard with Jake under him, both grunting loudly.

At first, my impression was of a man large

enough to be a professional wrestler, with long black hair that hung wild around his shoulders and a full beard and mustache. His body was solid beneath black jeans and a t-shirt. The more I looked, the more the man's true appearance came into focus. He was like the Orcneas in Wyrdwood, but more wild. Short tusks grew outward from the corners of his mouth, tipped with silvery metal that came to sharp points at the ends. His body became hunched, arms hairy and hands clawed, kind of like a werewolf except he wasn't shape-shifting. My sight was shifting, and the truth of him was revealing itself to me.

The man hit Jake in the face, several times in quick succession. My mind reeled, and I struggled to think of what to do. Then, the man lifted his head and looked right at me.

"Jake?" I cried.

Jake's face was bleeding, and he'd stopped fighting back.

I shouted, "Agate, get in the house," instinctively moving to put myself between her and our attacker. I watched him get to his feet, dread filling me. "Go!" I was only half aware of her dragging the first dog inside.

The man was in no hurry, smiling as he crossed the yard toward me. He didn't see me as a challenge.

I looked all around, searching for a weapon, and I spotted an ax stuck in a stump out in the yard. My body went into action, and I leapt off the porch, skirting wide around the man.

"Run, rabbit, run," he purred.

I ran, spurred on by the sound of him turning to follow me. The ground was uneven, and I stumbled but somehow managed to stay on my feet. Already gasping for breath, I made it to the stump and wrapped a hand around the ax. I pulled, but it didn't budge. I tried using both hands, but it barely wiggled.

"Fuck!" I cried. I felt more than heard him behind me and skirted around the stump to put it between me and him.

He was right there, eyes bright, grin crooked. With one large hand, he pulled the ax from the wood as if it were a knife stuck in butter.

The idea that he might hit me with it—cleave me to death with an ax—took my fear to a whole new level. I hunkered down, ready to run but knowing I had little chance of getting away from him.

Our eyes met, and I stopped blinking. I didn't know what he was waiting for until he turned the ax around, held it by its head, and handed it toward me. My jaw clenched. He wanted to play with me before he killed me.

My hands folded into fists, but they felt so weak.

I didn't dare take the ax. He waggled it at me, encouraging me to play along, encouraging me to fight back. When still I didn't take it, he threw it aside.

His body tensed. He was going to pounce.

Every cell in my body told me to run, but I didn't. I remembered the hag. I'd been able to repel it with my will—or so I'd been told. I lifted my hand

and pointed my palm toward the monster. My energy surged up from deep in my belly, and my willpower poured through the space between my eyebrows. I glared. My lips curled back, and I let out a long, low growl of intent.

For a breath, he paused, as if taken aback by my show of power.

I breathed in, preparing to yell at him to stay away, and then... He was *behind me. His arms encircled me, and I was trapped and terrified. Quick as that, he'd moved, and I hadn't even been able to see him do it. I expected him to hurt me, to kill me even. A second passed, then another. I felt his hot breath on my ear, his tusk scratching the side of my head. "Too slow," he said in a rumbling voice.*

I closed my eyes.

A loud thud sounded behind me, and the man's full weight pressed against my body, toppling me forward. My arms pinned, I had no control over the fall. I hit the ground and banged my shin painfully on the stump. The man landed on me, knocking the wind out of me. I gasped for air, but I couldn't breathe with him lying on me. Panic shot up my spine, and I stopped thinking clearly. I shoved at him to no avail. I had no leverage, flattened on my stomach as I was. A menacing darkness closed in over my vision, my breath still stalled in my throat. I couldn't—

The man rolled—or was rolled—off me. I felt hands on me, turning me over.

Jake said, "Breathe, Viv. Breathe!" In increments, I gasped the air deeper and deeper into my lungs until I was able to suck in a full breath. The wooziness receded.

I opened my eyes to blink up at Jake. He stood over me, brandishing his sword, his focus on the man lying beside me.

Our attacker was huge up close, easily twice as big as me in both height and width, and I was no dainty princess. His face and mine were parallel, and I could see every detail. He was unconscious, or pretending to be, with his eyes closed. His features were exaggerated, Neanderthal, with high cheekbones and a heavy forehead. Black eyebrows stood up in all directions, and long eyelashes fanned against his cheeks. Pockmarks marred his skin—what I could see of it around the thick beard and mustache. And the tusks. Celtic knotwork designs scrolled over the metal that tipped them, designs that continued as carvings along the lengths of the tusks themselves. They were surprisingly beautiful and delicate on such a brute of a man.

Jake said, "Can you move, Viv? Back away. He could wake up any time now."

So I did. I found that getting to my feet was both harder and more painful than I'd expected, but I made it. My shin was throbbing. I hobbled onto the porch and leaned against the wall. I glanced down at my leg—no blood. My jeans were intact.

It was just a glance, but when I returned my attention to our attacker, he was gone—there one second and gone the next. It was as if he'd become invisible. Or teleported away. His absence left Jake looking ridiculous, menacing an empty patch of earth.

"Shit," Jake said, standing up straight. He turned in place, looking for the man, and finally lowered his blade to his side. "We'd better get inside."

Neither of us said anything else as we gathered our composure, then Jake strode toward the front door. "I told you to stay in the house with Agate." He was angry and didn't even look at me as he opened the door and waited for me to precede him inside.

"I had to do something," I countered, trying not to limp as I went into the house.

Agate sat on the floor, wringing her hands. She had dragged Yogi and Boo inside while Jake and I'd been fighting. Both dogs were half-awake, lying beside Agate, and trying to lift their heads. One of them—I think it was Yogi—gave a weak bark.

"We need to go," said Jake. "Before he comes back." He yanked his jacket off a chair and put it on. "Do you have a suitcase, Agate?"

Agate said nothing. She crouched to pet the dogs.

Jake's voice took on an edge. "Agate, are you hearing me? We have to go."

"No, Jake," Agate said with calm determination. "I told you. This is my land. I can't leave it."

"That buggane wanted to kill you. Don't you understand? He'll be back." Jake was pacing up and down the length of the room, rubbing his temples.

Agate asked, "Why does he want to kill *me?*"

That halted Jake in place. He let his hands fall to his sides. "I wish I knew," he said. "I haven't figured that out yet. But I do know you wouldn't be the first. And until he's caught, you wouldn't be the last. We've had three other murdered kin, that we know of."

Agate continued petting the dogs. Tails thumped on the tile. "I'll reinforce my wards," she said. "If worse comes to worst, I'll go into the woods and hide there. He won't find me on my land."

"He did find you," Jake said. "That ship has sailed."

"I won't leave."

I watched them with growing consternation. Jake wasn't making any headway with her. A part of me felt like she was being stubborn as much because it was Jake trying to order her back to Wyrdwood as anything else. His earlier gentle tone had metamorphosed into a bullying command, and his frustration with her was showing. I wouldn't have been surprised if he'd picked her up and carried her back to Wyrdwood.

I limped toward Jake and said quietly, "Give her a minute to think. She wasn't expecting any of this." His eyes met mine, and we stared off. He blinked first, then nodded. I pushed him toward a chair. "Why don't you sit down and relax. Let me look at your face."

Agate brought a clean rag and poured a basin of warm water so I could clean Jake's wounds. He had a split lip and a cut over his eye. Both were swollen and bleeding. I tended to him in silence. No one else spoke either, and I felt the atmosphere in the room begin to settle.

Jake took the rag from me and used a clean corner to wipe at my chin. It hurt when he touched it, and the rag came away with blood. I must have hit it when I fell.

Gradually, Boo got to her feet and walked to her water bowl. Agate set out their homemade dog food and gave each of them a bone. They eventually climbed onto the bed with her, gnawing to their hearts' content.

I rinsed out the rag and wet it with cold water. My shin wasn't as bad as I'd feared, though it was already bruising. I held the cold rag against it. The pain dwindled to an ache. It still hurt to take a deep breath though, and I suspected I had bruised ribs.

Jake said matter-of-factly, "We can't stay here. The safest place for you is Wyrdwood."

From where she sat cross-legged on the bed, Agate shook her head, but her rejection of the idea wasn't as vehement as it had been.

I crossed the room and sat on the foot of the bed. With as little judgment in my voice as I could manage, I asked, "What about your baby, Agate?"

Agate sighed, and her shoulders dropped. Jake said nothing, for which I was grateful. We sat without talking further. I listened to the hum of the generator, the crackle of the fire in the stove, and the song of birds just waking with the breaking dawn. Under any other circumstance, I'd have loved to spend time in Agate's house. I imagined living there with Colin, a simple life, with dogs and books, sleepy mornings spent puppy-piled together in the bed.

"My dogs come too," Agate said.

I nodded. "Yes, of course."

Jake's phone dinged, and he pulled it out to check it. Striding to the front door, he said, "I need to make a call. You two get packed." He left, shutting the door behind him.

Agate did have a suitcase, and many things she wanted to take with her, most of which were for the dogs and the baby. She was exhausted, and so I helped as much as I could. We stuffed the suitcase full and used several shopping bags to carry the rest. As we were wrapping a large leg of venison in plastic wrap, Agate abruptly bent over, palm pressed into her lower back. She groaned loudly, and her water splattered on the floor at her feet. I rushed to her side.

"I thought the pains were because of all the stress." She was breathing more heavily than normal. "But I'm in labor."

She wanted to go to the bathroom, so I helped her there then returned to the main room. I opened the front door.

Jake was in the yard, talking on his phone. I called out to him, "Jake! Agate's in labor." He blinked at me with a startled expression, nodded once, then returned to his call. I didn't wait to see what he'd do. I went back inside, refilled the basin with water off the stove, and pulled a clean cloth from the cupboard. I knocked on the wall beside the bathroom curtain. "I have a cloth and warm water for you." The only reply she made was a long, low groan of pain.

◇

By the time Jake returned, Agate had made her way to the bed and was lying on her side with the dogs close.

I'd already read three articles on my cellphone about what to do if you have to deliver a baby and have no idea what you're doing. They all said to call the EMTs. So, I was on the phone with them when Jake came back inside. And he wasn't alone.

I told the operator, "Viviane Rose. I'm just a friend. Her name is Agate. I don't remember her last name. Yes, she's in labor."

The air in the house fled as Amalia stepped in on Jake's heels. Her white braid was made a fat halo around her head with tendrils escaping to curl around her face. She wore indigo-colored harem pants and a white tank top under a knee-length olive cardigan two sizes too big for her. She carried a tote bag woven from dried grasses. Coolly, she cast her cool gaze around the room. It latched onto me, and she scowled.

Into the phone, I said, "No, we can't get her to the hospital. Hold on, I can get you map coordinates for our location."

Amalia dropped her tote bag and strode toward me. She took my phone from me and said into it, "Never mind. The midwife has arrived. We don't need help."

She listened, eyes never leaving mine, then handed me the phone. "They need to speak to you. Tell them."

I stared at her, then took the phone. "Hello. Yes, I'm the one who called. Yes, the midwife is here. We're in good hands. No, it's okay. I'm sorry I bothered you."

The operator wished us luck, and I hung up.

Amalia took the phone out of my hand and threw it into the corner with vehemence.

I objected with an outraged, "Hey!"

Without warning, she put her hand around my throat and shoved me back against the wall. Her eyes blazed with icy fury.

"Amalia!" Jake cried.

"Mr. Lamb," she said without looking at him. Her grip on my throat was tight, already cutting off the blood to my head. I couldn't speak, and my face was getting tight. "You need to train her better."

I tried to pull her hand from my neck, but I was no match for her strength. I met her gaze and stopped trying. I was the baby rabbit, and she was the eagle. Her mercy was all that stood between me and death, and my primal lizard-brain knew it without a shadow of a doubt.

"Yeah," Jake said on a breath. "I will. I will. She's

a neophyte. It's my fault. Please. She gets it now."

Amalia put her face close to mine and said, "Never call Normals to handle wielder business." She pronounced 'wielder' like 'veal-duh.'

With one last shove, Amalia released me.

For the second time that day, I gasped for air.

"I'm sorry," I said, my voice weak.

Amalia screwed up her face in disgust and turned away.

A surge of mixed emotions replaced my fear. I bent at the waist, hands on my knees. My bottom lip trembled, and tears filled my eyes. I breathed out through pursed lips in an effort to regain control of myself. I wanted to curl into a ball and cry.

Amalia picked up her tote and went to the bed. She set the bag beside Agate and placed her palm against the baby bump.

Agate did not object. She said, "Thank you for coming."

Jake stepped up to me. Whispering, he asked, "Are you okay?"

I nodded and stood up. I could still feel the steel pressure of her fingers, and I suspected she'd bruised me. I touched my neck and swallowed.

"Where did she come from?" I whispered. My hands were shaking. I folded my arms on my chest and tucked my hands in. Of all the paranormal attackers who had come at me in the past few months, none had made me feel my mortality so keenly as that petite woman with the white hair and piercing eyes.

Jake replied, "Wyrdwood. I called her. She's the Midwife." The way he said it, I envisioned a capital M on the word "midwife."

"When did you do that?"

"Just now."

"Just now? How'd she get here so fast?"

Jake watched as Amalia pulled aside the sheet covering Agate. He said, "Magick," in a tone that implied I should have known that. *Duh.*

"So... Can she get Agate to a hospital with her magick?"

"No. Agate is not going to a hospital. Get that thought out of your head."

"Viviane Rose," said Amalia, every syllable a command for my attention, though she barely spoke above a whisper. "I need towels and a clean tray or plate."

A part of me wanted to fade into the wall, disappear where I wouldn't draw Amalia's notice. Another part wanted to shout at her that she couldn't treat me like that, that I hadn't done anything wrong. I hadn't—done anything wrong. Not by normal standards. And yet, in my new paradigm, I had screwed up big time. My inner child was sobbing with anger, fear, and contrition.

Ultimately, I was eager to get back into her good graces. I said, "Okay," and scurried off to do her bidding. I never wanted to experience her fury again, and the truth was that I wanted her approval. I was a mess, but at least I'd overcome the urge to cry.

"Jake," Amalia said. "Put the dogs out and prepare a bed for the baby."

CHAPTER 12

That birth was one of the most intense twelve hours of my life. Amalia focused entirely on Agate. She was fascinating to watch. Sometimes she'd trace her fingers along Agate's spine, and Agate visibly relaxed. Once, she spoke in a language I didn't understand, tucked between Agate's legs, almost as if she were calling the baby to come out.

It was an exhausting roller coaster ride for Agate. Back and forth to the bathroom. She threw up multiple times. As the day progressed, she grew more and more exhausted, mewling and crying when the contractions hit.

Watching her, I became convinced that I never wanted to have a baby. She was in agony, her body like a car without brakes that's gone off-road—downhill.

Jake took up a position at her head, supporting her upper body and encouraging her. There wasn't much for me to do other than keep the water boiling and bring glasses of fresh, cold water for them to drink.

The house became steamy and sweaty, a sauna of bodily aromas. We couldn't open any windows for Agate's sake, and so we shed layers of clothing instead.

It was a slow process until the very end when the baby's head emerged. After that, the birth progressed quickly. I stood by in wonder as the child came into the world.

It was a girl.

Amalia placed the baby on Agate's chest while she cut the umbilical cord. Agate spoke her name, "Ivy," and held her daughter to her.

Ivy was beautiful. So tiny. Pink and wrinkled, with a dusting of brown hair. Her cry filled the space under the hill, and I'd never felt so connected to life and nature as I did in those moments. I was so fascinated by Ivy that I failed to notice that Agate had gone pale, and her eyes had rolled back in her head.

"Take the child," Amalia commanded.

I hesitated, confused, and Amalia raised her voice. "Take the child."

"What's going on?" Jake asked.

I stepped forward and picked up the baby with shaking hands.

Agate's quick, shallow breaths stopped entirely. That was when I saw the blood spreading on the bed between her legs.

Amalia put pressure on Agate's abdomen and chanted in a language I didn't know. Her eyes were closed, her face set and determined.

In my heart, I knew Agate was dying.

Jake panicked, hugged Agate's limp body, and pleaded with her to breath.

All the while, the baby cried in my arms.

Outside, the dogs howled.

◇

At a certain point, Amalia gave up. She drew a complex symbol in blood on Agate's stomach.

Jake and I stood in a corner of the room, watching numbly as Amalia took her tools to the basin, poured in boiling water, and let them soak.

She took Ivy from me, placed her on the table, and cleaned her off with mechanical precision, as if she'd done it thousands of times. She swaddled her in cotton and a baby blanket. She gave the baby back to me, then washed the tools and put them away with the same steady movements.

I held Ivy against me, her little face calm and pink. It was comforting to me to hold her, and I rested my cheek on her forehead. I wanted nothing more than to keep her warm and comfort her.

"You're safe, Ivy," I whispered to her. "Don't worry. You're going to be fine."

"The father?" Amalia asked Jake.

"It was a Samhain celebration. She didn't know his identity."

Amalia nodded. "Honoring her ancestors. Good." She hung her tote on her elbow and came to retrieve Ivy from me.

I took a step back.

Amalia halted, watching me. She said, "I'll take the child to Wyrdwood with me. She will be safe there.

I'll find a home for her."

"It's okay, Viviane," Jake said.

Having been bombarded by so many emotions, I had slipped into a state of pure instinct, and I did not want to give Ivy up. I didn't know if I'd ever see her again, and my primal urge was to protect her.

Amalia reached for Ivy with authority. As if she'd read my mind, she said, "You can visit her when you get back to Wyrdwood."

I didn't resist.

Amalia lifted Ivy from my arms, tucked the blanket tightly around her, and covered her head lightly. She walked to the door.

The warm spot where Ivy had nestled grew cold, and I crossed my empty arms.

Jake stepped forward to open the door for Amalia, and as I watched, she took two steps across the porch, then disappeared. Just disappeared—in an instant. She didn't open a hole and fall into it as I'd seen Bella do. She just vanished.

Staring at the spot where Amalia had been, I couldn't stop shaking. "What now?" I asked.

Jake left the front door ajar and came to stand at the foot of the bed, looking down at the bloody mess that had been Agate. Amalia had left it all there.

Jake said, tone dour, "Now, we bury her."

I sat down heavily on a kitchen chair and buried my face in my hands. It felt like *my fault she was dead. Mine and Jake's. We had brought death to her door. We had saved her from one assassin only to have her die in childbirth. Fate had dealt a cruel hand, though there was one silver lining to it all. By saving Agate from the assassin, we'd saved her baby. That little lost lamb would grow up in Wyrdwood, and I vowed then and there to make sure Ivy was always safe, healthy, and happy. In a movie once, I'd heard someone say that if you save a life, then you become responsible for that life. I felt bonded to Ivy in a way I never would have predicted. I'd seen her take her very first breath.*

Much later, as the dogs and I stood beside Agate's grave, and Jake shoveled dirt onto her shrouded corpse, I remembered those last few minutes with Amalia, the midwife. I asked, "Jake? What did Amalia mean when she said Agate was honoring her ancestors?"

Jake leaned on the shovel, looking ten years older. "Some people believe," he said, "that if you conceive on a night when the veil between worlds is thinnest, then you have a good chance that one of your ancestors will reincarnate in the child. Samhain is one of those nights, Beltane, and either solstice." He took a deep breath before continuing. "For Agate, the conception was spiritual. She used magick to call the father of her baby. According to what she told me, she'd never met him before and didn't know who he was. Chances are, he had no idea what he was doing. He probably thought it was all a dream."

My eyebrows knitted in horror. "Isn't that rape?"

Jake scowled. "No. He didn't rape her. She knew what she was doing."

"Not her. Him. Did he give consent?"

Jake seemed surprised by the vehemence in my voice, and I could almost see his defensiveness rise. "Maybe he did. I never thought about it like that."

"Does this happen a lot?"

A dozen seconds passed before Jake answered. Finally, he said, "It's a tradition as old as the land. We presume that the magick won't call someone who isn't willing." He studied me. "Viviane, things work differently with our kith and kin. The traditions are sometimes cruel, but they haven't changed in thousands of years."

I snorted. "Well, maybe it's long overdue that our *kith and kin rethink those traditions.*"

"Maybe it is," Jake agreed.

I stared down at the freshly dug earth. Death was a high price to pay to bring back an ancestor. I was starting to see just how much I had to learn.

◇

Jake and I didn't stay long, but we did what we could to seal up Agate's home. We packed a bag of mementos we thought Ivy might want one day, and I spent as much time consoling the dogs as I did doing anything else. They knew. Yogi barely moved, his tail tucked tight against his body. Boo followed me around, her chin resting on my foot or leg. Neither of them would eat or drink. I found myself more than once crying—for Boo and Yogi, for Agate, for Ivy... For my mom...

Jake stayed busy, but he too was devastated. While going through Agate's things, he found an old high school yearbook.

"Look at this," he said, and I joined him.

Wyrdwood North High School. Their mascot was a Celtic-styled eagle. Jake opened the book and browsed through it. Everyone looked normal, human, even to my magickal sight. I assumed that's how photography worked. Then, Jake came to a photo of himself and Agate arm-in-arm, fists raised in triumph. They looked so happy and so young. It took my breath away. Jake abruptly broke into tears.

I put my arms around him and held him. He leaned into me. He was warm and heavy, body shaking as he cried. I petted his hair and rubbed his back, feeling my own misery grow as his washed over me.

"It's so unfair," I whispered, remembering how Agate had looked when she was dancing in the drum circle—so full of life, of Earth Mother energy. So beautiful. It just wasn't fair that such a joyous moment as a birth should be ruined by death. I hated how I felt.

Jake and I remained in the embrace, heads pressed together, exhausted. I was so worn out, emotionally and physically, that I didn't notice what was happening until I felt Jake's lips push against mine. His were soft, gentle, tentative. My whole being focused on that connection between us, on that intimate touch to my mouth, the way his head tilted, how his breath blew warm across my cheek. I responded without thinking, reciprocating the kiss. I wanted to cling to him, to push everything away except for how it felt to be close to someone. For me, it was more emotional than sexual. The embrace gave me an avenue through which to express my grief, and for the third time in twenty-four hours, I had my breath stolen—until I thought of Colin.

I pulled away, pushing against Jake's shoulders. "No," I said, and it came out far softer than I intended. I was breathing quickly, couldn't quite catch my breath. My head was spinning. "I'm engaged," I said.

Jake sat back and stared at me. He was working through what had just happened. With brutal honesty, he said, "He left you," and he wasn't wrong. As far as Jake knew, I hadn't seen Colin since he'd abandoned me to his murderous brother. He didn't know about Colin's visit.

I stood and crossed the room to look out the window. The day was darkening. We only had a few hours until sunset. "We need to go. We're running out of time, and I don't want to spend another night here."

What a long rollercoaster of a day it had been.

"I'm sorry," Jake said. "I wasn't thinking. That's not who I am. I just... It won't happen again."

I didn't have the energy to be angry with him or with myself. I said, "It's been an emotional day. It's a natural reaction to seek comfort. I'm not mad."

"Thank you." Jake stood and returned to packing.

◇

We covered the furniture with sheets, emptied the refrigerator and unplugged it, shut down Agate's generator, locked the front door and left. Jake agreed the dogs should have a new home at the haven, and we took them with us. We trudged back through the woods and across the clearing to the car.

On the way to the airport, we stopped at a pet store and bought two large crates, one for each of them.

Neither of us spoke much during the long flight home. I put in earbuds and listened to music while Jake worked on his laptop. Despite the silence, it felt like we had an intimate connection that hadn't been there before, as if our shared trauma—and the stolen kiss—had bonded us in a deep and lasting way. We didn't need to talk. He made sure I ate, and I cleaned up after him. It was pointless to ask, "Are you okay?" We both knew that neither of us were.

◇◇◇

CHAPTER 13

I'd never been so happy to get home as I was when we finally got out of the car at the Lost Lambs haven. Corona ran out to greet us, chattering about the dramas that had happened while we were gone and then promptly got distracted by the appearance of Yogi and Boo. I escaped to my room, drank two glasses of water, took a proper shower, went to bed early, and then crashed for almost twelve hours. I'd have slept longer if the knock on my bedroom door hadn't woken me.

Corona peeked in before I could get up to answer. "Decent?" she asked.

I grumbled something in response, then groaned loudly when Corona flipped on the light switch. With a hop and a skip, she dove into the bed beside me. It jolted my ribs, and they pained me. I grimaced.

Corona lay on her side, staring. "I heard what happened."

"I'm okay."

"I know." She just kept staring.

"What's up?" I asked, eyelids heavy.

"Data and DNA."

"What?" I rolled over onto my back and stretched carefully.

"My racial identity. I've got an appointment to

get mine checked."

"You're human, Corona," I said.

"No. I'm not. Not entirely. An' neither are you. Just because I was raised human don't mean I *am human.*"

"Okay." I put my pillow over my face to block out the light. "Well, I'm human," I said, muffled in the pillow.

"Rio says I'm selkie. They're seal people, shape-shifters, like mermaids, but less dumb."

"Mermaids are dumb?"

Corona pushed up onto one elbow. "Mermaids are Daphne. Selkies are Velma."

I moved the pillow aside and just stared at her blankly.

She said, "I found a place in Wyrdwood—a lab that does DNA tests for wielders." She beamed, eyes bright. "You should get yours done too!"

"I'm good," I said.

"You could find out who your ancestors were."

"It doesn't matter." I moved the pillow aside and turned my head to look at her. "It's not going to change who I am."

"It might help you find your magickal proficiencies. Like, if I'm a selkie, then I can become a seal."

"Can you become a seal?"

"Now? No. But I don't want to waste a bunch of time trying to become one if I'm *not a selkie. Duh.*" *She rolled onto her back, arms down at her sides. "Why don't you want to explore your ancestry?"*

I rubbed my hands over my face, wishing I could go back to sleep. "It's just not that important to me, Corona."

"It might be important."

"It's not."

Corona lifted all four limbs into the air, then dropped them back onto the bed. "I get it," she said. "It's like the steak. Ignorance is bliss."

"What?"

Tone serious, Corona said, "You *know the steak isn't real, but you don't care because it's good, and so you enjoy the steak when, really, it's all a fucking lie.*"

I sighed and rolled up to sit, feeling for my slippers. "Girl, get out of my room. I need to take a shower."

"I'm going to the lab later today, if you change your mind." Corona threw her legs high, then used the down-swing as leverage to roll herself to her feet. "See you laters."

"Yeah," I said and watched Corona go to the door, open it, and step into the hall. I had every intention of climbing back under the covers and going back to sleep, but Corona said, "G'mornin', Rio."

Rio came into view. "Good morning, dear," she replied.

Corona jerked her head toward me and said, "She's grumpy."

"Good to know." Rio entered my room and looked me over with an evaluating eye. "Are you all right?"

I remained perched on the edge of the bed. "Tired."

She shut the door behind her.

Having lost the hope of going back to sleep, I gave her a side-eyed look. "Did you want something?"

"Jake told me what happened. He asked me to check on you. You've been cloistered up here for a long time."

I glanced at the alarm clock. It was just after eleven. I said, "I needed to catch up on my sleep."

With her long dark hair down, Rio's demeanor softened, though her high-waisted pants and blouse were both tailored and professional. She moved to the window and pulled aside the drapes, letting muted daylight into the room. "Do you want to talk about it?"

I definitely did not. "Thanks," I said. "I'm good."

"You must be starving. It's almost time for lunch. Why don't you get dressed and come on down. I'll have Ayu make you something bolstering." Rio went to the door. "Say, in ten minutes?" She didn't give me a choice nor a chance to answer.

Once she was gone, I did get out of bed. Already the rawness of my memories and emotions was fading. I was exhausted, still. Even after having slept for twelve hours. It was as if I'd been beaten half to death, and my body was putting all my energy into healing my insides. I supposed that—from an emotional standpoint—that analogy was accurate. The thought of food—of fuel—drove me to shower, dress, and go downstairs. I wasn't in the mood to see anyone, especially not Jake, and so I was grateful to find the kitchen empty of everyone but Rio.

"Your sandwich is in the refrigerator," she said. "Roast beef."

My mouth watered. "Thank you."

Rio asked, "Have you heard from your grandfather? Your grandmother?"

"Grandpa sent an email to say he got home safely. I'll call him later today. My grandmother..." I hesitated before the lie, balking at it, "...is gone."

"Oh!" Rio said. "I'm sorry."

"It's okay. I never really knew her." That, fortunately, was the truth. I was grateful for the sandwich and doubly grateful when Rio didn't press me to make further conversation. We sat on stools at the bar, and she let me eat, reading something on her tablet.

As I was taking my plate to the sink, Rio said, "Why don't we take a drive? I have a surprise for you."

"A surprise?" I was suspicious.

"Something I want to show you." She stood from her stool. "I think you'll like it."

"Well, it's not like I have anything else scheduled today," I said with a touch of snark. "Do you know where Jake and the others are?"

She waved a hand dismissively. "We were all stuck for hours in what Jake called 'a debriefing.' He told everyone what happened in West Virginia. He gave everybody *tasks.*" *She did air-quotes on the* word "tasks."

"Oh," I said. "And your task was to babysit me?" That came out harsher than I intended.

Fortunately, Rio laughed. "Only to check on you. The rest is all me. Besides, you're not the only one who will benefit from this." As I turned toward her, drying my hands on a towel, she ushered me out of the kitchen. "Go on. Put on a jacket and some boots or sturdy shoes in case there's mud."

"Mud?" I found it hard to imagine Rio tromping through mud, but that wouldn't be the last time she'd surprise me.

◇

Rio was waiting out front when I emerged in my windbreaker and ankle boots. She had changed into jeans, several layers of shirts, and knee-high boots. She'd pulled her hair into a ponytail at the back of her neck.

"Let's go!" She had her car waiting there, a blood red, four-door sedan. "Get in."

She drove us back down the driveway to Snake Run Road, then turned east onto the lane that ran along the river, away from Wyrdwood and the sea. Before long, we pulled into a forest-lined side road that passed under a sign saying, "Slipper Stables."

I blinked. "Stables?"

Rio smiled at me and nodded. "Horses. You like horses, right?"

I did. I loved horses. I'd ridden throughout high school whenever I could afford it and even mucked out stables for less-than-minimum wage when I was a senior.

The forest parted, revealing a wide field. A trio of beautiful mavericks lifted their heads as we came into view. With a forested ridge behind them, and the blue sky overhead, it was as picturesque as it gets. Ahead, the ranch itself was a pair of longhouses, one for the horses, and one for the owners.

A man with tanned skin and dark hair met us.

"Welcome to the Slipper ranch," he said, offering us both hardy handshakes. "I'm the owner. You can call me Juan. Miss Rio, it's a pleasure to see you again."

"Juan," Rio said with a smile. "We'd like to borrow a couple of your beauties, if you wouldn't mind."

"Yes, ma'am. We have Sage and Missy—short for Mischief—saddled and ready for you. Why don't you come in and sign the paperwork, then you can be on your way. It's a gorgeous day for a ride."

The day, for me, had gotten even brighter. Rio and I signed the wavers, and she paid for the rental with a fan of cash. They offered us gloves, and I accepted with gratitude, tucking them into my coat pocket. The preparations all went by in a blur, my mind already on the horses. When we met them, I discovered mine was a strong and gentle creature, reddish brown with a wide streak of white down her face. I stepped toward her head, making sure she saw me as I approached and offering her the back of my hand to sniff. Her velvety nose brushed my knuckles, and my heart did a flip. "Sweet girl," I mooned at her.

"These mustangs are rescues," Juan explained, picking up a wooden box from beside the fence.

"Rescued from what?" I asked, petting down the horse's neck. Her name was Sage.

"From slaughter," he replied without preamble. "The government has eroded the laws protecting wild horses. People stampede them using helicopters, corral them, and then slaughter them to sell their meat."

My mouth dropped open in horror. How had I never known that?

Juan's jaw clenched, then he said, "The president wants to reduce government funding to the program that cares for the wild ones. We adopt and tame them to save them from the sausage factory." His tone dripped with disgust.

"That's awful," I said.

"All the corporations see is a chance to make money." Juan's gaze drifted out to the three horses in the pasture. "Here at Slipper, they run as free as they want."

"I'm so glad. Thank you." I lay my cheek against Sage's neck, breathing in her earthy smell. "Why do you call your ranch Slipper?"

Juan looked over at Rio, and she nodded to him. "Viviane is kin," she said.

The stable owner set down the wooden step beside Rio's mount. "The Sleipnir are a breed of eight-legged horses. Odin rides his into battle. They're almost extinct now. Less than a handful still exist, all in captivity. They were hunted and used for their speed. Normals can't see their extra legs, so they used to turn up at races all over the country. Anyone who bet on them was sure to win. It gave kin an advantage. Some people tried to breed them, but they don't work that way. You see, their freedom is directly tied to their well-being."

I had so many questions, but Rio interrupted my train of thought. "Mount up, Viviane. I'm sure Juan needs to get back to work. I can answer any questions you have as we ride." I watched her step up and swing into the saddle. Her horse shifted its weight but settled again as she found her seat.

"Thanks, Juan," I said. I didn't wait for the box but put my foot in the stirrup and slid up the side of the horse and into the saddle. My ribs protested, but I ignored them. A little pain was a small price to pay. Being on a horse felt like coming home, and as I bent forward to pet Sage's neck, I asked Rio, "How did you know I like horses?"

Rio laughed. "Don't all girls?" She clucked her tongue and kicked with her heels, turning the horse toward the path. I did the same.

The sun on my face felt magnificent, and the fresh air was going to my head. For a while, my questions fell away. We rode in silence along a path that skirted the big field and entered the trees, moving uphill on an easy slope. The pine trees around us had shed their cones and needles to cover the ground with them, making everything quiet.

The solitude and the quiet were exactly what I'd needed. Sage's rocking movement lulled me into an easy, relaxed state, and I breathed thick oxygen into my lungs. My thoughts drifted away with an almost meditative disconnection, and my troubles went with them. Nothing else mattered in that moment—not missing Colin or my mother, not my recent traumatic experiences, not the pain in my ribs. I became an extension of Sage, and through her, of the Earth, the sky, and the universe.

Eventually, Rio and I came to a cliff overlooking a lake whose dark blue waters sparkled in the sunshine. Layered hills gave the lake a scenic backdrop, and it was surrounded on all sides by thick evergreen forest.

"Fortunate Lake," said Rio, speaking for the first time since we'd begun our ride. "Let's water the horses." She dismounted and walked Missy down a path to the shore. I joined her, noting the animal prints in the dirt with fascination. I recognized raccoon, deer, some kind of large cat, what may have been a possum, and plenty of birds.

"That there," Rio pointed to a length of shore on the far side, "is actually an island, though you can't tell from this vantage point. It's a sanctuary for birds. No one's allowed out there anymore."

I acknowledged her with a nod and took a photo, for posterity. The island had various buildings nestled in an evergreen forest. They shimmered slightly in the sun, a visual effect I recognized as magick. "Why do they call it Fortunate Lake?"

Rio shrugged. "The lake was once a volcano. Many thousands of years ago, it blew its top. Maybe those who named it considered themselves fortunate not to have been killed by the eruption?"

The rim of the volcano had become cliffs surrounding the lake.

"Thousands of years ago," I said. "Can you imagine what these rocks have seen?"

Rio laughed and shook her head. "So much more than either of us can imagine." She went to her horse and unhooked her pack. She had brought a blanket and snacks. She laid them out, and we sat on the lakeshore. One of my favorite things about Rio was that she didn't need to make conversation. She was happy to just sit, stare at the water, and eat leftover breakfast biscuits with hunks of cheese in them.

Just as I was starting to get antsy again, Rio reached into her bag and brought out her tarot deck. I watched her with interest as she unwrapped the silk cloth and removed the cards. She began to shuffle, and in the process, one of the cards leapt out and landed on the blanket in front of her. I reached for it, asking, "May I?"

"Of course," Rio said.

The cards were printed, but they looked handdrawn. The front of the card showed a woman who looked remarkably like Rio, right down to the white streak in her otherwise ebony hair. She was dressed in an ornate gown and seated on a throne. The word written at the bottom was "Morrigan." When I turned the card over, I found the word, "Apfallon," worked delicately into an ornate knot design.

"What can you tell me about Apfallon?" I asked.

"It's a place," Rio said, still shuffling and watching me study the card. "To be more specific, it's an ancient magickal realm that sits perpendicular to our own. You can only get there if you know the way."

"Wow," I said. "Not what I thought you'd say."

Rio laughed. "You'd like it there."

"Is that where you're from?"

"Not any more." Rio's eyebrows pulled together. "My husband's people were exiled from there many generations ago."

"Exiled? Why?"

She snorted a soft laugh. "Politics. Territorial greed. Tyranny. The Fomor lost the war."

"You're Fomor?"

Rio reached out and gently took the card from me. "Only by marriage. I come from a long line of Morghaine. My ancestors remained neutral in the war, though maybe they shouldn't have." She slid the card back into the deck and resumed shuffling.

"And your husband..." I hesitated as I reviewed the question I was about to ask. *Is he normal? I laughed aloud at myself and said, "I don't know how to ask about his race."*

Rio replied, "I suggest you never ask that kind

of question unless you know the person well. And maybe use the word 'heritage' or 'lineage' instead of race. It's less charged." She didn't sound the least bit offended, and for that I was grateful. "A more general question might work better."

I said, "Such as... What's your husband like?"

She smiled her approval. "Yes, exactly. And in answer, I'll tell you that he's the patriarch of the Fomor. The king, the chief, the sultan, the raja in other words. He can be overbearing at times, but he loves me and our children with all his heart. Loves his people and hopes to one day lead them back to their homeland."

I was floored. "Wow. Seriously? Your husband is a king? Like, for reals?"

Rio chuckled. "Yes. For reals."

"Where?"

"In a place called Gehenna."

I'd heard of Gehenna. It was where Colin was from.

The implications rolled over me. "So that means you're a queen?"

In response, she nodded, eyes avoiding mine. "I am. But being royalty isn't what it used to be. I'm more of a figurehead these days. Please don't let that change anything between us."

"No, no. I wouldn't."

"Would you like me to do a reading for you?" Rio indicated the tarot cards.

"Sure. Why not?"

She handed me the cards. "Shuffle them, please. If you have something you want to know about, think about it as you're shuffling."

The deck was light. It had no more than two-dozen cards. "I thought tarot decks had a lot more cards," I commented.

"They can. The tarot are broken into two houses. The Major Arcana and the Minor Arcana. The Minor are for everyday things, like... Will I get the job I want? The Major deal with soul things, those aspects of your situation that have ties to the universe and to the very heart of who you are. I only ever do readings with the Major Arcana because I have absolutely no interest whatsoever in how your day will go." Her voice dropped in volume, but rose in intensity. "I want to know what's in your soul."

I laughed—as much with nerves as with amusement. "Well, all righty then," I said. "Let's see what's happening with my soul." I shuffled the cards. As I did, an image of Colin formed in my mind, and I wondered what we had in our future.

Once I'd finished shuffling, Rio cut the cards and turned the top one over on the blanket. The card said, "Lovers." It showed three people with their limbs interwoven within a Celtic knotwork frame. It was impossible to determine anyone's gender, but they were all naked.

I couldn't hide my surprise at that first card, and I wondered why it had three people in it instead of just two.

Rio said, "This reveals the nature of your question. It's complex. You have a love unfolding but it hasn't yet come to fruition. Your heart isn't fully open yet, and it's hard to find the path to happiness."

Me and Colin, I decided. Definitely was complex. I nodded in acknowledgement.

Rio turned the next two cards, placing them so they made a triangle with the first one at the top. The left-bottom card was "The Tower." It showed a dramatic scene filled with lightning and fire. The tower in the picture was crumbling, and people were falling from its windows. The right-bottom card was "The World." In it, an angelic figure hovered over a lush landscape where beings of all kinds had come to see her. I spotted an orcneas, a satyr, and a man with pointed ears among the foxes, birds, lions, and other animals.

Rio said, "These two describe your current situation. The one on the left is outgoing, but still presently affecting you. The one on the right is incoming and will be affecting you for the foreseeable future. Outgoing is the Tower. It indicates a big change in your life, one that you probably hadn't expected."

I joked, "That's my nominee for the understatement of the year."

Rio continued, "The World is the opening of a door. Your world is growing bigger. Your view of reality is expanding. Your role and influence—in both your own life and the lives of those around you—are being amplified. This is affecting the love story you have unfolding. This may seem scary." She tapped the Tower card. "But the World tells me that change needed to happen."

I kept wanting to say, "Wow," but I refrained.

She lay down three more cards in the bottom row, forming the base of the pyramid. "This row reveals the foundation of your situation, the soul's undercurrent." She indicated the one on the far left. "Your past." It was The Moon. It showed a giant full moon against a field of stars, reflected on dark blue waters. Also in the water was a face. The angle made it appear as if my own face was reflected there. It was just hazy enough that I could imagine it was me.

"You've always been intuitive in a special kind of way, but you've kept it hidden." The middle card on that row was The Star. Rio picked it up and handed it to me. "This," she said, "is your present. It's your rebirth from the roots of Yggdrasil."

A naked woman was climbing from the thick roots of a Tree of Life. The tree's roots interwove with its branches—more Celtic knotwork without beginning or end. While all around was darkness, she herself glowed, and her hair had a life of its own. The only stars in the scene shone in her eyes and hair, twinkling sparks of magick that came from inside her.

Rio didn't have to say anything more about that card. I understood the symbolism of a new beginning, a new identity, and hope.

I handed the card back to her, and she replaced it in the spread. We both looked to the third card in the row.

"Your future," Rio said, resting the tip of her index finger on the Strength card. "You'll find a new kind of strength with the support of your lover," She touched the Lovers card again. "It's all intertwined. Your strength is inside you, but it reaches its fullest expression with the one you love. Things won't be easy, but you'll have what it takes to overcome your challenges and make the right decisions. You'll become a savior to others through your love."

She sat back in silence. I studied the cards, putting it all together in my mind. It sounded like Colin and I would be okay, and that left me with a warm feeling. I said, "So, the prognosis is good, Doc?"

Rio laughed. "Very good indeed. Keep doing what you're doing." She gathered up the cards and returned the deck to its box. She said, "I have to visit the ladies' room in the bushes before we head back. Keep an eye on the horses, won't you?" She headed up the trail toward the top of the cliff.

"Sure," I agreed. "I'll be here." I glanced over at the horses. They had their heads down chewing on tufts of grass.

I thought about how my life had been turned upside-down in such a short time. Back at Malum Center, my world had been so dark. Now, it felt brighter—despite my mother's death. I was no longer looking down a steep, darkened staircase. I was free and sitting in the sunshine. Colin had visited me, and I knew I'd see him again. Nothing could keep us apart for long. And I allowed myself to think about the fact that I had magick. The world was so much bigger than it had been before. So different from what my limited viewpoint had made it out to be. I closed my eyes, breathed deeply of the fresh air, and thought, *Mom would be happy for me.*

I had no idea how much time passed, lost as I was in my own reverie, but a voice startled me out of it. A voice inside my head.

Viviane. I need to speak with you. We don't have much time.

I turned on the blanket to find Nathan at the crest of the path. His black wings flapped in small movements to keep him aloft just above the ground. He descended until he was standing. My adrenaline surged.

"Why are you here?" I asked, aware of my teeth grinding.

Don't be afraid.

"I am not afraid of you," I said, emphasizing every word. I got to my feet.

The horses whinnied and side-stepped a little.

You don't need to speak aloud, Nathan said. Your gift lets us dialog. Which is lovely, actually. With most people, I can only eavesdrop on their thoughts—most of which are beyond boring. You have no idea the crap that goes through—

I took a slow, deep breath and thought at him with all my might, *LEAVE ME ALONE!*

Hey! No need to shout! Nathan met my gaze

without faltering. His feathered raven hair was a mess on his head, disheveled by the wind, and his black trenchcoat rippled about him as if wishing for flight. He didn't hide his wings, but they relaxed down his back.

He thought, *I know who killed your mother.*

"Who?" I said aloud on a gasp, forgetting to just think it.

As if he sensed he was back in charge, Nathan clasped his hands over his stomach and turned to the side. Stalling. Stretching out the moment. *There is so much you don't know, liebchen. You're still soaking wet and wrinkled from the Normal bath you've been living in. A newborn. I couldn't possibly explain generations of politics and prejudice to you in the time it takes that woman to get her knickers down for a piss.*

I thought at him, *Just tell me who did it.*

Nathan waved his hand, *It wasn't your precious Colin.*

I never thought it was.

Oh. Why not? He was there too.

I left the horses nibbling at reeds and walked purposefully toward him. *Tell me, Nathan, or I swear to god...*

Which one? he asked, almost as if out of habit and curiosity.

Which what?

Which god will you swear to?

My frustration was making itself felt in the heat

in my cheeks and the thrum of my heartbeat in my neck. Aloud, I said, "Nathan! Just. Fucking. Tell. Me." I paused a beat, then added, "Please." On the last word, I felt myself melt a little, my grief crashing over me like a wave. One of my feet slipped on the rocky incline, and I stumbled. Having crossed half the distance between us, I halted in place, waiting as he studied me. *Please, I repeated I my mind.*

His thought came as a whisper, You won't like it.

I don't care. Tell me.

It's quite like Romeo and Juliet, though less poetic, he said, dragging out the words. Your and Colin's story was foretold. Your destinies are entwined, and anyone who gets in the way of that—

A shot rang out, making me jump and gasp. It echoed briefly, and the horses whinnied in fear.

Nathan dropped to his hands and knees.

I peered around, but saw no one. My gaze returned to Nathan just in time to see him fall forward into a heap on the ground. He didn't move. Breaking into a run, I scrambled up the path and made it to his side in seconds. At first, my mind didn't fully comprehend what I was seeing. He was lying facedown in the dirt. His mouth hung agog, and he was staring straight ahead. A thick red stain was spreading from under him, a stream of blood that made its way downhill and began to pool in a little dent in the earth. His wings were gone, and he looked so humanly fragile. Broken.

In the distance, I heard Rio shout, "Viviane? Viviane!" She burst out of the trees further along the path, jeans unbuttoned, shirt untucked.

I knelt to feel for Nathan's pulse, moving my fingers around, searching—but not finding it. I forgot to blink. I forgot to breathe until Rio's hand landed on my shoulder. Someone cried out in anguish. At first, I thought it was me, but then Rio ran around to Nathan's side and rolled him over. With one violent sob, she broke into tears and bent her body over his.

"Nathanatos!"

CHAPTER 14

I took a step back from Nathan's body and fumbled through dialing Jake.

"Viviane," he answered.

"Jake—Jake." I couldn't catch my breath. I tore my eyes from Nathan, bent over, and stared at the ground, panting.

"Viviane, what's going on?"

"Somebody shot Nathan," I managed. "He's dead. We need help."

"Where are you?"

"Slipper Stables. But we rode out to the lake. Fortunate Lake."

"Okay. Are you safe?"

"I don't know."

"Okay. Stay there. We're on our way." As he was hanging up, I heard him yell, "Hilda!"

I couldn't stop shaking. "They're coming, Rio."

Rio was sitting on the ground, a look of shock on her face. "Did you see?" she asked, sounding numb. Her eyes lifted to mine, and I saw she was anything but numb. "Did you see who did this?"

I shook my head. "It came out of nowhere. I heard...I heard it. That's all. And then, he..." I felt like I should be doing something, but I didn't know what. I searched the tree-line again but didn't see anyone or anything.

Rio was pulling Nathan into her lap, not unlike a Pietá. "I have to take him home," she said as she tugged on his body. His blood stained her clothes and her hands. It was heartbreaking to watch. When she had him settled in her arms, she raised her gaze back to mine. I saw her lips move, but I couldn't hear what she said. It didn't matter because a second later, the ground opened up beneath her, and she fell through the hole in reality, taking Nathan with her.

The hole disappeared the moment they were through, and I was left alone, dumbfounded, beside a bloody stain on the grass. I burst into tears.

◇

I heard a distant buzz well before the ATV emerged from the forest and headed toward me. I was standing with the horses, pulling warmth from Sage's body. I waved at the approaching vehicle. It had no roof and four seats, with Jake in the backseat, Hilda front passenger-side, and Juan driving. They bumped across the uneven ground and slowed nearby. Jake stood, holding onto the roll bar, well before the ATV came to a full stop. He leapt out and strode toward me. The only hesitation he allowed himself was when he noticed the blood stain. Then, he was beside me, pulling me into his arms.

I melted against him, tears overwhelming me again.

Juan pulled the ATV over and turned it off. Hilda stepped out.

"Where's Nathan?" she called, turning in place.

"Rio took him," I said, my voice muffled against Jake's chest. "She... She opened a hole and fell through it with his body."

Jake called to Hilda, "Rio 'chuted him away. They probably went home."

"Yeah," I said, once again feeling like I might regain control of myself. I pushed away from Jake's body. "That's what she said. She said she was taking him home." I swiped at my tears with the backs of both hands. "I'm glad you're here." My voice broke a bit.

Jake released me from the hug but kept his hand on my shoulder.

Juan came over to us. "No need to call the Sheriff. No body, no crime."

"Agreed." Jake bent to look me in the face. "Viviane, are you sure he was dead? Maybe his family could heal him?"

I nodded. "I'm sure. Rio was sure too."

Jake's expression was dour. "Let's get you back to the haven. You're probably in shock."

Shocked was exactly what I felt—the urge to cry so close to the surface. I let Jake guide me into the front seat of the ATV and help me to buckle up. My whole body was still shivering. Hilda pulled a wool blanket out of the back and draped it around my shoulders. It smelled like horse.

Juan and Hilda rode Sage and Missy back to the stables. Jake drove me in the ATV. I wrapped my arms around myself, hugging the blanket closer. I felt weak and feverish, as if I'd been in a terrible accident. I supposed I had, except it was no accident. Whoever had shot Nathan, had done it on purpose. Of that, I was certain.

At the stables, Jake and I switched over to his car. He turned the heat on, including the heated seats, and the tension began releasing my abused muscles. With one hand, Jake rubbed my shoulder and neck.

While we waited for Hilda to catch up, he asked, "How many shots were there?"

"Just one. That's all it took."

Jake nodded, thinking, his hand warm and strong as it kneaded my muscles.

"Jake," I said, the fog in my brain starting to clear. "What's Rio's relationship to Nathan?"

Jake licked his lips before answering. "She's his mother," he said.

So I was right. The pieces were coming together. "And Colin? Is he hers too?"

"Step-son," Jake replied, watching me closely. "Colin and Nathan shared the same father."

"The king of... Gehenna?"

"The ruler, yes."

"So that makes Colin..."

"The heir to the Gehenna empire. Now that Nathan is... well, gone."

"And Rio's a queen?"

"'Queen' is such an outdated title, but she's definitely the matriarch of the Fomor, by marriage. She comes from the Morghaine lineage. You could say they're royalty too."

"Do you know who Colin's mother is?"

Jake shook his head. "No. Just that it's not Rio."

"Why didn't you tell me?" I asked. "Why didn't she?"

Jake huffed a sigh. "When you're new to the magickal world, it's easy to get overwhelmed. She asked me not to tell you who she was, and I honored that."

Hilda and Juan rode up and dismounted. Hilda handed Missy's reins to Juan, patted the man heartily on the back, and then walked toward the car.

I slid into the dark water of my own thoughts. So much death. Mom, Agate, and Nathan. It was too much. Something was happening. I knew it couldn't be random. I remembered how Nathan had looked, lying in his own blood, face dead slack—and then I remembered him sitting with me and Corona in the rec room at Malum, with his funky socks—black with purple stars—and that crooked grin of his. I remembered his cruelty when he'd kidnapped me and had his driver break Corona's arm.

A crow flew down and landed on the fence, and I was reminded of seeing Nathan in the top of the tree, the way his coat had rippled around him, and how he'd morphed into a raven and flown away. Unlike Colin's, his black wings had been inky black. No rainbow colors mixed in.

Hilda climbed into the back seat, and Jake directed the car down the long driveway.

I turned in my seat to watch the crow shake out its feathers and peck at something on the wood. There was nothing magickal about it. Just an ordinary every-day bird. It pooped, and I heard the ghost of Nathan's laughter.

◇

By the time we got back to the haven, I was feeling calmer—somewhat numb, even. Corona met us outside, eyes widening when she saw us. She helped me out of the car as if I were an invalid. I wrapped my arm around her shoulders as we crossed the drive to the front of the house.

"So, Nathan's dead?" she asked quietly.

"Yeah. Somebody shot him."

"Damn. Who'd do that?"

It was the question of the century, and I certainly didn't have the answer. My mind was churning over the possibilities. I said, "He was about to tell me who killed Mom."

"What?" Corona looked up at me.

"He didn't get a chance to, before... You know." She nodded.

I said, "He didn't do it. That's what he said."

"You believed him?"

"I did, yeah. He said Colin and I were destined

to be together."

Corona snorted through her nose. "Everyone knows that."

I held the front door and let her precede me into the haven's big living room.

Amalia was there, standing with her hands folded in front of her. She tilted her head when I met her gaze, sniffed, then said just loud enough for me to hear, "You smell like death." Her voice had the rustle of dry leaves.

A flash of anger lit me up. I was too tired and raw to filter my words. Before I could stop myself, I replied, "Something tells me you like that smell."

The only sign she'd even heard me was that her white eyebrows rose. We stared at one another for a moment, then I diverted the conflict by asking, "How's Ivy?"

She relaxed back and replied, "She's well. She's in good hands."

"I want to see her," I said.

Amalia nodded. "All right. Not today."

"No," I said. "Not today." I thought of the tiny body I'd held in my arms, so fragile and innocent. I wanted her to be safe and wished I trusted Amalia to keep her that way.

"C'mon," I said to Corona, pulling her along toward the hallway. I needed the sanctuary of my room, a shower, and fresh clothes. I hadn't even liked Nathan—not entirely—but seeing someone murdered so violently had shaken me to the core.

Corona understood. She said nothing until we were well out of earshot of Amalia. Only then did she say, with surprising clarity, "This new paradigm we've tapped is dangerous in ways we can't begin to comprehend. I don't understand how everyone goes through normal life with all this just outside the bounds of their vision. Do you know the parable about the blind men and the elephant?"

"Huh uh," I replied with a small shake of my head.

"It's ancient Buddhist wisdom—a parable—about some blind men who come across an elephant for the first time, and they're feeling it. You know, 'cause they're blind."

"Got it."

"The one who touches the trunk thinks an elephant is like a big snake. The one who touches its leg believes an elephant is a tree, and the one who touches its side thinks the elephant is a wall. And so on. That's how it is to be Normal, I think. Maybe you feel a portion of magick, but you never see the whole thing. You're blind, and you misinterpret it. You explain it away, trying to fit into your little tiny normal boxes. But you and me, we've had our eyes opened. Now, we need to keep our minds open too."

"What do you mean?" I asked.

"I mean... An elephant is a lot bigger and more dangerous than any one of its parts, and we're still only feeling up a leg."

I said, "I wish I'd never learned about the elephant," and I meant it. I'd been almost happy before. "I just want a normal life. I want to settle down with Colin, have some kids, and live happily ever after. I never asked for this magickal bullshit."

"Not true."

"Excuse me?" I pulled back and looked down at Corona.

"You don't want a normal life. If you did, you'd have given up looking for Colin. Except you were never really looking for Colin—or not just Colin. You were looking for an answer. And the question was far more personal than whether Colin was alive or dead. Do you know what the question is?"

"No." I didn't like the uneasiness her words were stirring inside me.

"'Who am I?' That's the real question." She and I stared into each other's eyes. She continued, "You and me, we're the same. No parents. Weird reality. Faux schizo. You even fell for a guy who had *amnesia. Maybe because you understood how it felt to not know who you are. Our lives tell a story, and yours definitely does not read 'Normal.'*"

I sighed and pulled Corona along. "I need a shower."

We crossed the walkway to Cedar House and climbed to the second floor. Outside my bedroom door, Corona asked, "Why are you here instead of in hiding with Colin?"

"That wasn't an option."

"Maybe. Or maybe you're afraid to find out who

Colin really is."

We entered my room, and while I'd had every intention of undressing and showering, the bed called out to me. I flopped down on it and curled into a ball. I *had been afraid, when I thought Colin might have a wife and kids hidden by his amnesia. The truth—that he had wings—was surprisingly easier to handle.*

"Have you heard from Simon?" I asked.

Corona landed in the armchair. "No. Not since we left the Center."

"Malum Center seems so long ago now," I said. "Like a different life. The laundry. Julio."

"In a way, you had amnesia too."

I hugged myself. "And ever since things changed, people have been dying. Polly, Mrs. Dufour."

"That was the hag."

"But what if the hag was working for someone? What if this is all connected?" When Corona didn't reply, I continued, "An assassin came after Agate. If we hadn't been there, he'd have killed her and her baby."

"It's good you were there."

I didn't feel good about it. "She died anyway," I said. *"Why is this happening? And why not me?"*

"Why not you what?"

"Why kill Mom? Why Nathan? Why not me?"

"We know it wasn't dumb luck," Corona said in a dour tone. "In the Matrix, nothing is random."

◇◇◇

CHAPTER 15

Eventually, I found the energy to shower and dress in clean clothes. My body felt weak and chilled, like I was coming down with a cold. More than anything, I had a yearning for a hot cup of tea, so I went to the kitchen to make one.

To my surprise, Rio was there. She had pulled her hair back into a severe bun at the nape of her neck, and she was wearing a black pantsuit with a midnight-blue blouse. She was sitting at the counter with her hands around a mug, and though she didn't look at me as I entered, she said, "The water's hot, and I left out the box of teas for you." As if she'd known I was coming.

"Thank you," I said and set about making a cup of tea for myself. I didn't know what to say other than that.

Fortunately, Rio took the lead. "Nathan is with the family now."

"Good. How are you doing?"

"It is what it is."

"I didn't know he was your son."

Rio looked over at me, expression unreadable. Neither of us said anything more until I took a seat at the bar with my tea in hand. Then she asked, "Why was he there?"

I breathed in the steam rising from my mug. "He said he knew who killed my mother."

"Who?"

"He didn't get a chance to say."

"You talked to him?" Rio's eyes were rimmed with red and her mouth turned down.

"In my head," I told her. "He and I could talk—telepathically, I suppose."

"You mean you could hear him?"

"Yes, and he could hear me too. Two-way. He said that was unusual."

"Yes, it is. It means one of your abilities is emerging. That's a good thing." Her tone was matter-of-fact. "If you'd like, I can help you hone it. With training, you could use it even without seeing the other person."

"Really?" The idea of Rio training me felt much more acceptable than having Jake train me.

Rio's voice sounded in my head. *Try with me. Can you hear me? Shades of her grief wafted along with the words.*

I nodded and thought at her, *I hear you.*

Ayu came into the kitchen, greeting us both with a solemn, "Hello." She went to the coffee pot and began setting it up to brew. "I made muffins this morning. Blueberry chocolate chip. Help yourselves."

"Thank you," I said.

Rio thought to me, *Are you able to eavesdrop on people's thoughts?*

Not that I'm aware of.

Try. See if you can hear Ayu's thoughts.

I had a brief pang of concern about the ethical ramifications, but then Rio encouraged me with a wave of her hand. I took a deep breath and made my shoulders relax a half inch more. I "listened" for Ayu's thoughts. Leaning forward, I closed my eyes to concentrate and repeated, *Ayu, Ayu, Ayu, in my head. Dead silence. Nothing.*

I can't, I thought at Rio.

Try again. Except this time, don't push. Just imagine a channel opening between you and her. Imagine your third eye opening like a camera lens and point it at her. Be receptive.

I gave it another shot, doing as instructed. The middle of my forehead tingled, but none of Ayu's thoughts came through—until abruptly, I thought maybe I heard, *...milk, two sugars... It was so quiet I might have imagined it. My own thoughts might have filled in the blanks. I stopped and turned to Rio.*

Maybe, I thought at her.

Rio regarded her tea, then slid off her stool. *No worries. We'll try again later. Right now, I need to talk to Jake. She left without good-bye, and I grabbed a couple of muffins to share with Corona.*

◇

Over the next few days, I worked with Rio to improve my "wifi," as Corona called it. I learned that I could use the relaxation techniques Richard had taught me during our hypnosis sessions to get into the right frame of mind, and before long, I was listening in on Ayu's thoughts about what to make for dinner. Rio had me try to send a thought to her while she was on the far side of the haven. I chose to send the number 42, and after three failed tries, the fourth one worked. I was starting to understand what it should feel like to both send and receive thoughts, and so it was getting easier to make it happen. I practiced on Corona, with her permission, though her thoughts tended to include technical, computer-related terminology that I didn't understand, and she couldn't hear mine. That old demon, Ethics, kept rearing its ugly head too, and I wasn't entirely uncomfortable eavesdropping on Jake or Hilda.

More than once, Rio tried to help me reach out to Colin. I wanted *that to happen, badly. The closest I got was seeing a vision of him in a yellow kitchen with white lace curtains. Beyond the window, I could see the ocean through a stand of pine trees. Colin was frying eggs on the stove. I didn't hear his thoughts, but Rio was encouraged that I'd seen a vision of him. She called it "jumping the moon," and said it was likely that my soul had been in the room with him, wherever he was. I walked around the rest of the day as if I had clouds for shoes, convinced that Colin was nearby.*

◇

Several days passed without incident. I didn't see Rio and assumed she was dealing with Nathan's funeral. I hadn't been invited to it, which was a relief. I thought a lot about Colin and wondered if he knew his half-brother had been killed. I wished more than anything that I had a way to contact him, and often, I reached out with my mind—trying to get him to hear me. If he did, I got no response.

Corona had been more restless than usual. We went down to the ocean shore on multiple occasions, just to walk, talk, and breathe. On one of those occasions, Corona had said, "Have you ever wondered what it would be like to return to the womb? Start all over again? Come out with a new life—a new you?"

"Like reincarnation?" I asked, bending to pick up a tiny bead of green sea glass.

"Yes, but without dying. You just stop being the you you are right now, and you become the you you were always meant to be."

It sounded terrifying to me, and I told her so.

"It wouldn't hurt," she said. "Not much, at least. You're only afraid because you don't know who you really are."

"And you do?"

"Not yet. But soon. I feel it coming. It's how the caterpillar must feel when it's making its cocoon. It knows something is coming, but it can't really know what, right? It's like that." She threw a bit of driftwood out into the waves. It soared over the water and then was swallowed up. "The caterpillar has to take a leap of faith—big faith—that it's doing what needs to be done."

"I think the caterpillar just gets tired of eating leaves and wants everyone else to leave it alone so it can sleep."

Corona laughed. "No, that's you."

If I'd been paying closer attention, I'd have known she was up to no good, but I was consumed by my own problems. I didn't see what she was planning until the morning I found the note in her room. It was lying on her pillow, and it said,

Don't worry about me. I've spent enough time in my cocoon. It's time for me to come out and find my people. Viv, if I don't make it back, you can have all my stuff. Please get online and tell autochthon at iberberian.com that I'm gone.

I took the note straight to Jake. "What do you think this means?" I asked him.

He read it with a dark look on his face, then pulled out his phone, and dialed.

I started getting nervous, because *he was nervous.*

"Hilda," he said. "Meet me at the house as soon as you can. Corona's run off to find the selkies."

"She did what?" I asked when he'd hung up.

Jake went to his desk and unlocked a drawer. "It's possible that Corona has at least one ancestor who was one." He took a holstered handgun from the drawer and looked it over, checking that it was loaded.

"You need a gun?"

"Possibly," he replied. "The selkies prefer to keep to themselves, and they may not welcome Corona with open arms if she approaches them." He hooked the holster to his belt and then grabbed his jacket off the chair.

I followed him out through Holly House to the front, where we ran into Hilda and Rio.

"You know where she went?" Hilda asked, falling into step beside Jake and heading for the car. I trotted along behind them.

"Not exactly," Jake replied. "But I have a guess. Viviane, why don't you go toss her room. See if you can find any clues to where she went."

"No, I want to come with you."

Jake stopped in place. Hilda paused a couple steps later. They both looked back at me.

Hilda sighed as if I were bothering her.

"You can't," Jake said. "It's very possible she's gone somewhere you can't go. You'll be much more helpful if you stay here."

"I don't understand."

Hilda snorted, "So what else is new?"

Rankled, I reverted to the habits of my laundry days and said, "Fuck you, Hilda."

The surprise on Hilda's face was satisfying.

"Viviane," Jake scolded.

Rio moved to stand beside me. "I'll explain it to her," she said. "Go on."

"Thanks," said Jake. He took me by the shoulders and looked me in the eyes. "Viviane, you have to trust me on this. We'll get her home. Call me if you find anything." He didn't wait for a reply but turned and walked quickly to the car. Hilda followed in his wake.

I watched them drive off, and Rio came to stand beside me. "Don't worry," she said. "If anyone can get through to rabid selkies, it's Jake. Because you're a stranger, and mostly human, your presence would only rile them up."

I went back inside to Corona's room, hardly caring whether Rio followed me or not. Jake was behaving as if finding Corona were a matter of life and death. My heart pounded as I stared around at my friend's belongings.

Almost immediately, I found the report on her DNA. It was lying on her bed, upon the manila envelope in which it had arrived. It took me a minute to understand what I was reading.

Corona was half human and half selkie. In the comments section, it noted how unusual it was that she had no other magickal DNA represented. Unlike other species, it said, selkies tended to breed almost exclusively with their own kind or with seals—rarely with humans.

Rio appeared in the doorway and leaned there.

"She's *half selkie," I said.*

Rio nodded as if she'd already known.

I sat on the bed. "Tell me about them, please?"

"Well," Rio replied, moving into the room and taking a seat in Corona's desk chair. "Let's see. What do I know about selkies? I know they're one of the oldest races. They originally come from the Norwegian Sea and the lands that surround it. They're shapeshifters. They have their own religion. Most of the time, by choice, they live in seal form, but occasionally they'll shift into human form. They don't get along well with humans—for obvious reasons, the primary one being that humans have historically hunted, killed, and eaten their kin."

I thought of Corona and her fascination with the ocean. Her pear-shaped body, sweet face, and big brown eyes. It made sense. "So she's gone looking for them, and Jake's afraid they won't accept her?"

"Or that they won't even give her a chance to tell them she has selkie blood. She can't shapeshift, so she has no way to convince them of her sincerity. They might think she's just another mermaid wannabe."

"Mermaid wannabe? Is that a thing?"

"Among humans, it is. They have the misconception that magickal beings are all sparkles and hot sex."

"I see."

Rio picked up a pamphlet on the desk and looked it over. "This is where she went. We should tell Jake." She leaned toward me and reached out with the brochure. It was for a protected site called Seal Cove. Humans weren't allowed within a certain perimeter, though they could eat in the overlooking restaurant or walk along the boardwalk to observe the wildlife.

I called Jake.

"Viviane?"

"She's got a brochure here for Seal Cove. That's may be where she's going."

"Shit," Jake hissed.

"What?"

"She's as likely to get arrested for trespassing as she is to find a selkie," he said. "Okay. Thanks. We're on our way."

After I'd hung up, Rio said, "Why don't you try to reach her. With your ability."

"You think I could?"

"Maybe. Lie back." Rio got up and sat on the end of the bed. "Close your eyes and imagine Corona." I did as she instructed. "Don't impose a location on her or anything like that, just see her face. Feel her energy."

I took a deep breath and let it out with intent, using everything I'd learned on Richard's therapy couch to help me go deeper. The hypnosis sessions with him had always felt more like meditation than anything else. I quieted my mind and focused on counting backwards. At first I heard all the sounds around me—Rio breathing, the birds outside, the buffeting of wind against the windows... I felt Rio's hand rest upon my ankle.

Then I fell away into silence and darkness. For a moment, I didn't remember why I was there, but then I saw Corona's face looming out of the darkness.

Different sounds leaked into my consciousness. They were nothing I could identify at first, more a roar with the occasional whisper. I followed the sounds, flying through my own mind as if I were astral projecting. I was a spirit freed from my body.

I realized I was hearing the ocean, the ebb and flow of waves, and the call of birds. Corona's thoughts began to take form in my mind. *Hiya, I heard. I'm Corona. I'm like you. Hi. Hello. I felt her emotion, though dimly, like an echo. She was excited.*

The sound of the water grew louder, closer. *I'm like you, Corona thought. We're family. Wait! Where are you going? Can I come? One moment, she was happy, exalted even, and then something changed. She passed through a moment of confusion. What are you doing? What's going on? On the other side of the confusion, terror emerged. I felt her thoughts shift. She was fighting, struggling. No! I don't want this! I felt the moment she realized she was going to die. Her entire being rejected it. She fought. Don't breathe! Swim up! No!*

My connection to her was broken. Too abruptly. It shocked me awake and shaking, back in my body, undoubtedly wide-eyed.

"What happened?" Rio asked.

"She's drowning."

◇◇◇

CHAPTER 16

I dialed Jake as I ran out of the haven. I didn't wait for him to say anything but was calling his name as he picked up. "Jake! Jake! Jake!"

"I'm here," he said.

"She's in the water. She's drowning."

"Okay, I'll find her. Stay there." He hung up.

"No way in hell," I said, shoving my phone into my pocket. I was running down the driveway toward the garages where they kept the haven vehicles. It was all a blur, focused as I was on getting to the seashore as soon as possible. I grabbed keys and a car and took off down the road. It had been awhile since I'd driven, but I wasn't thinking about that. I just needed to get to Corona. I took a curve too fast, and the car fishtailed a little. I was forced to slow down as I descended toward Wyrdwood. That may have saved my life.

Another vehicle came out of nowhere behind me and slammed into my rear bumper. The car *did spin out that time, and I was flung sideways against my seatbelt. The violent explosion of airbags obscured my vision and hit me in the face. It happened so fast. One second I was cruising along, and the next I'd lost all control.*

The car spun off the road, hit a tree on the passenger side, and spun around it before coming to an abrupt halt. I sat there as my mind caught up with what had happened. The airbags collapsed. My knee hurt where I'd banged it on the underside of the steering wheel and my previously-injured ribs were on fire, but otherwise I didn't seem injured. I felt for my phone, found it, and started to dial 9-1-1.

The window beside me exploded inward, glass flying everywhere. I screamed and cringed away from it.

A big, hairy hand reached in through the window, grabbed the phone away from me, and threw it aside. I looked up into eyes so terrifying I screamed again.

My attacker wrapped its hand around my throat.

I clawed at it, trying to get it loose. The angle was awkward, so it wasn't entirely blocking my air. I fought, managed to get hold of a pinkie and bent it back with all my might. I felt it pop.

My attacker roared, the sound of a furious animal, and released me.

I fumbled to undo my seatbelt, then scrambled across to the passenger side of the car. The window there had shattered. I tugged on the handle and pushed.

The door wouldn't open.

My attacker banged loudly on the roof. I jumped and screamed.

Through the windows, I glimpsed the torso, moving around the back and coming toward the passenger side. The figure appeared to be female, a black mass, broad and strong, hairy arms exposed. Wearing black jeans and T-shirt. She resembled Agate's attacker—a misshapen monster on two legs, with a face—what Jake had called a "buggane."

As she moved toward the front passenger side, I crawled into the backseat and tried the rear driver-side door. It wouldn't open, either. I'd just realized that it was locked when the woman bent and put her face through the open window. She roared at me. Her mouth was a wide maw with red flesh and large white teeth, incisors long and sharp. Her head was huge, almost filling the entire window opening, and as she roared, she pushed against the car, rocking it.

I just about wet myself.

Hand shaking, I fumbled to unlock the car door. My heart was beating so hard, it felt like it would break out of my chest. With a glance, I saw my attacker turn to come back around to the driver's side. The lock clicked, and I shoved the door open. I landed on the ground in a heap and immediately began crab-crawling backwards, turning and trying to get to my feet to run. Escaping was the only thing on my mind.

The woman roared again.

My knee burned hot and a sharp pain burst there, but I wasn't going to let that stop me. I used a tree to stand and started moving. I had no idea where I was going. I just needed to get away.

I headed into the forest by the side of the road. I hobbled forward, putting as much distance as I could between me and the assassin. In my mind, that's what the woman was—an assassin—and I had no doubt that her goal was to kill me. She was the wolf, and I was the lamb.

I ran, tripped, got back to my feet, and ran some more. My breath came in raspy, painful gasps. My ribs burned. I could hear her crashing through the brush behind me, following but taking her time, tiring me out—the smart predator.

I fell again, and my muscles felt like loose ribbons. I couldn't get up.

I heard her, though I couldn't see her. My instincts told me to hide. Glancing around, lungs burning, side-stitch adding to the pain in my ribs, I spotted an especially large tree trunk. I hoped that if I could get behind it, and if I could be quiet enough, maybe she would walk right on by and think she'd lost me— maybe even give up.

I went down on my knees, stifling a gasp when I bumped my injured knee. I did my best not to put any weight on it as I crawled to my hiding place and settled down to wait with my back against the trunk. I willed myself to breathe silently, listening.

A fist-sized rock lay on the ground near my foot. I picked it up and wrapped my fingers tightly around it. Exhausted, but armed, I waited.

Rio! I thought, trying to reach her. Rio! I need help! I got no response, felt no sense of connection to her. I considered trying Jake but decided not to distract him from helping Corona. She needed him.

I was alone.

The assassin moved through the trees behind me, not bothering to hide her presence. She breathed with snorting, animal grunts, and occasionally sniffed loudly. I scooched, keeping the tree between me and her as she advanced.

The one I needed was Colin. He could fly me out of her reach. I did my best to quiet my mind and focus on him, but the assassin was closing in, and every sound she made broke my concentration.

And then the assassin stopped moving. I listened intently, heart hammering. I was barely breathing, my throat tense with the fear that I might cry out in spite of myself.

A twig snapped just behind the tree, and I froze—all but the hand holding the rock, which was shaking uncontrollably. She was so close that when she roared, it felt as if it would burst my eardrums. The sound echoed through the forest. Birds flew up from the tops of the trees. My stomach clenched, and I made myself as small as I could, pleading desperately to Colin to come save me. *Colin, I need help! Colin!*

Her face came around the tree trunk, a wide grin spreading that awful maw. She'd found me.

I lashed out with the rock, hitting her as hard as I could right on the bridge of her nose. The grin gaped, and she roared again. She reared back, and I took off. I stumbled when pain stabbed through my knee and it gave out, but I managed to grab hold of a tree and stay on my feet. I limped as fast as I could, moving deeper into the forest. Behind me, her grunting and growling receded with each of my steps.

Then, she went silent. I stopped by a fallen tree to catch my breath and listen. I didn't hear her, so I climbed over the trunk to put it between me and her, then hunkered down. My ears were alert for any sound, so I was surprised when I felt a heavy hand land on my shoulder. I twisted and looked up to see her face covered with blood. Her black hair was a halo of tangles, twigs, and leaves. Her strong jaw worked as she gnashed her blood-stained teeth. Her eyes were dilated, the irises golden halos around big, black centers.

Her fingers dug painfully into my shoulder, and I tried to hit her again with the rock. The angle was wrong, and the blow glanced off her arm.

"Let me go!" I shouted. "No!" I wiggled and twisted. Her grip on me loosened, and I managed to free myself. I landed on my back, looking up at her as she loomed over me, her hands on her knees. I scrambled backwards, away from her, and she had the audacity to laugh as she reached for my ankle.

I cocked my arm back and threw the rock as hard as I could, straight at her face. I heard it hit, but I didn't stick around to see where. As quickly as I could, I rolled onto my front and was moving forward even before I was fully on my feet. My knee screamed bloody murder, but I ignored it. At that moment, I didn't care if I never walked again. I was determined to survive.

I barreled blindly through the trees, driven by hot panic.

She kept up, but didn't gain on me. With each step, she grunted, starting slow and gradually gaining speed.

In my head, I thought as loudly as I could, *COL-IN! PLEASE! I NEED YOU! The thought became a whimpered pleading again. Colin... Please...*

I glanced back over my shoulder—I couldn't see her, though I heard the crashing of the underbrush, the pounding of her feet, and her animal snorts—and because I wasn't looking where I was going, I ran straight into something big and hard, and only mostly solid. A pair of thick arms wrapped around me, and I screamed. I beat at the muscled chest with both fists, squirming to be free of the vice grip on me.

"Viv! Viv, it's me!"

It took far too long for the words and the voice to sink in through my panic. When the proper neurons finally fired in my brain, I thought, *Oh, thank god! It was Colin.*

I rested my palms against his chest and locked my gaze on his face. On each panted breath, I tried to spit out the words to explain what was happening.

"It's... She's... Killer... I..."

The assassin came into view.

I said, "Let's go..."

The woman charged. Colin shoved me aside, and I fell to the forest floor, banged my elbow on a tree root, and hit my injured knee on a rock. The pain left me reeling, and I hovered on the verge of passing out. I watched the fight through a veil of tears, desperately wiping at them and holding onto my knee in an effort to will the pain away.

Colin threw the assassin to one side.

She got up and hit him square in the chest, sending him flying. Magick sparked in the air, and with it came the smell of ozone and burning hair. Several sparks of light—some blue, some green, and some gold—lit up the trees. It didn't last long, and when all was said and done, Colin stood over the assassin, who had fallen to her hands and knees. She stayed down, gasping and moaning.

Colin demanded, "Who sent you? Who do you work for?"

"Who says I work for anyone?" growled the woman. She spat blood onto the ground.

Colin thrust a hand toward the woman, and she let out a yelp that sounded like a dog in pain. "Who do you work for?"

Clutching at her chest as if she could dig the pain out of it, the woman shook her head.

Colin rotated his hand to the right, drawing another series of cries from the assassin. His face was a mask of cold determination.

"Colin, stop," I said, though my voice came out weak, and he either didn't hear or chose to ignore me.

"Tell me," Colin commanded.

"Thu!" the woman said. "I work for the Thu."

Colin's face darkened even more. "Why?" Just for good measure, he rotated his hand a bit more, causing the woman to fall completely to the ground and curl into a ball. She wept.

"For Apfallon," she said. "She is a threat to..." She sobbed, closing her hands into fists against her chest. "Apfallon."

Colin let out a slow, audible breath. His eyes had gone completely black, and his jaw was set so tightly that his dimples had become deep valleys in his cheeks. He looked at the woman with murderous intent and no mercy.

"Colin!" I yelled.

The assassin saw it coming too and raised a clawed, hairy hand to plead with him. "No! She said—"

Colin let out a shout, like a martial artist's battle cry, lifted both hands high over his head and brought them straight down. A ripple cut through the air. He didn't touch her, but her neck snapped. The sound of the bone breaking and the sight of her head tilted at that unnatural angle turned my stomach. I leaned forward, vomiting uncontrollably. That became the only sound in the forest in the wake of the woman's death. I retched and coughed. I sputtered. I'd never felt so awful in my life—until shadows rose up from the ground around us. They took solid form, and we were surrounded by a dozen black, dog-like creatures. They hunkered down and growled.

Colin turned in place, hands out at his sides, ready to defend himself. He took a step toward me and said, "Don't move, Viv."

I don't think I could have moved if I'd wanted to. My hackles had gone up, and I could feel the beasts eying us. It had grown darker in the forest, the sun making its way downward. The red-orange, fiery glow of eyes blinked all through the trees.

"I'll get us out of here, Viv, but we'll have to move fast." He took another slow step toward me. "Get ready to take my hand."

The blood was rising in my head, making the scratches on my face throb. I readied myself, attention locked on Colin. I saw his wings appear, though they remained low against his back.

One of the devil dogs growled—a big one, probably the alpha.

Colin took another slow step toward me. He reached down to me, and I reached up toward him. Our hands connected, and he latched onto my wrist with a strong grip. His wings spread wide.

A flash of light coursed through the trees and hit Colin in the middle of the back. It bent his body, and I saw the surprise on his face just moments before he went slack. He collapsed onto my legs, unconscious.

"Colin!" I froze, looking him over, trying to understand what had just happened. "Colin!"

Strong hands grabbed me under the armpits. Two people, one on either side of me, dragged me away from Colin. I screamed and struggled weakly. I used what fight I had left in me—which wasn't much and certainly wasn't effective. My captors held me down on the ground.

Several large people dressed in rags—hunched and deformed—had emerged from the trees, walking right through the ring of growling dogs. Four of them converged on Colin and each took a limb. They picked him up and carried him away.

I kicked and clawed at my captors, called them names. I cursed them—to no avail. All I was doing was hurting myself. My strength gave out and I was forced to stop.

The raggedy people hefted the body of the dead woman who had attacked me and took her away too.

"Relax, Viviane," said a sophisticated, male voice from behind me. "We're not here for you. We were never here for you."

I let that sink in, gradually allowing my muscles to relax. I asked, "Then what were you here for?"

"Him."

"Colin? Why?"

"He's been trying to gain access to Apfallon. We cannot allow that."

"Why not?"

His voice remained cool as he replied, "The Fomor are the enemies of the Thu. They're unredeemable monsters, twisted and dark. If we gave them the chance, they'd kill every single Apfallonian so they could claim the realm for themselves."

To me, Colin was anything but a monster, whereas this Apfallonian was a pompous, prejudiced, and cruel asshole. I said, "I don't understand."

The owner of the voice crouched down behind me. I tried to turn my head to see him, but all I got was a vague form in my peripheral vision. He said, "Let me put it to you in the most basic of ways. Apfallon was once the home of the Fomor. Colin is Fomor. Many generations ago, however, the Fomor lost the war over control of Apfallon. They refused to bow to their new masters and were cast into Gehenna—the bleakest realm we knew—as punishment."

"Gehenna is bleak?"

"It's the land where the dead go to await sorting. To be fair, they've made the place their own. They herd the spirits of the dead and mete out punishment to those who deserve it."

I needed a moment to take that in. Neither Colin nor Rio had told me much about their homeland. I'd imagined it was like Wyrdwood, not what he described.

"And Apfallon?" I asked.

"Apfallon is the holy grail of lands. Pristine. It exists in a pocket realm, safe from Reality. We hide from Normals, but we don't need to hide from wielders."

"Fomor are wielders. Why can't they just go there?"

"Their blood is cursed. No one in their bloodline can cross the barrier into Apfallon. The blood itself bars them from crossing the border without permission. You, of course, are welcome to visit any time. Just come to Fortunate Lake and take the boat to the center island. When you step ashore, you will be in Apfallon." The other person holding me—the one who hadn't spoken—stood, signaling the conversation was coming to an end.

I demanded, "Let Colin go!" I twisted to look at the man holding me. He wasn't what I'd expected. He was darkly beautiful, no older than twenty, with short black hair. He wore a navy-blue double-breasted trenchcoat with large silver buttons. Kohl lined his eyes, emphasizing their depth and the dark brown of his irises. I was taken aback by his long thick eyelashes. His lips had a blush, as if he were wearing a subtle lipstick.

"I can't do that," he said. "He needs to spend some time in the grist mill, learning his place well enough that he goes back to his Fomor swamp and tells them to never try to enter Apfallon. That is, either he'll tell them himself, or his body will bear the message. Frankly, as far as I'm concerned, one less Fomor is one less hassle."

"Please. You don't have to do this," I said, resorting to near-begging.

"You'll get over him."

The next thing I knew, he grabbed the back of my neck with one hand and closed the other over my face. I smelled pine and grass on it. He squeezed, my mind screamed Colin's name, and that was all.

◇◇◇

CHAPTER 17

I dreamt I was running through the forest. Beasts and creatures rustled in the undergrowth around me, and no matter where I turned, there were only more trees, red glowing eyes, and snarling threats.

I awoke abruptly and sat up straight. The pain in my knee brought my mind to immediate clarity.

"Simon?" I asked. "Are you here?" It was a faint hope, and I wasn't surprised when he didn't respond. It'd been weeks since I'd left Peoria and last spoken with him. "Where the hell are you?" I moaned.

I was still on the ground in the forest, and I was alone. Time had passed and the sun had set completely. Darkness enfolded me, obscuring anything beyond my immediate vicinity, and I realized I had no idea which direction was home. A chilly mist was working its way through the trees, and I buttoned my jacket to the top. When I explored my knee, I found it swollen and sore to the touch.

"Dammit," I said aloud. I was alive, but Colin and his captors were nowhere in sight. They'd left me there to die of exposure. "Assholes!" I shouted at the trees.

Without bothering to get up off the ground, I began working through the situation. The Apfallonians, otherwise known as, "The Thu"—I whispered it aloud—had taken him because he was a Fomor, and according to them he'd been trying to get into Apfallon. For that, they were going to make an example of him. "Assholes!"

Delayed fury and frustration made me shake.

My phone rang, its musical chime surreal in the dark forest. It was twenty feet or so to my left, hidden. I pushed up onto my one good leg and hobbled toward it. "Keep ringing," I begged. "I'm here." A sharp branch poked me in the head, making me rear back, and when I touched the spot, it stung and my fingers came away wet. Cursing and determined, I put my hands up to protect my head and continued toward the sound.

It went silent.

"Wait, call back." I took another step or two in the phone's general direction but was afraid I'd go too far. I tried to imagine where it might be and bent down, feeling through the prickly pine needles and fallen branches. "Call back! Please call back." For the first time ever, I'd have been happy if it were a telemarketer.

Then a single chime sounded. The caller had left a message, and that one little bing guided my hand the last few inches to it. "Oh, thank you." I held the phone to my chest like a cherished kitten, on the verge of relief tears. Suddenly, I had a connection to the real world again.

Rio had called, and I jumped out of my skin when the phone rang again. I answered right away.

"Hi, I'm lost in the woods."

There was a pause, then Rio said, "Viviane? Where are you?"

"If I knew that, I wouldn't be lost." I heard the urgency in my voice.

"All right, don't panic. Let me get help. Hold on."

I was about to hang up to save battery power when a man's voice came through the line. "Miss Rose. Let's get you home, okay?" I recognized it as Mr. Jorgenson, the CEO of Lost Lambs.

"Thank you," I said.

"Tell me what happened."

So I did, as quickly as I could manage, emphasizing the fact that the Thu had kidnapped Colin.

"Okay, okay," said Mr. Jorgenson when I ran out of breath. "First things first. You say you were driving west on Snake Run Road when your car went off the road?" Through the phone, I heard a door slam and an engine roar to life. "That should be easy to find. We're heading that way now."

"We have to call the police," I told him. "They're going to kill Colin."

"The police can't help. Just hold on. Our first priority is to get you to safety."

"They weren't after me," I said. "There was a war and a curse, and the Fomor are exiled." I realized I was babbling, and I remembered one of the last things Nathan had said to me, *I couldn't possibly explain generations of politics and prejudice to you... I wished he'd tried. Maybe if I'd known sooner, I could have done something. I was grasping for the reins after the horse had already left the barn.*

Rio's voice came through the phone. "There—I see it."

Mr. Jorgenson said, "We found the car, Miss Rose, so we're close. I want you to open the map app on your phone. You know how to use it?"

"Yes, of course." I felt like a dumbass for not having thought of that myself.

"Share your location with me, and I'll come to you."

I did as requested.

A noise in the dark startled me, and yet again, my heart rate sped up.

"Hurry," I whispered into the phone.

"I'm on my way," Mr. Jorgenson said. "I'm close."

I rocked myself in an effort to calm down.

Mr. Jorgenson is in the woods. Rio's voice came into my mind. You're safe now.

They took him, Rio, I told her.

I heard, she thought. The Thu can be brutal.

I thought to her, *They said it was because he tried to get into Apfallon.*

If he did, then he must have had a good reason, Rio said. He knows the risk. You can't get in with Fomor blood unless you have special dispensation from the Apfallon queen.

What are they going to do to him?

Rio hesitated before replying, then just said, *Don't worry about that now. I'll let his father know he's been taken. There may be a diplomatic resolution.*

I heard someone large moving through the brush. The beam of a flashlight swung back and forth. "I'm here," I shouted.

I got to my feet—my one foot—and half-hopped half-limped toward the light moving from tree to tree.

"Miss Rose?"

"I'm here!"

Mr. Jorgenson was a knight in shining armor, wearing a scowl, when he appeared through the trees. He came straight to me, and seeing that I couldn't walk well, he asked, "May I carry you?"

"I'm not dainty," I told him.

"Not to worry," he replied. "I inherited my grandmother's strength."

He handed me the flashlight, picked me up like I was a child, and carried me all the way out of the woods.

Rio was waiting by the car they'd arrived in. Its headlights illuminated the car I'd driven, and my stomach did a flop when I saw the damage, the broken glass, and the indent made on the roof by the woman who had attacked me.

The vehicle that had hit me was gone.

I huddled against the tall solidity of Mr. Jorgenson, feeling small and weak.

"You're injured!" Rio cried when she saw us.

"I banged my knee pretty good," I said.

I felt Mr. Jorgenson's voice rumble in his chest when he said, "I'll call the doctor when we get back to the haven."

Rio opened the back door for us, and Mr. Jorgenson put me down on my one good foot. I hopped into the back seat.

"What do we do now?" I asked, once everyone was back in the car.

I met Mr. Jorgenson's eyes—one blue and one purple—in the rearview mirror. He then looked to Rio, who said, "There's nothing that can be done."

"But Colin..."

Rio said, "Hush now. Just rest. We'll figure this out once we know you're safe and sound."

I was grateful to be alive. "Thank you for coming to get me. Both of you."

In the rearview, Mr. Jorgenson gave me one of his half-smiles, and Rio turned to look at me over her shoulder. She said, "Oh, child, it's no trouble. You've had quite a day."

She was not wrong, and I felt it deep in my bones.

When we got back, I saw myself in the mirror. Dried blood streaked down my face and neck from scratches, eyes hollow, skin too pale, hair tangled with sticks, pine needles, and broken glass. I looked a fright. When I undressed, squared bits of glass fell out of my clothes. I took a shower, washing it all away. As I watched the dirt and blood slide down the drain,

I lost the last of my strength, and the sobs overtook me.

Again, I thought, *I'm in way over my head. Why does this have to be so hard? All I wanted was to be with Colin and to be happy. Was that too much to ask? I remembered something Lenore had said to me, "The only people living a trouble-free life are dead."*

◇

Rio was waiting for me when I came out of the shower wrapped in a towel. Despite my protests, she insisted on helping me put on my pajamas. The only consolation to my modesty was that she turned her back while I put on my underwear.

"I turned up the heat for you," she said. "It'll get toasty in here soon. Mr. Jorgenson has phoned Dr. Beaulieu and says he's on his way."

"Isn't that the coroner?" I asked.

Rio helped me into bed. "Yes. But he's also the best wielder doctor we have. He'll have you up and running in no time."

I was exhausted, but I had every intention of staying awake. "Is Jake back? Did he find Corona?"

"Not yet. He has Hilda and Booker with him." I guess she saw the worry on my face because she said, "Corona's smart and more powerful than she knows. You don't have to worry."

I *was worrying. About Corona. About Colin.*

I said, "It's like we're in some kind of guerilla warfare. People are dying all around us. The monster that attacked me—I think she was just a soldier or mercenary. It was planned, Rio. Is this how it is all the time here?"

"No. There just seems to be a convergence of energies intent on creating chaos right now." She placed an ice pack wrapped in a towel on my knee. "You're lucky to be alive. The Thu can be ruthless."

"They didn't want me. They wanted Colin. I was just the bait. Somehow they knew he'd come to save me. And when he showed up, they ambushed him."

Rio pulled the covers up and tucked me in like a child. She sat beside me and took my hand.

"Rio," I said gently. "Would they kill him?"

"The Thu?" she replied, considering. "Yes. They're rabid about keeping the Fomor out of Apfallon. They see us as inferior."

"Even after all this time? Why?"

Rio sighed again as if the story were a weighty burden. She said, "The Thu took Apfallon from the Fomor, and conquering us was a hard-won prize. We fought to the end. Both sides lost many people in the wars."

"Wars? Plural?"

"Yes, there were more than one. The first time the Thu tried to take the Fomor's land, the Fomor won. The second time, the Thu won, and in retaliation, they cast the Fomor out. Since then, the hate has passed from generation to generation, and they're still unable to open their doors to us. Fomor ancestors, their gods, and their stories are rooted in Apfallon, and yet they can never return. Some of my people see Apfallon as our rightful homeland. They're as obsessed about getting in as the Thu are about keeping us out."

"That sucks," I said.

"Yes. Although things are changing. Occasionally, a Fomor and a Thu will fall in love. Have children. There are also arranged marriages meant to keep the two lineages intermingled in order to avoid another war. It's the magickal version of the Cold War. Treaties signed. Mutual destruction assured. However, it's the offspring of those arranged marriages who will save us all. I cling to that belief."

"I hope you're right. But for now, how are we going to get Colin back?"

Rio said, "We'll figure something out. It will require a strong dose of humiliation and diplomacy." She sat up a little straighter, then added quietly, "I can't lose another son."

"It's so complicated."

"Family is complicated."

An ancient grudge—how was I supposed to save Colin from that? It was so new to me, and yet, this had all been happening—all along. Behind the veil. Out of sight. I was the woman I'd seen in Rio's tarot card, emerging from among the tree's roots and seeing the world for the first time. I ached to crawl back in—back into the warm womb in which I'd lived most of my life, where ignorance was bliss. But there was no way back, no way to unknow what I knew.

Amnesia, I thought, would be a blessing.

"Viviane," said Rio, interrupting my thoughts. "Do you think you could try jumping the moon to Colin? You did it once. If you could do it again, you could maybe see something that would tell us where he is."

"I can try." It was a good idea, though I immediately experience performance anxiety. I closed my eyes and tried to focus my breathing. I repeated Colin's name in my head like a metronome. *Colin. Tick tock. It took me awhile.*

The first time the bed fell away beneath me, I jerked awake, startled. It took me a moment to refocus. I was so tired. When next I felt the bed drop, a horrible thought crossed my mind. *What if I see him dead? I recoiled from the idea and came wildly awake again, heart hammering.*

Rio watched this happen two more times before she said, "You can't let the fear of what you'll see paralyze you, or you'll never see anything. Find your courage, Viviane. Colin needs you to be strong. *I need you to be strong. You have to find him, no matter where he is or what's happened to him.*"

I knew she was right, but I was so afraid. I blew out a few breaths through pursed lips to try to calm myself—in through my nose, out through my mouth—closed my eyes, and tried again. I repeated in my head, *Colin, I'm here. Colin. I'm coming. Colin,*

Colin, Colin. Tick tock.

A knock on the door jerked me back to my body.

"Mother fucker," said Rio under her breath. She patted my hand, then stood and went to the door. It was Dr. Beaulieu. He hunched a bit as he entered, though he wasn't any taller than me. He wore a khaki trench coat and his thick black hair had its usual sheen of oil or pomade. His wrinkles rearranged into a smile as he approached the bed.

"Good evening, Miss Rose," he said. "I've been led to believe you have suffered an injury to your knee."

I pushed up to sitting, my back against the headboard. "Yeah. I just hope it isn't too bad."

"Well, let's take a look, shall we?"

I rolled the covers off me, set aside the ice pack, and pulled up my pajama pants leg. It didn't take him long, and he only caused me to squeak in pain once. His diagnosis was that it was badly bruised but nothing more.

"This," he said, uncapping the small jar of cream, "is a combination of arnica and other magickal herbs. Are you allergic to anything?"

"No. I don't think so."

"Well," he grinned. "We'll find out if you are. Rub this on twice a day, when you first get up and then again twelve hours later. Do this for the next five days. Don't stop just because the pain is gone. You need to see it through, or the pain may come back." He opened the pot. "I'll put some on now. I recommend you wrap the knee, for two reasons. This salve stains, and also, it'll keep it in place on your skin."

I watched the doctor's wrinkled hand rub the salve onto my knee—so gently. He had an experienced touch, and I found myself wondering if he preferred working on living or dead people. Dead people, I presumed, didn't twitch when he hit a sore spot.

Once that was done, he wrapped the knee loosely with a stretchy bandage. I had him look at my ribs and was surprised when I saw the watercolor of bruising on my side. He rubbed the cream on them and wrapped them in bandages.

"All set." He covered me back up and squeezed my toes. "Best thing for you is rest. I'll leave you to it."

"Thank you for coming out so late, Doctor," I said. He saluted me with two fingers, then left.

Rio went with him, to see him out, and I scooched back down into the bed. I had to try again to reach Colin. I closed my eyes and slowed my breathing. I counted down from a hundred, timing each number with an exhalation. I felt the world shrink around me. My consciousness turned internal. I saw Colin in my mind's eye, the man of my memories, his curly red hair so alive, his eyes so bright, and his smile so damn charming. I remembered kissing him and holding him against me, the feel of his naked body, his warmth, the way his neck turned red when he was turned on, how his erection felt pressed between our bodies as we embraced—all the aspects of him that I would never forget.

Blood. It exploded in my mind and washed away the memories, replacing them with a different scene. Colin was seated, his hands and wings tied behind his back. His face and upper torso were bloodied and bruising. A wave of horror washed over me, and in its wake came a wave of relief. His head was hanging forward as if he were unconscious, but he was breathing.

Colin! I thought at him. Colin, can you hear me? Colin?

He made no indication that he could.

I wasn't sure how long I could stay, so I scanned the room around him, looking for any clue to his location. The room was dank and gray, concrete floor and cinderblock walls. It had a window high on the wall, and when I willed myself to it, I could see out. Security lights on the building lit an overgrown lawn. It had once been a beautiful garden but had been allowed to go to seed. A statue stood on a pedestal, a jaunty satyr—half goat and half man. It played a Pan pipe and danced. One of its pointed ears had broken off, and the tip of the pipe was long gone. Ivy grew up over him, clinging to his legs and mid-section like emerald adornment. A sparse stand of white birch ringed the edge of the garden. Beyond, a body of water shimmered, reflecting the moonlight.

I willed myself back to Colin. *Colin, I thought. I'm here. I love you. I love you so much. I'll be back with help. I promise.*

Still, he didn't react.

The door to the stark room opened, and the

form of a man appeared just outside. A male voice said loudly, as if wanting Colin to overhear, "I think we should just put an end to the heir and send his body back to Gehenna as a warning."

"Yeah, that'll teach 'em." said another male voice. "Fuckin' Fomor."

They laughed.

Without preamble, I snapped back to my body and came alive with a jerk, their laughter echoing through my mind.

"Any luck?" asked Rio. She'd come back in while I was away.

I rolled out of bed, intent on doing something. Anything.

Rio asked, "What are you doing?"

I told her what I'd seen and heard. I hobbled to the closet and pulled out clothes to wear.

"I know that place," Rio said. "Are you sure you should be walking on that?"

"I'm sure." Truth was, the salve had done its job. My knee, while still painful, wasn't as bad as it had been, and I was bound and determined to find my fiancé.

Rio said, "Jake and the others aren't back yet."

"What about Mr. Jorgenson?"

"He's gone to help Jake. You sure you want to do this?"

"Positive."

"All right, then. It's us or no one. Just you and me, kiddo. But between us, I'd say we have enough magick to take on the entire Apfallon army." She launched into active mode, rushing ahead to warm up the car.

I finished dressing, then made my way downstairs. I paused in the living room when the fireplace crossed my vision. The iron poker would make a good weapon. As I closed my hand around the cold metal and pulled it free of its stand, I knew I wasn't normal—never had been and never would be. I just had to accept it—or lose Colin forever.

CHAPTER 18

The haven felt completely empty and silent. I wondered what was happening with Corona, my worry about her adding to my worry about Colin. I thought about calling Jake, but I couldn't risk dragging him away from helping Corona. Instead, I paused by the phone table to scribble a quick note.

Colin kidnapped by Thoo. I didn't know how to spell it at the time. Rio and I rescuing him. House by lake / White birch, garden & satyr statue. And I signed it "V."

Rio pulled up to the front of the house. I didn't even bother to lock the front door but rushed to the car and climbed in. Rio took off the moment my butt was in the seat, spinning out gravel. I slammed the door shut and put my seatbelt on.

Rio took one look at the fireplace poker and said, "Good call."

"What's the plan?" I asked.

"First, we have to find him," Rio replied. "I think I know that house. I've seen a statue like you described. It's an old manor on the other side of Fortunate Lake. The side where Apple Island is. It's how you get to Apfallon, so it's basically right next door."

"The island in the lake where..." I let the sentence dangle, but in my head, I finished it with: ...

where Nathan was killed.

Rio chose a less painful memory, finishing for me. "Where we picnicked. Yes."

"That's Apfallon?"

"Yes. The island holds the gateway to it."

"Why didn't you tell me before?"

Rio shrugged. "I didn't want to overwhelm you."

"At some point," I said, "people need to stop babying me. It isn't working out so weeeeelll."

I held onto the oh-shit bar as she whipped down the snaking road, her headlights careening off trees. I had one foot on an imaginary brake, and my heart skidded around the curves too. Memories of my own accident shot adrenaline through my system.

"Please," I choked. "Slow down. Just a little."

Rio glanced over at me, thought about it, then nodded. "Sorry," she said. Then added, "Breathe." She slowed enough that I was no longer ready to jump out of my skin, and I focused on the trees rushing by.

"Once we get to the house," she said, "we'll park some distance away and sneak up, see what we can see."

"Okay," I said.

"I'm hoping he won't have many guards, since he's tied up and..."

She paused, so I finished it for her, "Injured."

"Yes."

Instead of turning toward Wyrdwood, she went in the other direction, up into the hills.

We drove in silence for long enough that the

questions and worries in my head began to over-whelm me. *What if we can't overpower them? How many will there be? Will there be monsters like the one who attacked me in my car? I gripped the poker tightly. What if Colin is already dead?*

To get out of my head, I asked, "What about the Fomor? Can't your people come and help us?"

Rio glanced over at me, then shook her head. "I spoke with his father. The baboon won't lift a finger to help him. He might even make it worse. He's furi-ous with Colin. Colin's been branded a traitor."

"But he's his father."

"Yes, well," Rio said dryly, "family—common blood—doesn't mean as much among some people as it does to humans. Or maybe it means more. Betrayal is unforgivable."

We passed the turnoff to Slipper Stables and continued up into the mountains. I tried closing my eyes, counting down, slowing my breathing, but before I could jump out of my body, my stomach churned with discomfort. Car sickness. I opened my eyes wide and took a deep breath, willing the nau-sea to recede. At least there weren't any more hairpin curves.

"We're almost there," Rio said, slowing to pull onto a dirt side road.

I thought back to the hag who had attacked me at Malum and how Corona, Simon, and I had made the decision to go after it before it could kill anyone else. It wasn't my first rodeo, so to speak, though I certainly didn't feel like an expert at handling dangerous situations. Then, I remembered how I'd fought the buggane assassin at Agate's cave-house in the woods. I'd also prevented Nathan from strangling me by shoving a needle in his eye. I was dumbfounded by how often this kind of thing was happening to me, but the realization also bolstered my confidence. I could do this. I could save Colin and maybe not get killed in the process.

Rio pulled over to the side of the road and turned off the car. "If I'm right," she said, turning to drape her arm over the back of my seat, "then the place where they're keeping him is just through there." She pointed to the woods lining the road. "Why don't you try jumping the moon and see what you can see. I'm going to get a glimpse of the house."

"Wait, what?" I stared at her. "Don't go up there by yourself. What if they catch you?"

"I can always 'chute away if I need to, but I'll be careful. I won't get that close." She reached for her door handle. "I'll come right back. If I'm not back in fifteen minutes, take the car and go." She climbed out, then turned back to say, "Try to jump now that we're closer. Maybe you can get more information about where he is and who's guarding him."

I nodded, determined to do as she requested.

She shut the door quietly, then walked around the car and into the forest. She disappeared completely in the darkness, and I realized she didn't even have a flashlight—probably for the best.

My anxiety doubled, but I had to do my part. I rested my head back and began the process of going under. It took me a few minutes to focus my mind and cut out my own distracting thoughts, but I eventually managed. *Colin. Colin, are you okay?* It felt like how your tongue probes a sore tooth, except it was my consciousness probing for Colin.

Viv? A whisper of a thought came back to me. I wasn't sure I'd heard it at first.

Colin? Is that you? Where are you?

I'm in a cellar, in a house by Fortunate Lake. Number 444. Get help, Viv.

How many of them are there?

Just two, I think. Get help. Is Lamb there?

No, Jake's busy. It's okay. We're here. We're coming to get you.

No. This isn't that simple.

I understand. Your step-mom and I are going to get you out.

My step-mom?

Rio. She's here with me.

Viv, you have to leave right now! You don't—

I felt the connection drop, like a balloon that broke its string and was buffeted up and away by the wind, irretrievable. I opened my eyes. I'd felt a flash of pain right before we'd been cut off, as if someone had hit him or... I didn't want to think about the possibilities.

I got out of the car, iron poker in hand, and headed into the woods. My eyes had adjusted somewhat to the darkness in the car, and it was a clear starlit night, so I wasn't completely blind—thank goodness. I crept along, favoring my sore knee, feeling my way carefully, and more than once I got snagged on or poked by a branch. The house wasn't too far back. I began to see it through the trees and took more care not to be spotted.

"Viviane," came a hissed call. Rio crouched behind a tree at the edge of the yard. I made my way to her.

She asked, voice low, "Did you see anything new?"

I whispered, "No. I talked to Colin, though. He said it was number 444, and there are only two people guarding him."

"This is the place then. When we passed the mailbox, I noticed the address."

"Did it say who lives here?"

"No. I don't think anyone does. It's run down. What do you want to do?"

I studied the two-story house. It looked to have been built in the middle ages. It was made of stone and mortar, and it tilted on the land, as if one end had sunk a bit. It didn't have many windows, and the ones it did have were small. Two large stone chimneys bookended the north and south walls, and I could see the white birch, overgrown garden, and lake beyond it. The front of the house faced the water, and a black sedan was parked at the bottom of the driveway on the side closest to us.

"This is definitely it," I said, confirming what we already knew. "I'm going to see if there's a way in. You wait here, and I'll text you when I know I can get in. Then you create a distraction."

"How do you want me to do that? They'll know me if they see me." She pointed to herself. "Well-known wife of the czar, remember?"

"Right." I looked around, searching for something. An idea occurred to me, and I asked, "Can you fly? Like Colin and Nathan?"

"No. They get that from their father."

"Oh. Well, what *can you do?*" I asked.

"I affect elements," she said. "Earth, fire, air, water."

The nearest chimney was releasing a steady stream of smoke.

"What about the fireplace?" I asked.

"Yes. I can make it burn hotter. Or less hot."

"Hotter, I think. While they're dealing with that, I'll sneak in, find the stairs to the basement and free Colin."

"Sounds like a plan," Rio said.

I turned to look her in the face. "Wait for my text. Make the fire, then you get out of here. Okay? Go straight back to your car and leave."

She looked surprised.

I explained, "I don't want anything happening to you. Colin can fly me out once I've freed him."

Rio's mouth set in a straight line. "Go now!" She said, waving me off with her hands.

I looked back at the house, took a deep breath, and began to work my way through the trees to where I could approach the house without being seen.

CHAPTER 19

I was not an action hero. Sneaking around that house felt more like high school shenanigans than actual danger. I'd dabbled in Ninjitsu with a boyfriend when I was in college, but his knowledge of the art was as much fantasy as fu, as much woo as wushu. Flirting had definitely been one of our practice drills. However, he did teach me the basics of stealth. I'd used the skill numerous times to sneak back into the house after curfew.

The first window I checked wouldn't budge. When I peeked in through it, I saw the living room. A man sat on the couch, feet up on the coffee table, scrolling on his cell. He had long, uncombed hair and an untrimmed beard, his head a mass of scraggliness. He turned to look straight at me as if he had sensed me there.

I ducked and froze, my heart racing.

When nothing happened, I kept going. The next window was slightly ajar, and when I pulled it out, it swung open. Inside was a bedroom, and the door was closed. I hefted myself up onto the sill and crawled in. As I was bringing my other leg in, something wrapped around my ankle from outside. It felt like a hand, but hairy. I bit down on the urge to cry out and kicked. My heel landed, and I kicked again. Whatever had hold of me let go. I pulled myself inside as quickly as I could, landed on the floor, and crab-walked away from the window. No one appeared in the frame, and I figured he'd gone around to catch me inside.

I had to hurry, so I texted Rio, *FIRE NOW. Almost immediately, I heard a woosh followed by a shout of surprise outside the bedroom. Chaos erupted from the living room, the two men shouting at one another and cursing.*

I took that as my cue to crack open the door and leave the bedroom, moving away from the noise. I needed to find the door to the cellar, and my best guess was that it would be in the kitchen. I didn't know where that was, but it wasn't a large house. A short hallway stretched away from the living room, with the stairs on one side. I paused to check a door under the stairs. A closet.

The kitchen, as it turned out, was at the end of the hall. It was small with olive-colored appliances. Faded gingham curtains hung on the one window, and a rickety old laminated table with metal legs stood in the corner covered with fast-food containers. A door in the rear opened to the outside, but none led to a cellar.

The cacophony in the living room was growing louder, and I began to smell smoke. I wondered if I'd miscalculated or somehow missed the cellar door.

"Get a bucket! Water!" shouted one of the men.

"Where?" asked another, voice also raised.

"From the kitchen, moron! Under the sink!"

My heart leapt into my throat. I was trapped—unless I went back outside. My only hope was to get out the back door before those thudding footsteps reached the kitchen. I hurled myself at the door. Fortunately, it was unlocked and opened on the first attempt. I slipped out and shut it behind me. The short set of stairs outside tangled my feet, and I tripped and landed face-down in the mud at the bottom of them. I scrambled up and pressed myself against the house.

"Found it!" a man yelled from the kitchen. The sound of running water seemed to go on forever.

That's when I saw the cellar doors. They were on the outside of the house, and I felt like an idiot for not checking there first. A relieved idiot. With a glance back at the kitchen door, I hugged the house's exterior wall and ducked below windows, making my way to the cellar doors. They were old and weather-worn, but they weren't locked. I pulled one side open. It was enough to let me step in.

Rio's words, "It's us or no one," whispered through my mind again, and I girded my loins, as they say. I hunkered down to avoid hitting my head on the door frame and carefully descended the stone steps. The inside was pitch black. I took out my cell and turned on the flashlight app. This presented a problem. I still had the poker in one hand and now I held my cell in the other. This left me no hands to hold onto the railing. The stone steps were old, worn, and uneven. I moved carefully, but quickly. The people inside the house knew I was there, and it wouldn't be long before they got that fire under control.

My phone illuminated the area directly in front of me, pushing back the darkness much better than I'd have expected.

"Colin?" I whispered. "Are you there?"

I heard a rustle of movement, then a clunk, then grunting. I shone the light in that direction and found Colin just as I'd seen him in my mind. I hurried across the basement, tripping once on an unseen obstacle and almost falling. I set the poker down and pulled the gag out of his mouth.

"Viviane," he gasped, relief and urgency in the exclamation. "Hurry! Untie me!" They'd bound him with twine wrapped numerous times around his wrists and ankles. The rough string was stained with his blood where it had rubbed him raw. I found the knot, but had to set down my phone to use both hands. I couldn't see, and the twine frayed my fingernails. The knot was too tight for me to undo, and I had nothing to cut it with.

In a panic, I picked up my cell and turned the light on the scene around me, looking for anything I could use. A bench stood in the corner with an anvil on it. An anvil meant tools. I hurried over there, walking right through a spiderweb that stuck to my face and tangled in my hair. "Ah!" I frantically wiped it away, refusing to think about where its maker—and/or her offspring—might have gone.

"You okay?" Colin asked, trying to twist to see me.

"Yeah," I said. "Just a spider web. I'm okay." My head itched, though I was pretty sure I was imagining it. Or so I told myself.

"Hurry!" he hissed.

The bench was covered with dust, but it had abandoned tools and other detritus lying on it. I found a screwdriver, a wrench, some old car parts, a box of dirty nails, and a saw. I picked up the saw. It was the kind you use to cut branches and boards. Its handle was old-fashioned, made of wood, and the blade had seen much better days. Some of its teeth were missing. I didn't trust that it was sharp, but all I needed was to get through one strand of twine, and then I could unravel it from there.

I lay my phone on the floor, light facing upward, and tackled the bindings. The saw didn't want to cut cleanly through the twine, but I worried it enough that I got it to fray and then to break, freeing Colin's hands. I set to work on his legs while he rubbed his wrists and tugged the gag off completely.

"How did you find me?" he asked.

"It's a long story," I said, scraping the twine with the saw. "They know I'm here." The bindings broke, and Colin's hands joined mine to help unwrap his legs. Once he was free, he stood and took my hand. "Let's go." I barely had time to grab my phone before he was pulling me toward the steps. Then just as abruptly, he halted in place. My forward momentum caused me to bump into him.

"Oh, no," said a male voice by the steps. He had

no real emotion in his voice. "We're too late. The brat has broken free. His woman has risked her own life to save him."

Colin tensed.

"Too bad," the man continued. "The Fomor will sit his ass back down if he knows what's good for his woman." With all the bow-legged confidence in the world, he descended the stairs. In the dark, it was difficult to see his features, but he was huge.

A second man, the one with wild hair, appeared in the doorway, backlit only by the velvet blue of starlight. He had Rio with him, gripping her by the arm. "And what's good for his wet nurse."

My breath caught in my throat.

Colin let go of my hand and rushed the man coming down the steps. He threw his whole body forward.

It took a second for my brain to catch up, a time during which several blows were exchanged between them. I remembered the poker. I'd set it down by the chair. Urgently, I turned and used my flashlight to search the floor.

Colin grunted in pain, then the other man huffed out his breath and flew back into the far wall with a crash.

I found it.

The fighting shifted once again to the steps, but this time, it was different.

"I got this," said the wild-haired man, coming down the stairs. He had pulled a sword and jabbed it at Colin.

Colin backed away, doing his best to dodge the onslaught of attacks. The basement wasn't big, and it wouldn't be long before the man had Colin cornered.

"Colin!" I cried and held out the poker to him. He glanced once, then twice, between dodges, and took the poker from me with a flourish. He parried the next stab. The clash between the two weapons rang off the stone walls.

"Get out of here," Colin hissed at me. "Go!"

The swordsman was intent on Colin, unable to turn his back. I tucked my cell into my pocket, and darkness closed in again. I needed both hands to pick up the chair. My intention had been to get behind the swordsman and hit him over the head with the chair, knocking him out. Colin, Rio, and I would then escape back to the car and safety.

I skirted around the sounds of fighting, keeping the chair in front of me like a lion tamer. I made it into position and raised the chair with every intention of following through, but the chair suddenly became doubly heavy. I realized then that the first man—the swaggering, bow-legged, giant man—had latched onto one of its legs and was pushing it back against me. I needed to see, so I let go of the chair with one hand and pulled out my cell.

The man emerged from the darkness then, on his feet. He put his nose close to mine and snarled at me. I saw his face then. It was deformed, with unnatural cheekbones and a caveman forehead. Patches of fur grew on his jawline with mangy irregularity. His breath hit me, a sour stench that made me gag. I lost track of what was happening as my entire being recoiled from him. Two steps back, and I came up against the wall. I was trapped. The man put one hand against the stone by my head and loomed over me. The chair was pressing into me, between our bodies, and the leg bit into my thigh. I wiggled to free my leg, but it rubbed hard against my thigh as it slid across it.

He pushed himself harder against the chair, crushing me between it and the wall. I expected to hear my ribs crack.

I looked into his eyes—bloodshot and reddened, black at the center, evil. I knew in that moment that he had every intention of killing me, and maybe even eating me. The thought hit me like a bucket of cold water, and my "flight" reflex shifted into "fight." I lifted my cell phone and shone the light directly into those malevolent eyes.

The man groaned, recoiled, and released some of the pressure on me. I took the opportunity to shove the chair to the side and slide out from between it and the wall. The shift put the man slightly off-balance, and I barreled into him to add to his tilt. The chair clattered against the wall, and the man stumbled. I ran for the steps.

I caught a flash of steel reflecting my flashlight, and then the strangest sensation of something penetrating my body, my stomach. I froze, but then was tugged forward as the blade that had entered me was pulled out again...and re-inserted in a different place. Pain crashed down on my spine, and my legs gave out. I banged my head when I hit the floor.

CHAPTER 20

I heard Colin call my name as if through deep water. Then, he was there, cradling me against him, and I tasted blood. My mind scrambled to understand what was happening, and I relived it again.

Rio had come out of the darkness into the light of my cell. She had just stood there, a granite expression on her face. The flash of steel had reflected the light, and then she'd stabbed me. Not just once, but twice.

Rio's lips had been a tight line as she'd pulled her weapon out of me. She'd touched her fingers to my lips, and I'd felt a lingering tingle of magick. Then Rio had screamed. I'd wanted to scream too, but my lips could only tremble.

"Oh gods, Viv," Colin groaned, his hands exploring my stomach, applying pressure.

Rio appeared beside Colin, looking worried and upset. Tears streamed down her face. Damn, she was good. She touched him and said, "We have to get her help, or she'll die."

I tried to speak, to tell Colin not to trust her, but I couldn't. My mouth just wouldn't do what I wanted.

Colin was panting and wild-eyed. "Tell me how."

"Fly her to the lakeshore," Rio said. "Summon the boat. The druids will save her. She's a daughter of

Thu. Hurry. There's no time to waste."

I felt Colin pick me up in slow motion, the world moving around me. We climbed out of the cellar to stand under a field of twinkling stars. I felt the moment he opened his wings and lifted into the sky.

I was so cold. I hid my face against him, my thoughts a nest of vipers twisting and twining around each other. One particular one kept raising its terrifying head. *I'm dying.*

Colin landed on the lakeshore, his boots crunching in the rocks. He set me down gently on a small patch of grass, and his warmth left me, dissipating into the fog that was crawling off the water. He put both hands around his mouth. The sound he made resembled the *om from yoga class, deep and resonant, extended as long as his breath held out. He'd called three times before the head of a black dragon broke through the fog. It was the prow of a boat shaped like a Viking longship, but in miniature, no bigger than a large rowboat. It had a sail as dark as the night.*

A man's voice called, "Fomor, you are not welcome here. Turn away or face the consequences."

Colin shouted, "She's Thu. You have to save her!" He returned to me and sat beside me, pulling me into his lap and holding me against his chest. If he was warm, I could no longer feel it. "I don't need to go. Just take her. Save her!"

My vision was collapsing at the edges, my breath growing difficult to pull in.

The man said, "If this is a trick, you will pay dearly."

"It's not. She's dying. Please!"

I heard the boat touch the shore, then splashing and footsteps.

An unfamiliar face appeared in my range of sight, a man with long elegant ears and golden hair braided and wrapped around his head in a knotwork pattern. He looked into my eyes, then turned his attention to my torso. "She's been stabbed," he reported to someone. "It is a mortal wound."

"Let me see her," a woman said. More splashing. More footsteps.

My eyelids were closing as a woman's face came into view. Shock and concern marred her expression. I didn't have time to recognize her before my eyes closed. But I heard her breath huff in surprise, and she said, "It's Viviane Rose. Carry her to the boat. Now!"

Colin let them take me, and he stayed behind. I had no voice to object one way or the other.

The woman sat beside me, her soft fingers brushing across my forehead and cheek. No one spoke. The gravity of the moment quelled the need for words.

Later, I learned that the moment I entered Apfallon, the ancient Fomor curse was broken.

◇◇◇

CHAPTER 21

I slipped in and out of consciousness over the next twenty-four hours.

At first, I was lying on a concave rock, feeling the indents eroded in its surface with my fingertips. Spirits circled around me in green flowing cloaks that occasionally lifted on the breeze to reveal naked skin beneath. They chanted and rubbed scented oils onto my body. Magick danced across my skin, sinking in, and reconnecting separated tissue. The pain subsided quickly, though it never fully went away. My head ached, and my belly ached more. I could feel my heartbeat in my scalp. I focused on it and was grateful.

Later, I lay in a bed with four posts and a canopy of translucent fabric. A beam of sunshine fell across my cheek, warming it. Heavy quilts covered me to the neck, but I was otherwise naked. Sore and stiff, I could move only a little—just enough to straighten or bend my legs.

Next I awoke, I was still in bed, to the distant sound of music—a guitar or perhaps a lyre being strummed. The song carried peace and tranquility with it. I felt my stomach and discovered linen bandages wrapped all around my mid-section. The area of my wounds was still tender to the touch and hot, but for the first time, it felt possible I was going to survive. I fell back asleep wondering where Colin was.

Later, a person came in, wearing a chiffon caftan in marbled shades of brown and green. Its hem danced just above brown leather sandals. So beautiful, and yet so androgynous I couldn't tell whether the person was a man or a woman. They were carrying a tray with a basin of steamy water, fresh white washcloths, and bandages. They kept their eyes down as they moved around the bed to set the tray on a table by the window. Their long mahogany hair—as fine as silk—hung straight, parted over each pointed ear. For a moment, I thought I'd fallen into a Tolkien novel.

The person—*elf?—pulled back the covers, helped me to stand up, and wrapped me in a fluffy white robe.*

"Where am I?" I asked.

The being lifted large violet eyes to me. "Apfallon," they said with a gentle smile, "in Gliton Manor. I am Meenan, your caretaker." Their voice was a breathy alto.

"Thank you, Meenan," I said. "You're very kind."

Meenan blushed. "I'll leave you to your toilet. When I come back, I'll bring your breakfast." They left the room, closing the door behind them.

It was good to be on my feet again. I relieved myself in the portable commode's chamber pot, then used the warm, moist cloth Meenan provided to wash up. It smelled of lavender.

As if sensing the moment I was done, Meenan returned with a tray of food. "I will change your bandages first, and then you can try to eat. If you're not too cold, I can open the window and let in the fresh air."

"Thank you."

Meenan carefully pulled off the old wrap. It stuck in places where blood and other fluids had dried, but not a lot. My wounds were red and angry, but closed, already turning to scars. There were two— one an inch-long line and the other a ragged three-inch line. As I stared down at myself, I remembered the blade going in, out, then in again. I remember the hard expression on Rio's face.

"Am I okay, Meenan?" I asked. "I mean..." I touched my fingers to my skin near the wound.

Meenan nodded and patted my shoulder. "Yes. The damage was deep and serious, but we mended it in time to keep you from losing all of your blood. You'll be weak for a while. Perhaps you won't be as perfect as you were before, but you will be alive."

I laughed on a soft breath. "I've never been perfect, but I'm glad to hear that. I thought..." Memory of the moment I realized I was dying hit me again, and the remembered fear made the words catch in my throat. My eyes filled with tears.

"Shh, shhh, shhh," Meenan said, hand rubbing my upper arm. "Death lost. This time."

I sniffed and blinked back the tears. "Thank you." All I wanted was to go back to sleep.

◇

On the second day, I tried to reach out to Colin with my mind, but it felt as if there was a barrier between us. I could hear the thoughts of people in the manor, like background noise with nothing coming fully into focus, but I couldn't touch Colin. And so, I brooded on him and on Corona, thinking and fretting about them. I was restless all morning. I doubted the Thu had sent word of my condition. Colin probably thought I was dead. Who knew what Jake thought— what Rio had told him.

When Meenan came in, I leapt at the chance to ask, "Did anyone tell my fiancé I'm okay?"

"Your fiancé?"

"The man who brought me to the lake? Colin Aubrey? Can I get a message out to him?" I knew the answer to that. I had no idea where Colin even was— or if he was even all right. And then it occurred to me that, if he could, Colin would check with Jake for news on my condition. I asked, "Or maybe to Jake Lamb?"

Meenan replied, "The man from the haven."

"Yes. And ask him if Corona is okay?"

"Corona?"

"A friend."

Meenan's head tipped in a considering gesture, then they said, "Perhaps you should write the note yourself. If the mistress approves, I can have it delivered to Lost Lambs. Would that suffice?"

Immediately, a weight lifted off me, and I breathed a sigh of relief. "Yes. Thank you." I paused a beat, then added, "Who is the mistress?"

"She will visit you soon."

More questions jostled for dominance in my brain, but none of them gained any traction. I took each moment as it emerged from my foggy mind, tracking Meenan and following their instructions.

Meenan finished changing my bandages and helped me to the chair by the window. I was glad to be out of bed, and the food smelled delicious, but the view out the window captured my full attention.

It was magnificent. My room looked down upon an enclosed courtyard. I was on the third floor. Curving paths formed swirling patterns made by a mosaic of colored stones on the ground. The walkways circled garden patches, some with blooming azaleas, some with fruit trees—cherry, apple, pear—and a wide array of berry-laden bushes. All beautifully planned and tended, it was as pleasing to the eye as ripened fruit was to the tongue.

The walls around the courtyard were casement windows, revealing the room interiors beyond them. Each room had a unique decor, and they appeared lived-in. Some were bedrooms, others were offices or sitting rooms. One had an easel with a canvas whose painting I couldn't see. People moved around in the rooms. They were dressed in modern clothes, to my surprise. Meenan had set my expectations with their Middle-Earth elfen style.

The smell of the cheesy scrambled eggs and buttered oatmeal tugged on me. I took my time and savored each bite, watching the lawn as I did. I couldn't eat it all, but what little I did manage was enough.

In the meantime, Meenan changed the linens on the bed and tidied the room. "Are you cold?" Meenan asked. "Would you like me to open a window? Or, perhaps you'd rather return to bed?"

"I can sit here for a bit," I said. "Please do open one." I watched them do so, then asked, "Do you know when I'll be well enough to go back?"

"That is not something I can predict. You will know when you're ready." With that, Meenan put their palms together and touched them to their third eye. It was a gesture I had come to recognize as a blessing upon parting. I watched them head for the door.

"Thank you, Meenan," I said, putting as much sincere gratitude into the words as I could. "May I have something to write a note with?"

They faced me, made the gesture again, and then left. Shortly, she returned carrying paper with flower petals pressed in among the fibers and a silver ink pen of modern design.

I set about composing a note to Jake.

Later, Meenan confirmed that the message had been delivered, and Jake had sent back a reply.

Viviane,

I was happy to hear you're all right. Everyone was worried, though Rio assured us you were in good hands. She told us what hap-

pened. I've arranged to visit you tomorrow. I hope you're feeling up to it.

I haven't spoken to Colin, but Rio has said she might know how to reach him.

Corona is back at home. She'll be fine. I'll let her tell you the details, but suffice it to say, she had quite an adventure. She's lucky to be alive. I don't know how you knew what you did, but it saved her life. We found her and pulled her from the water before the tide turned for the worst.

Send word if you need anything at all. I'll have Carrie pack a bag for you, and I'll bring it when I come.

Feel better soon,
Jake

◇

By the third day, I was feeling much better, able to walk around on my own, make my way back and forth to the bathroom, shower, and eat full meals. I had just dressed with the intention of going down to the courtyard for some fresh air and exploration when a knock sounded at my door.

"Come in!" I called, turning toward the visitor, thinking maybe it was Jake.

To my surprise, it was Lenore, the octogenarian proprietor of the *Poetry, Prose, and Poe bookstore.*

"Hi," I said. All other questions or comments

fled as I got a good look at her.

Lenore was no longer the fragile old woman at whose tiny house I had dined. She stood straighter, head held high. She looked no younger, but she didn't move as if her joints pained her, and she had lost that hunch that comes with old age. She didn't have her cane and obviously didn't need it. Perhaps it was an affectation when she was in Reality. Perhaps she actually needed it there. She lifted her chin and smiled at me, her turquoise and copper eyes shining.

She was dressed all in ivory, an elegant pantsuit with a calf-length duster over the top. A beaded pattern spread downward from the mandarin collar, the tiny bits catching the light when she moved.

"How are you feeling?" Lenore asked. Even her voice was stronger.

"Better. Thank you."

"I'm sorry I couldn't come see you sooner. Do you have everything you need? Has Meenan been attentive enough?"

"Oh gosh, yeah," I replied, and then it hit me. "You're the mistress of Gliton Manor."

"I am."

"You're the one who saved me."

Lenore nodded, still smiling, and moved to one of the two chairs at the little table. "It was a spur of the moment decision."

What did that mean? I thought. Does she regret her decision to save me?

She gestured to indicate I should sit down

across from her, and once I was situated, she said, "I'm sorry, but I do regret it."

She heard my thoughts! I thought.

Lenore smiled. In my head, I heard, *Yes, it's a family gift.*

Then aloud she said, "We need to discuss the repercussions of that decision, and there's so much I need to tell you now that you're here."

My nerves jangled, and I clasped my hands together in my lap. "Like what?"

Lenore lifted her chin so high she had to look down her nose at me. She narrowed her eyes and said, "Like who you are and why saving your life was perhaps the worst thing I could do."

CHAPTER 22

L enore gazed out the window at the courtyard below. "Tell me the truth," she said. "Did you allow this?"

"Allow this? Allow what?"

She faced me, her expression harsh, eyes cutting. "Did you let them hurt you? Let them bring you here at death's door?"

"You mean *on purpose?*"

"Maybe you did it for love of that Fomor? I might be able to forgive you if you did it for *love.*"

My voice dropped almost to a whisper. "I had no idea what was happening. Colin had been kidnapped, and I was trying to save him." My voice rose, accusatory. "You're the ones who were torturing him."

"Who told you that?"

"Rio. Colin's step-mom. She was helping me free him, but then..." I remembered the moment when she'd stabbed me, the look on her face so hard.

Lenore gasped and closed her eyes. I knew then that she'd been in my head with me. She crossed her arms. "I knew it. I wasted too much time thinking about what to tell you, how much of it to tell you. *When to tell you. I should have done so as soon as you arrived."* She opened her eyes and studied me.

I waited for her to continue but was ultimately

forced to break the silence. "Tell me what?"

"The truth about your ancestry and why it puts you in danger."

I nodded. "Okay. Now's as good a time as any."

Lenore was picking at a hangnail on her thumb. It began to bleed, and she put it in her mouth. Then, as if realizing what she was doing, she tucked it behind her back. She said, "I'm Moira's mother—your great-grandmother." She said it as if she were relaying the time of day, but it knocked me back.

"What?"

Lenore held up a hand. "Hold on tight. That's the tip of the iceberg." She let me think for a few seconds, then added, "You were foretold."

"Excuse me?" I was getting irritated. "What does that even mean?"

"Many generations ago, our ancestors—the Tuatha dé Danann, the Thu—fought many wars. Some we lost, some we won. During it all, we made mortal enemies of the Fomor and took Apfallon from them."

I nodded. "I've heard all this."

"What you may not know is that the Fomor are devious murderers. All our attempts to find a diplomatic truce with them have failed. They cling to the belief that one day, a child of mixed human, Fomor, and Thu blood will open the door to Apfallon for them. That day has come, and that child is you."

I had a sinking feeling. I asked, "The curse?"

"Broken." Tears streamed down Lenore's face. "The moment I brought you into Apfallon to save your life, it opened that door. It's only a matter of time before the Fomor army is upon us."

I shifted uncomfortably. "I didn't know."

"I see that." Lenore closed her eyes and dipped her chin.

"It was Rio. She used me. Oh my god. I'm so sorry."

Lenore snorted a wry laugh. "Don't be sorry. They put their plan in motion before you were even born. In hindsight, I see that now. And none of it matters anymore. What's done is done, and now we must prepare for the consequences of our gullibility."

A quiet knock came at the door, and Lenore called, "Enter."

Meenan had brought us tea and danishes on a tray. They took one look at us and hurried their steps. They set down the tea, poured two cups, and then put the back of their hand to my forehead. "She's pale," they noted, glancing over at Lenore with concern.

"She's fine," said Lenore. "The tea will help. Thank you."

I wrapped my hands around the warm teacup and smiled at Meenan. "I'm okay. Thanks."

Lenore waited for Meenan to leave before she said, "Family..." She paused, presumably searching for the right words. "Magick is interwined with our very souls. It's a form of grace. Because of it, we never truly die."

She was losing me. I didn't understand, and she could see it on my face. She held up a hand to stall all the questions banging on my teeth.

"We reincarnate within the same lineage." She emphasized her next words, scrutinizing me, "For example..."

She paused for dramatic effect, then finished, "You are my mother reincarnated."

I froze. Then, I laughed. Surely, she was joking. With sincerity, she said, "I'm *not joking.*"

I sat back in my chair. "Oh. You're not?"

"No. Not even a little. It's not a metaphor. It's not a joke. It's not an exaggeration. It is fact."

"Okay." A question clawed its way to the surface. "I don't remember any past lives." Even as I said it, I knew that wasn't true. During my regression sessions with Richard, I'd gone too far back one time. I'd seen myself in a verdant valley surrounded by rolling hills and a palace whose parts shifted around as I watched. There'd been people there in Regency attire, dancing on the lawn. Though I could still see it all in my mind's eye, I'd chalked it up to my imagination, as had Richard.

"Yes," said Lenore, a smile in her voice. "That was a memory." She was still in my head, and it was starting to bug me.

Lenore said, "My mother's name—your name—was Victorina, and she was the reincarnation of her own grandmother. In that way, we can trace our lineage all the way back to the primal gods."

We sat in silence. She put two large teaspoons of sugar in my tea and served me a cream-cheese danish with cherry jam. It looked homemade and beautifully imperfect.

I asked, "How do you know?"

Lenore picked at the crust of her own danish but didn't eat it. She said, "It has always been this way. It's true for anyone who has magical blood. Occasionally, one of us remembers the past life or displays aptitudes that match."

I thought, *Will I ever remember my past life?*

Lenore answered me aloud. "Some do. Some don't. It happens less often with those whose blood is mixed. Like yours. Your soul is Thu, and you have Thu blood, which is our line. But you also have human blood from your grandfather and Fomor blood from your father."

"My father was Fomor."

"Yes."

"And you think they plan to attack Apfallon?"

"Invade it, yes. The Fomor have never been content with sharing the land, even though there's always been plenty to go around. They will—again—try to kill us all so they can have it to themselves." She spoke with sadness and resignation.

My stomach did a complete flop. "Holy shit," I said. "That's why you should've let me die. If you had, the Fomor curse would still be in place. And I'd have been reincarnated."

Lenore nodded. "Yes. I saved the one at the expense of the many. I saw the blood and your face as white as a sheet, and I reacted just as they intended me to. So now, Apfallon will pay the price."

"Shit."

"They'll destroy Apfallon rather than share it with us."

I watched her as she turned to look out the window again.

"I have friends who are Fomor," I said. "We can talk to them. We don't need all this ridiculous Medieval bullshit. This is the twenty-first century."

"And yet wars rage throughout the normal world based on ancient grudges and territory disputes. This is no different. Many will die." She made her way to the door. With her hand on the knob, without looking back, she said, "I have to prepare. You and I, we have our work cut out for us."

"We?"

Lenore looked over her shoulder at me. "Yes, Viviane," she said. "We. Your mother is gone. Your grandmother is gone. *You are all I have left. You were the key that unlocked the door and let the enemy in. You owe us. We can't let whatever comes through that door massacre our people." Her jaw tensed. She opened the door and left.*

One name sat bitter on my tongue, "Rio."

◇◇◇

CHAPTER 23

Two days later, the black sailboat with the dragon figurehead dropped me and a driver onto the Reality-side of Fortunate Lake. Though Lenore had advised against my leaving the healing sanctuary so soon, I was determined to get back. The driver—a taciturn man wearing black jeans and a faded flannel shirt—walked with me to where Lenore had parked her SUV, and then he drove me to the haven.

I and my two tote bags of clothes, bandages, salves, soaps, and gifts I'd collected while at Gliton manor had been deposited at the base of the stairs to Holly House. I waved the driver away and stood there, looking up the ridge at the houses, the trees, and the stairs. I was shockingly glad to be back.

Climbing the stairs with my bags took my verve right out of me. I leaned against the front door to rest, rang the bell, and gave up on martyrdom.

Jake himself answered the door and lifted me off my feet as he pulled me into a hug. "You're home!" he said, the relief audible in his voice. "Jesus, I wasn't sure we'd ever see you again." Though the hug squished me painfully and lasted a bit longer than was respectable, he did eventually release me. "How are you?" he asked, looking me up and down.

"I'm better," I said, happy to see him. "They took good care of me."

"I figured they would when I heard what had happened." Jake's expression darkened as he remembered.

"I have a lot to tell you," I said.

He looked at me with a worried expression. "C'mon in." He picked up my totes. "Ayu's going to want to feed you, and Corona's going to jump on you..."

"Like you did?" I teased.

He smiled an apology. "Did I hurt you?"

I shook my head. "Thanks for letting me know Corona's okay. She *is okay, right?*"

"Oh yeah," he said. "She's fine. She got herself in a lot of trouble, but she made it. I'm sure she'll want to tell you the story herself." Jake set the bags down and stood there, looking awkward. "Kitchen? Couch? Bathroom? What do you need?"

"Anywhere we can talk." That ended up being the seating area by the fireplace. Ayu came in with a tray of coffee, and Jake lit a fire while she fussed over me. She left again with a promise to deliver pesto-chicken sandwiches.

"Has Rio been here since that day?" I asked once Ayu was gone.

"Once," Jake said, unsuspecting. "But that's not unusual. Why do you ask?"

I didn't know how else to say it but to blurt it out. "She's the one who stabbed me."

"What?" I heard disbelief in his voice, but it didn't last. Understanding dawned, and his eyes narrowed.

"She was betting that Lenore wouldn't let me die," I explained. "And it worked. The Fomor curse. It's broken."

"Holy fuck," Jake said, courtesy filters smashed.

"I think she killed Nathan too." My head felt heavy. I looked down at my hands. "I think Nathan was going to tell me who killed my mom. We were talking in my head. Telepathically, I guess. Rio can do that too. I think she was listening, and she... She shut him up." Though it had been tickling the back of my brain ever since she stabbed me, I hadn't yet said it aloud. The words themselves felt like burrs on my soul.

Jake whispered, "Her own son."

"And Mom too, I think." I nodded. "Apparently, she'll go to any lengths..."

"To break the curse," he finished for me.

I nodded again. "Yes. And now it's done. She's won."

Jake shifted over to sit on the couch beside me. He took my hand. "That's a problem for tomorrow. Right now, I'm just grateful you're okay and you're home."

I squeezed his fingers. "Me too." We sat in silence for a moment, just holding hands. I pulled away first, sat back, and picked up my coffee mug.

Jake said, "Colin came to see me."

"He did? And you told him I was alive?"

"Yeah, I told him."

Another wave of relief washed over me. "Thanks," I said. "What'd he say?"

"He said to tell you that he's dealing with family stuff and that he may not be able to see you for a while."

"Did he say anything about Rio?"

"He didn't stay long enough for a conversation."

"I don't think he knows," I said, "that Rio set all this up."

"He's a smart guy. He'll figure it out."

I nodded, "Maybe. I think he was as fooled by her as I was."

"I hope so," Jake said. "For your sake."

The idea that he might have been in on it terrified me. I could not let myself believe that.

Jake said, "She duped us all. I'm sure he'll be in touch as soon as he can."

As soon as it was cool enough, I finished my coffee with greed.

Corona's squeal made me jump. She came flying out of the back hallway and would have leapt upon me if Jake hadn't been so quick on his feet. He wrapped an arm around her waist and held her at bay.

"Careful!" Jake warned. "She's injured."

Corona brought her physical enthusiasm down about fifty notches, but her voice still sounded over-caffeinated. She hit me with a barrage of questions even as she gently draped herself over my shoulders, giving me no time to answer any of them, and smooched my cheek over and over a dozen times until she had me giggling.

◇

Later, in the solace of my room, I took a nap. I dreamt of the manor at Apfallon. I was roaming the halls, with their carved wood panels and thick wool carpets, looking for something I couldn't find. The manor became a maze. I was lost and growing panicked. A roar sounded behind me, and I recognized it as the assassin who had attacked my car. I saw again the clawed hands, the tangled black hair, masculine mutton chops, and the gaping red maw. She was right in my face, and I was backed against a wall. I stared straight into her eyes, those black pits ringed with gold.

She spoke. "I could've been beautiful," she said. "I could've been you."

Her hand reared back, preparing to rake down my body. I cringed...

My scream woke me. I pushed up on my elbows and scanned the room. I was alone. The light was waning outside, an orange blush rising over the blue sky in the West. My belly ached, and I lay back down. I focused on my breathing and pulled the covers up to my chin.

The last time I'd woken up screaming, I'd been in Malum Center. Colin had been missing, and in my nightmare, I'd watched him drown, his hair floating around his head, mouth open wide in a silent scream, eyes staring but not at me. At nothing.

So much had happened since then. Colin had turned up alive and well, and my whole world had turned upside down. I'd discovered real magick. I wasn't crazy. I'd never been crazy, and apparently my sanity was genetic.

I had the urge to do something productive, so I threw back the covers. I took a long hot shower and put on a pair of sweats, a soft, oversized sweater, and thick wool socks. No bra. I was as comfy as I could make myself. With an unexpected surge of energy, I tidied my room and changed the sheets on the bed. As I carried the laundry basket down to the basement, I thought of my Mom and her stories. She was Thu, but she'd been living in Peoria with my human grandfather. My grandmother had changed her identity to throw off our enemies, and I was the result of a fling with a Fomor named Chance. I had no idea who he was.

I set the basket on top of the dryer and started filling the washer with water and detergent. The sounds took me back to Malum Center. They were a soft echo of the roar in the Center's laundry room. I thought of my coworkers, Julio, Jax, and all the others I'd worked with. I thought of Simon who'd been absent for weeks. He'd missed all of it, and I knew he'd have wanted to be there if he could. I wondered if he even knew Mom was dead.

I thought of my best friend Lettie, left behind in Peoria, and vowed to call her the next day. I had no idea what that conversation would be like. I couldn't tell her any of it, nothing real about my life. My heart ached for that, and it occurred to me that maybe I shouldn't call. Maybe I should just let her go.

Today, you're pain. Tomorrow, a stain. The old laundry motto drifted up from the depths, but it held new meaning for me. I'd left my whole life, my entire old self, behind just like that. *Bam!*

It would have been easy to cut everything out of my life except Wyrdwood, but I had too much invested in Reality. Abram had returned to Peoria without me. He was my anchor. My get-out-of-jail-free card. And the truth was, I couldn't cut Lettie from my heart, not even if I'd wanted to. She was a part of me. I'd have to find a way to tell her everything. I missed her too much not to.

I preferred to stand with one foot in Reality and one in Wyrdwood. Maybe that was my true destiny. Maybe I could be the one to bring Wyrdwood—kicking and screaming—into the twenty-first century.

Tick tock.

I looked up at the clock on the wall and realized it was dinner time. I shoved all the dirty laundry into the washer, closed the lid, and hustled back up the stairs. As I turned off the basement light, I thought of Ayu's cooking, and my stomach growled.

THE END FOR NOW

◇◇◇

Appendix

O nce again, as she did quite often in those days, Bella Rosenblum, née Moira Gliton, crouched over the oak slab in the forest clearing. A chill permeated the night air, causing her breath to escape in visible streams. Tears ran down her face as she gazed into the water in the scrying bowl.

Lenore, Viviane, Abraham, and Kushala sat around a dining table. Lenore and Kushala appeared so fragile with age—but then, they were well over two hundred years old each. The years caught up to them whenever they left Apfallon.

Bella hadn't spoken with her mother since Viviane was born, thirty-three years earlier. To everyone she'd ever loved, Bella was dead. It broke her heart again to see her mother and her granddaughter dining together for the first time. She yearned to be there with them, but there was no going back. Not yet. She had to see her work through to completion. For the time being, she remained a spectator, watching remotely from her hiding place. When Viviane and Abraham left to return to the Lost Lambs haven, Bella cleared the water and returned to her tiny cottage in the woods to write down what she'd witnessed.

Every night, she trekked out to the place of

power where the ley lines intersected. She set out her bowl and whispered a new incantation, a new name. Her magick caused the water's surface to ripple, then settle, revealing the person whose name she spoke. She collected visions of other people's lives like treasured puzzle pieces that helped her understand the complexities of the political environment in Wyrdwood—albeit in a chaotic, piecemeal way that often confused her as much as it enlightened her.

Bella had to be circumspect about her choice of target. Some people might sense the intrusion and trace it back to her. For this reason, she poked around the periphery of Viviane's social circle like a dog sniffing for overlooked crumbs.

◇

"Corona Bachmeier"

Corona leaned against the short wooden fence intended to keep tourists off the beach at Seal Cove. The late afternoon sun glimmered on the surface of the Pacific Ocean. A small herd of seals lay sprawled upon the rocky beach, soaking in the day's last warming rays.

She spoke into her phone, holding it so it was filming the beach, "Otto, look at them all."

"Awesome," answered a man. "So what are you going to do?"

"I'm going down there," Corona replied, "and

I'm going to introduce myself."

"You sure it's safe?"

Corona laughed. "What're they gonna do? Swarm me and eat me? Maybe if they were zombie seals."

"They might be zombie seals. It's hard to tell at this distance."

"You're makin' shit up. They're not zombies," Corona said. "But some of them might be selkies."

"Yeah, about that," Otto said through the phone. "I've been diggin' since you told me about this selkie shit."

"What'd you find?"

"Lots more of the popular mythology. Scottish origins. Seal skins. Shapeshifting. You know, typical wiki dreck."

"So why'd you bring it up?"

"'Cause I found out there's a scientific word for shape-shifting—*therianthropy. And there's enough people who believe they're of mixed species that there's a Psychology term for it—clinical lycanthropy—and it's not just for werewolves. It's a kind of psychosis where the patient experiences 'species dysphoria.' Like, you're not the species you were told you are.*"

Corona turned the phone so the camera was on herself and glared into it. "Fuck you, Otto. I'm not psychotic."

Otto stared back from the screen, dark eyes wide. He shook his head. "No, dumbass. That's not what I'm saying. I'm saying that it's a Thing, capital T, trademarked. If enough people believe it, then it's got to be real, right? And it's just the Man keepin' us minorities in our place. Homogenization on a mythic level. They even got a name for it in the Psych textbooks. I mean, shit, they didn't even remove homosexuality from the official list of psychological disorders until the late '80s. And that's not the 1880s, that's the 1980s. You grock?"

"I get what you're saying."

Otto smiled. "Knew you would, Trin."

"Normals are limited," Corona said.

"Not me."

"No, not you. All the others. It's like, I know selkies are real. D.N.A. doesn't lie. I'm a selkie. Well, half-selkie. It makes sense. It explains why I never fit in anywhere."

"Who do you think was the selkie? Your mom? Or your dad?"

"My dad was painfully, stubbornly human, so it couldn't have been him. Besides, he drowned to death, so..."

"There's a metric crapton of stories about human dudes who stole a selkie's skin and forced her to have sex with him to get it back."

Corona scoffed. "I don't think my dad was devious, perverted, or smart enough to do that. I'd bet my mom got him drunk and seduced him on the beach. She was prob'ly his first."

"Now who's makin' shit up?"

"Yeah, I'll never know the truth."

"You never talk about your mom. You know what happened to her?"

Corona shrugged. "What memories I have of her could just be wishful thinking. They're warm and cuddly and unrealistic. According to my dad, she dropped me off at his place when I was about a year old. Abandoned me. I don't think he knew I existed until she showed up with me."

"Damn. You sure you're his?"

"I'm sure. I totally got his German genes." Corona sighed and shifted the phone to her other hand. "I better get going. The sun's going down."

"You think your mom could be alive?"

"Maybe." Corona laughed. "Maybe she's one of those harbor seals down there." A surge of excitement made Corona take a deep breath. "Gotta go, Otto. I'll call you when I get home."

She didn't wait for his reply, but hung up, stashed her phone in her pocket, and climbed over the fence.

A rough and craggy bank surrounded the beach, and Corona climbed down it crab-style, using her butt as an anchor. The beach itself consisted of smooth stones of all sizes. An orange one caught her eye, and Corona bent to pick it up. *Agate, she thought, studying it. It had been polished by years in the tumbling waves. She pocketed it.*

Someone shouted, and Corona looked for the source. A group of boys stood at the fence some distance down the beach, throwing rocks. They laughed and jeered, though Corona couldn't make out exactly what they were saying. They directed their rocks at a seal lying on the water's edge. When one of the rocks hit it in the back, the tip of a rear flipper flipped up, but it did nothing else.

Corona broke into a run and shouted, "Hey! Cut that out, you stupid little shits!"

The boys ignored her.

"Stop it!" Corona called. She skirted around the main body of the herd, but the seals didn't seem too bothered by her. One or two grumbled loudly, and a couple others moved away, but the rest just stared at her as if she were the most interesting thing to happen to them all day.

A boy in jeans and a gray hoodie spotted her and pointed her out to his friends. They hesitated, then all took aim one last time and let their rocks fly.

"I'm gonna call the police!" Corona shouted.

The boys laughed.

Corona stopped, watched them jostle each other as they ran off and out of sight, then turned toward the seal. She approached it cautiously.

"Hey, hey," she said. "Are you okay? Those mean boys are gone."

The waves lapped up over the seal, but it didn't move to get to higher ground.

With each step, Corona got closer until finally she understood why. A barbed fishing hook had pierced the seal's side. Blood ran down its fur from the wound. The fishing line attached to the hook had gotten wrapped around the seal's body, pinning its front fins to its sides and cutting into it.

"Oh no!" Corona cried in horror. She made soft cooing sounds as she approached the injured creature, hoping not to scare it too badly.

The seal was exhausted, and the incoming tide was about to overtake it.

Corona said, "Don't worry. I've got you. I won't let you drown." She knelt beside the seal and took hold of it by its hind-flippers, spinning it around, and pulling it up higher on the shore. Crouching down, she examined it. Its fur was white with black and dark gray patches. It was panting and snorting out its nostrils.

"I've got you," Corona said, wondering how she was going to cut the fishing line. She didn't have a knife. A glance around told her there wasn't anyone to help her. She could call for help, but that would take a long time. "This is going to hurt."

Before she could rethink her decision, Corona bent down and bit into the fishing line where it was attached to the hook. She tasted brine and smelled the copper of the seal's blood. A rising panic urged her to hurry, and she bit through the line. Her own breath was coming more quickly.

Corona sat back on her heels and said, "There. Just a little more." She took hold of the barbed end of the hook, hesitated only a moment, then closed her eyes, and pulled it on through. It caught briefly on the rounded end where the line had been tied, but with an extra tug, Coronal managed to pull it free.

The seal cried out in pain, a woeful sound like nothing Corona had ever heard.

"I know, baby. I know. I'm so sorry." Corona petted the seal's fur. "It's gone." After a moment's pause, she set about unwrapping the fishing line. She was forced to roll the seal, but the animal didn't complain any further.

When finally, the line was off, Corona picked up the hook and stepped back.

The seal lay there, panting and shaking, then turned its head to look up at Corona.

"It's okay," Corona said. "You're going to be okay." She took another step back so as not to frighten it any more than she already had.

Another step and then another... Corona walked right into a person, the one standing behind her. She squeaked in surprise and rolled to the side.

A man stood there, naked as the day he was born, but much more muscular.

"Oh!" Corona cried. She was at a loss for words.

"What are you doing to that seal?" the man asked.

"I...I..." Corona held out the fishing line and hook still in her hand.

The man looked down at it with a scowl. "Get off this beach, and don't come back." His raised dark brown eyes back to Corona's and added, "Now." His voice was low, but firm with smooth strength.

Corona licked her lips, digging deep for courage. She lifted her jaw and asked, "Are you a selkie?"

The man narrowed his eyes then walked without answering toward the sea.

"Wait!" Corona cried. "I'm like you. I'm a selkie too." She took two steps in the same direction, and the man halted abruptly.

He did not look back when he said, "Go home." He turned his head so his ear faced Corona, paused as if waiting for a reply, then continued walking. The ocean waves splashed over his ankles.

"I am. Please. I can prove it." Corona took a step for each of his, keeping up with him. "My mother was a selkie. Would you just... talk to me?"

Stopping in place where the water hit him at his knees, the man faced Corona, expression dark. "You want to know us," he said. "You want to learn about your heritage and explore your culture." It wasn't a question.

"Yes, I do. Please. My name's Corona. I'm magickal, and I took a DNA test in Wyrdwood that said I was half selkie."

The man studied Corona for a couple seconds, then his mouth spread into a wide smile. "Well, why didn't you say so." He called out toward the ocean, "She took a DNA test."

To Corona's surprise, several pairs of eyes rose from the ocean, some human, some seal. They peered out at her, silhouetted against the setting sun. Corona waved at them and smiled, the familiar excitement flowing up her spine.

"Hiya," Corona said. "I'm Corona. I'm like you. Hi. Hello."

"Come," said the man. "I'll introduce you."

Corona hesitated. "Into the water?"

"Why not? It's where you belong, isn't it?"

"I've never..." Corona didn't know how to put her thought into words.

The man finished her sentence for her. "Changed?"

Corona nodded.

"Relax," the man said. "We've got you." He turned around and walked into the water. When it was up to his waist, he lowered himself into it and began to swim out. "Don't be afraid," he called back. "You're a selkie, right?"

Corona stared after him, frozen in place.

The others stayed where they were, watching her with just the top halves of their heads above the water. When the man had drawn even with them, he turned and faced the beach, treading water, waiting.

Corona felt her heart in her throat. As she debated what to do, a string of Hollywood wisdom came to mind, and she said, "This is your last chance, Corona. After this, there is no turning back. Take the blue pill, the story ends. Take the red pill, you stay in Wonderland and learn just how deep the rabbit hole goes." Before she'd finished speaking, she was stepping forward.

The ocean water sent goosebumps up her legs and down her arms. It chilled her to the bone, but she ignored it. With her eyes locked on the selkies, on her people, she walked into the water. When it was up to her waist, she slid down into it and swam forward, right up to the man waiting for her.

"What now?" she asked.

A crooked smile tilted the man's lips, and he disappeared down under the water.

Corona looked around. One by one, the others did the same thing.

A hand grabbed Corona by the ankle and dragged her under. She barely had time to suck in a quick breath before the water closed over her head. When she opened her eyes, the cold of the water hurt them, and she closed them again. The hand on her ankle was pulling her through the water. She couldn't tell if she was going down or out or in or what? When her breath started to give out, she began to panic.

This isn't right, she thought. What are you doing? What's going on?

Panic shifted into terror. Corona kicked out against the person holding her. She opened her eyes and tried to find the surface. It shimmered high overhead, painted blood red by the setting sun.

No! I don't want this! Her lungs were imploding. Her muscles spasming. She kicked again and felt the grip on her ankle release. Don't breathe! Swim up! No!

She tried to breathe.

A wave of black consumed the scarlet light, and Corona's world turned upside down and inside out.

Her strength abandoned her, and her last thought was, "Otto's gonna be mad."

The ocean moved around her, swirling, moving her legs for her, and she felt a hard nudge against her side. It pushed her through the water. Light began to leak in through her eyelids, and another push moved her again.

Nothingness enveloped her, cold and as loud as the crashing of waves.

Corona felt a band wrap around her, crushing her chest, and still the ocean was unforgiving. She couldn't hold on any longer.

◇

Pain exploded in Corona's chest, and the urge to heave racked her body. She puked up water, felt it surge out through her nose, crashing up from her lungs. And when she inhaled, the frigid air burned her.

Corona could do nothing but shiver, retch, and suck in air that made her cough and sputter painfully.

Gradually, she became aware of someone seated on the rocks beside her, and she managed to open her eyes, blink back the blur, and see who it was.

A young woman sat there, no older than Corona herself. She was nude, her skin pale in the twilight. Brown hair streamed down around her face, flat to her head, and spread like seaweed over her shoulders. She had huge brown eyes, canted with worry, and she hugged herself with long, slim arms. "You're alive," she said, her voice a warm alto.

"Who?" was all Corona could manage, but already she knew the answer to her question. A wound in the woman's side continued to trickle watery blood, and red welts marked the path of the fishing line that had bound her.

"Corona!" someone shouted from a distance. A gunshot rang out.

The selkie looked up in fear and immediately began to get to her hands and feet, moving backwards toward the water.

"Wait!" Corona rasped, throat sore. "I want to be your friend."

Backing away, already up to her knees in the water, the selkie hesitated.

Another gunshot sounded.

The selkie launched herself into the ocean.

"Stop," Corona whispered, the delayed emotions of what she'd experienced reducing her to sobs. "Sto-o-op..."

"Corona," said Jake, crouching down beside her. "We've got you. It's going to be okay." He took off his coat, helped Corona to sit up, and wrapped it around her. It was large enough to engulf her small form. "Are you hurt?"

All Corona could do was cry.

Jake picked Corona up in his arms. "She's frozen. Let's get her to the car."

Hilda fell into step behind him with a hissed, "Fucking selkies."

◇

"Jake Lamb"

"I assure you, Mr. Rose," said Jake Lamb into the phone, "Viviane and Gisèle are safe here. Richard Reuter will have to go through me to get to them." He paused, listening, then said with a touch of impatience, "He's called you three times? Well, you did right by not revealing their location. Have you considered taking out a restraining order on him yourself? I mean, I know Viviane has one in place, but if he's harrassing you..."

Lamb's computer pinged.

"Uh huh," Lamb said, listening. "Uh huh." He grabbed his mouse and clicked open his email. A new one had arrived. He opened it and read.

Jake,

Thank you again for allowing me to visit your facilities. I enjoyed seeing the important work you're doing. I'm reaching out today to get your help with one of my patients. Perhaps you can help me find her. She has run away from both the Malum Center and her family.

You remember Viviane Rose, the young woman you met in my office? The one who suffers from schizophrenia and is prone to

hearing voices that give her commands. If
you know anything about her whereabouts,
please contact me ASAP. I'm frantic with
worry as is her grandfather.
      Professionally yours,
      Richard Reuter

Jake hadn't heard a word Abram Rose had said over the previous minute. He shifted in his chair, sitting up straighter, and said, "Mr. Rose. I'm going to have to go. I assure you that Viviane is protected here. Richard can't get to her. I give you my word."

He paused, listening, then said, "Okay. Yes. I will. You take care now. We'll talk again soon."

He hung up and turned to the computer to reply.

Richard,
      It was my pleasure hosting you here at
the Lost Lamb Haven. I hope you can incor-
porate some of what you saw into your own
practice.
      I'm afraid I haven't been in touch with
Viviane since I left Peoria. I doubt she would
contact me, if she even has my details. Have
you considered contacting the police?
      Please let me know how it turns out.
      Best regards,
      Jake Lamb.

◇◇◇

Thanks for Reading
WW06242020

Leave a review. If you enjoyed this story, please take a moment to give it a review. It's the kindest thing you can do for the authors you love and who love you back (like me!).

Read more. A peripheral novella to this book, titled "Charlie Darwin Or, The Trine Of 1809," is available as a free download at WyrdwoodAngel.com/charlie.

◇

Join our growing community by signing up for the Wyrdwood email list. We'll send instructions for how to connect with other magickal readers just like you. Sign up now.

Know anyone you think would like this story?
Please let them know about it!
They'll appreciate that you did and so will I.

And, in appreciation, here's a sneak preview of the next book in the *Wyrdwood Welcome series*.

◇

HEXING THE MOON

Wyrdwood Welcome Book #3

Sneak Preview

I stood at the threshold to Purgatory—Gehenna. A long hallway stretched out before me—the proverbial tunnel. The light at the end of it did little to illuminate my way. Instead, it whitewashed the details of what lay ahead. The back of my neck twitched, and my shoulders clenched in dread. I felt certain someone—or some thing—was watching me.

Oddly—or perhaps not—the corridor reminded me of Vince Malum Residential Living Center. It made sense that my Purgatory would resemble my own personal Hell. Doors lined the walls, and everything sat askew, as if tilted or twisted. I had no desire whatsoever to explore what lay beyond those doors. I tightened my grip on the fireplace poker in my hand and kept my focus on the path ahead.

Something brushed the back of my shoulder, and I jumped. I nearly turned to face it, but I knew the rules. Bella had explained them very clearly. I must not look back until I was in the light.

"No matter what," she'd said.

"What will happen if I do?" I'd asked.

"You'll lose your way." That was all she'd said, but her dire tone made the warning clear.

Colin had said, "I'll be waiting for you in the light."

My legs didn't want to obey me. Though my mind was telling me to move forward, my body wasn't on board.

I blew out a breath through pursed lips. "C'mon, Viv," I told myself. "You've got this. Just take a step. One foot in front of the other." The words reminded me of the song from *Santa Claus is Coming to Town, and I said it again, to a little tune. "Put one foot... in front of the other." My voice came out weak and shaky. "And soon—"*

Something hissed behind me. My breath hitched.

Eyes wide, I strained to hear.

Whispers. All around me.

"It's her."

"Sweetness."

"She's here."

And those were just the tidbits I could make out. A hum of voices all around me wove together to create a blanket that threatened to suffocate me.

Of their own accord, my feet started moving. Panic had me by the neck. I broke into a run, making a break for the light—the mysterious light that held unknown danger—and maybe my Colin.

A sharp pain erupted in my ankle, then another on the back of my head. Something had hold of my hair. I wrapped my hand around the snagged hair even as I leaned back. My feet kept going, and I almost went down. I yanked my hair free just as I reached my tipping point and somehow managed to both stay upright and remain facing forward.

I swung the iron poker wildly behind me, not knowing at what. The poker didn't contact anything, and I felt the strain in my wrist as it whipped around at an awkward angle.

The whispers rose up around me. "Pretty."

"Golden."

"She's ours."

I shouted, "Get away from me!" My center dropped an inch or two, and I readied to run again. I gritted my teeth and locked my gaze on the light at the end of the hallway—the tunnel. It didn't seem any closer than it had when I'd first arrived, but at least I wasn't turned around.

A sibilant wind blew up from behind me, lifting the hem of my coat and the ends of my hair. It was hot and smelled like the sewer. So thick, it made me gag. I put my free hand over my nose and mouth.

Something tugged at my coat sleeve.

That was it. I was done. I pulled free and ran full bore toward the light. If there was anything beyond it—inside it—it had better be ready to catch me because I wasn't stopping.

I sprinted. The sound of my feet slamming on the tile echoed in the empty hall. The rasp of my breath gained speed as the hallway stretched and what physical endurance I had was put to the test.

The iron poker in my hand kept grazing or pinging off the wall, creating loud noises that startled me.

The beings with their grabby hands and terrifying whispers kept pace with me. I slapped at fingers that grabbed, felt claws cut into my legs, arms, and scalp. They were herding me like a cow toward slaughter. The poor cow thought salvation lay at the end of the corridor. Going back was never an option.

I barreled forward for what seemed like an eternity, ignoring the pain in my side, the burn in my throat, and the fear that I didn't have it in me to continue.

My steps slowed to stumbling, and I leaned forward to keep whatever momentum I had going.

"Colin!" I cried, wanting—needing—help.

I had to stop. Black dots danced at the edge of my vision. I put my hands on my knees and panted hot, fetid air. I couldn't get enough. I was suffocating. My legs gave out, and my vision went white.

The last things I remembered were the dirty tile floor rising up toward me, a sickening vertigo, and a single thought:

Being dead sucks.

TO BE CONTINUED...

Grab *your* copy of Hexing the Moon today.
http://wyrdwoodangel.com/HexingTheMoon

About the Author

Angel Leigh McCoy has worn many faces, told many stories, loved many people, and lived many lives. Through it all, writing has been her one constant.

Angel is a spark of creative force behind the epic Dire Multiverse and the darkly fanciful Wyrdwood project.

She's an award-winning video game writer, having worked on "CONTROL," IGN's Game of the Year 2019. Prior to that, she spent ten years weaving intricate tales for millions of *Guild Wars 2* fans. As a writer for White Wolf's *World of Darkness,* she created stories about vampires, changelings, mages, and werewolves.

◇◇◇

Sign up for my mailing list to get
the latest Wyrdwood news and fun.
(http://wyrdwoodangel.com/newsletter)

◇◇◇

Copyright

https://www.wyrdwoodangel.com/

◇◇◇

The Wyrdwood Welcome trilogy is comprised of:
Stalking the Moon (1)
Jumping the Moon (2)
Hexing the Moon (3)

All available now.